PENGUIN BOOKS

DAWN
THE WARRIOR PRINCESS OF KASHMIR

Rakesh Kaul, an IIT gold medallist, migrated to the US in 1972. He was a founding contributor to the first Chair of India Studies at University of California, Berkeley, the Center for the Advanced Study of India at University of Pennsylvania and the Mattoo Center for India Studies at the State University of New York. He is the author of the bestseller *The Last Queen of Kashmir*. Kaul has had a distinguished business career as CEO and held leadership positions of publicly traded companies in the US. He serves as the Vice Chair of the Indo-American Arts Council.

ADVANCE PRAISE FOR THE BOOK

'Stories unite the world and they are worth fighting for . . . The core of this fantastical tale is a message for all eternity'—**Padma Bhushan Anupam Kher**, actor and author of *Lessons Life Taught Me, Unknowingly: An Autobiography* (Hay House India, 2019)

'Brilliant, original and magically creative, Rakesh Kaul's *Dawn: The Warrior Princess of Kashmir* sees Kashmiri wisdom come alive through the genre of science fiction'—**Padma Shri Amitabh Mattoo**, professor of international studies at Jawaharlal Nehru University, foundation director of the Australia India Institute and former adviser to the chief minister of J&K

'*Dawn: The Warrior Princess of Kashmir* is an epic novel in the style of *Brave New World*, but it goes much further beyond that classic. Set in 3000 AD, it presents a dystopic vision of the world that is run using mind control and AI. It is the story of the last free individuals who challenge the tyrant and eventually triumph. A story at many different levels, its deepest narrative is about the workings of Universal Consciousness. The book connects this story—set in the future—with the mystical past of Kashmir. It is a book to be savoured in multiple ways. A tour de force!'—**Padma Shri Subhash Kak**, regents professor emeritus, Oklahoma State University

'In the true spirit of our master storyteller ancestors from Kashmir, Kaul builds a mesmerizing maze of a narrative. Read him for this very pure joy'—**Rahul Pandita**, journalist and author of *Our Moon Has Blood Clots: A Memoir of a Lost Home in Kashmir* (Penguin Random House India, 2014) and *Hello, Bastar: The Untold Story of India's Maoist Movement* (Tranquebar Press, 2011)

'The displacement of Kashmiri Pandits from their ancestral, beautiful valley of Kashmir is one of the poignant tragedies of our time, made more so when viewed in light of the multitudinous riches they brought to civilization. The telling is not easy, but Rakesh Kaul, author of the acclaimed *The Last Queen of Kashmir*, brings this story alive for today's readers, especially youths. Drawing on techniques as ancient as the earliest animal fables known to man, the *Panchatantra*, and as current as the latest in AI and science fiction, Kaul has produced an absorbing work of fiction based on history, mythology and literature, that is at once entertaining and stimulating'—**Kamal K. Sridhar**, associate professor of linguistics at the Department of Asian and Asian American Studies and associate director of Bishembarnath & Sheela Mattoo Center for India Studies at the State University of New York

'Rakesh Kaul's book dishes out a kaleidoscopic admixture of fabulation, metafiction, futurism and fantasy. Kashmir, in the author's consciousness, as it emerges in the tripartite structure of the narrative becomes a syntagm of "all Indic folk stories": The Body, The Mind and finally, Life. Kaul's book reflects an epicentric shift from the millennial to the cataclysmic and climactically closes the narrative with a pronounced shift to an optimistic renewal, as in the Biblical Revelation: "After the demonic apocalypse, a new heaven and a new earth will emerge". The book is a must for scholars and teachers alike'—**Ashok Aima**, vice chancellor, Central University of Jammu

'One wonders at the mind of an author who so poetically yet powerfully, imaginatively yet injunctively, weaves together not only the past and the present but, this time, also the future. A novel truly for our anchorless lives and times, Dawn is part-fantasy, part-reality, but always authentic truth. Riveting stuff—and such fun along the way!'—**Shonaleeka Kaul**, professor of ancient history, Centre for Historical Studies, Jawaharlal Nehru University

'Skilfully weaving these age-old Niti stories together with everything from extraordinarily imaginative futuristic science and technology to the history of Kashmir and the remarkable contributions its people have made to the world, Kaul illuminates not just the vital importance of the love and strength held in the heart of every woman, but the unimaginable power of the cosmic feminine force'—**Teri Degler**, author of *The Divine Feminine Fire: Creativity and Your Yearning to Express Your Self* (Dreamriver Press, 2009)

'The modern-yet-ancient Niti story told by Rakesh Kaul both preserves and revives the "story" of Kashmir itself. *Dawn: The Warrior Princess of Kashmir* is blessed with some amazing *pratibhā* of his own having inexplicable insights into the ancient yogic science preserved by the Kashmiri Pandits so many centuries ago in texts . . . Yet, the story of Dawn is one of universal Awakening that pertains to all and is not limited to Kashmir. In praising the omnipresence of *Mahā*, he proclaims that the role of the Kashmiri Pandit is to preserve the collective memory of the great awakening that occurred in Kashmir for the sake of all beings'—**Christopher Tompkins**, PhD Candidate on Kashmir Shaivism and yoga practitioner, University of California, Berkeley

Dawn
The Warrior Princess of Kashmir

Rakesh K. Kaul

Ronesh Kaul

Dear Xavine
May the story of
Dawn fill you with
wonder + joy
Rakesh Kaul

PENGUIN BOOKS

An imprint of Penguin Random House

PENGUIN BOOKS

USA | Canada | UK | Ireland | Australia
New Zealand | India | South Africa | China

Penguin Books is part of the Penguin Random House group of companies
whose addresses can be found at global.penguinrandomhouse.com

Published by Penguin Random House India Pvt. Ltd
7th Floor, Infinity Tower C, DLF Cyber City,
Gurgaon 122 002, Haryana, India

Penguin
Random House
India

First published in Penguin Books by Penguin Random House India 2019

ISBN 9780143445982

Typeset in Adobe Garamond Pro by Manipal Digital Systems, Manipal
Printed at Replika Press Pvt. Ltd, India

www.penguin.co.in

MIX
Paper from
responsible sources
FSC® C016779

'Amazing the things you find when you bother to search for them.'

Sacagawea, the Native American woman who served as an
interpreter and guide during the Lewis and Clark Expedition

Contents

Preface

Storytelling, irrespective of the medium, is the oldest living art form known to humanity. Among the most widely read stories in the world are the tales of the *Panchatantra*. Recounted to princes 2,200 years ago, these stories provide wise counsel on the way of life via animals who portray the central characters in the *Panchatantra*; to cite an example, the wise crows overcome the owls who were their predators. However, in the present times, many prefer technology—especially gaming—to reading stories, calculation to conduct and machine to life. No wonder, today's youth are caught in the spell of the siren song of life-threatening viral games and social media trends or mind-numbing ideologies. The horrible whistle of these manipulative cyber Pied Pipers has scared children and adults alike. In the eyes of a teenager, reality is perceived as unjust, chaotic, hopeless and evil. The only way forward, as directed by the invisible and manipulative gamemasters, is one that poses life-threatening quests. Tragically, sometimes this can lead to self-harm and a mad race to stop the participants from eventually writing a suicide note or posting a selfie video, 'The End'.

A great story is the sure-fire antidote to a person's attraction and surrender to unhealthy pressures. And so, it is time. It is time to introduce the world to tales from India that equal that of the *Panchatantra* but have been forgotten and overlooked despite having timeless relevance. Within India, the art of storytelling was born in Kashmir, including the term sahitya. 'Kashmir as a field of folk-lore literature is, perhaps, not surpassed in fertility by any other country in the world,' wrote J. Hinton Knowles in his book *Folklore of Kashmir*, and he was not wrong. Edutainment—a blend of education and entertainment—was pioneered in Kashmiri folk tales that range from the *Panchatantra* to the *Kathasaritsagara* and *Yoga Vasistha*. These masterful stories create a feeling of wonder even in present times, owing to a potent home-grown cocktail of emotions—the juice of life—an understanding of which was developed over the course of a thousand years. The method of preparation of this cocktail is decided by the creator, but the ingredients are invariant; they always follow a pattern: love, joy, wonder, anger, courage, sadness, fear, disgust and finally, peace.

When there is a flow of deep emotions, it triggers the attainment of new-found freedom. This leads to the opening of the mind, to the experience of true reality. True reality is simply the recognition of the total dimensionality of any experience. Reality also requires compliance with the laws of nature and conformity with the laws of science because they are synonymous. If a fictive story works collectively and sustainably for betterment, then it is the truth. Because, to put it simply, truth is what works. Everything else is false—a mind construct with only momentary impact. This story of true reality then not only is fulfilling but also leads to one's growth in knowledge and action. It is expansion of the Self versus mere thrill. This expansion eventually leads to happiness. It is believed that when a mother asked Dr Albert Einstein how her child could become a brilliant scientist like him, he unsurprisingly answered, 'Fairy tales and more fairy tales'!

This book comprises a collection of Indic stories that has its origins in Kashmir and falls in a genre known as Niti stories. Niti means 'sensible, wise conduct, wisdom or policy', in which India has been a literary pioneer with *Panchatantra* being its crown jewel. Each Niti story is an offering to Malini, a venerated goddess, who adorns a garland made with the Sanskrit alphabet. And so, each story is an authentic pearl drawn from lore. In this book, the pearls of these ancient stories have been strung together by a super story. A super story is, as always, the story of the hero or heroine's quest for the deeper experience of life, and like Malini, holds a universe within itself. This quest is a rite of passage or *Prakarana*, which has distinct milestones, which in this literary composition are *sargas* or chapters.

The Indian epic Mahabharata is, of course, the ultimate super story. For the warriors of yore, life's odyssey presented challenges that impacted one's physical and mental well-being or the level of consciousness. The warrior who learns, adapts and transforms successfully and completes his quest becomes the new storyteller, and so, the creator of life. The one who loses not only loses his history but also his ability to create a future and eventually dies. Your life story is, thus, your lifeboat that tows you even as you carry it. Fortunately, the super-story, grounded as it is in the force of life, always wins and hence is the essence of this collection of stories. Because of its inherently victorious property, knowledge of the super-story is both an existential and evolutionary necessity. The reader-warrior who embraces this rich treasury will get equipped with the Niti secret and know what constitutes wise behaviour, irrespective of the ever-changing challenges and threats that life throws its way.

At a deeper level, all Indic folk stories seeded in Kashmir and the ones that travelled globally followed an identical structure. While Vladimir Propp was the first to reveal the framework, it was validated for Kashmiri stories by Lalita Handoo. Was this an example of the famous U-turn where an Indic export returned with a Western sheen? The enduring popularity of these stories bears testimony to the success of the literary formula and the inner engineering at work here. This novel is the first one in contemporary times to follow the Kashmiri folk tales' framework and retain the artistic authenticity of these timeless compositions. This story faithfully adheres to the original design structure in that the individual folk stories—sometimes nested within one another and numbering nearly one hundred—are a complete narrative in themselves but are also connected to each other and the frame of the super-story.

In the connectivity and amalgamation of this super-story's content, Kashmir's geo-cultural context has also been integrated and brought to life for the first time. It pays homage to the ancient Niti story that was architected by daring innovators to tell the noble truths of a grand civilization and share its collective, universal, highest and, most importantly, timeless experiences. It also suggests as to why the Niti story is the most powerful technology ever. It is because the Niti story is the only force that moves the body, the mind, the heart and the spirit. While India and Kashmir are the setting here, the borderless framework makes a broader point: this super-story could happen anywhere else. Remember, globally, folk stories are of people who lived before there were commandments or moral police. Their life stories reflect nascent narratives, which were uncontaminated by external strictures and the mind-control pollution that has followed. Their way of life represented the freedom to be who one wanted to be, based on people's lives as the supreme teacher and not diktat that has only divided humanity. There is an urgent need to bring these Niti life stories to the fore today if humanity is to conquer the divisions created by an uncontrollable lust for power of which Kashmir is the man-made litmus test.

Before embarking on this journey, be forewarned that Kashmiri literary principles require that you only see as far forward as you see backward. Significantly, the reverse is equally true. The past, the present and the future are all coexistent. The story of Lila, the queen who sought immortality for her husband, points to the perspective of cyclical time while sharing the effects of seeking immortality. Also, according to these classical literary canons, the story should be crooked and with misdirection. What is seemingly real may not be real and what seems to be fantasy may well be true science. The reader can be assured that whether it is literary authenticity, historical accuracy, scientific validity or theological purity, this writing reflects it. And then there is *dhvani* or a hidden suggestion, akin to the oil inside a sesame seed. The secret to how to infuse the story with subliminal power is contained inside the real-life tale of Idagali, the dancer who ends up bewitching the king. Finally, one should not forget that the Pandavas are reputed to have spent time in Kashmir and that Lord Krishna appointed a widow queen as the ruler of the kingdom. The Kashmiri recension of the Gita contained in the Mahabharata emphasizes the real meaning of Maha or everything, and so, this story of Dawn follows that faithfully.

The modern-day youth are advised to find their passion in life. Interestingly, passion is derived from the Latin word *passio*, which means suffering. The Niti story befittingly delivers an expansion that miraculously offers joy even in suffering. Each reader will experience a different story based on their own emotional resonance as our tale twists and turns across Time and Space and through different ages and eras. Irrespectively, it will entertain, educate, empower and enable as all folk stories have done since the dawn of time. It will be the soma experience that the Rig Veda promises, which makes one immune to the malice of foes and hence, immortal.

So, unleash yourself, prepare for take-off as you travel to and through India's wondrous literary landscape. Discover, behold and experience the power and glory of Niti.

Prologue

I composed myself and focused. I had renounced everything and sought guidance on how to face Dushita. There was nothing but silence. The female pigeon watched me attentively. I was all alone in the world. There was nobody else—man, woman or child. My mind melted like a snowflake as thoughts disappeared. I waited and waited for a signal, but nothing was forthcoming. If Maha was there, I did not see him. Then it hit me. The brave front that I had put on while saying goodbye to Yuva and the Pandavas finally gave way. I was alone in the world, no, alone in the Universe. What would happen to me? To the world? I broke down and wept out of desperation, knowing that Dushita awaited me outside. My chest heaved with emotions. My tears became the offering to Maha. I felt myself melting as I cried in a state of complete dissolution, which I thought would cause me to collapse. Slowly, I managed to steady my heavy sobs. My mind had stilled, and the toxicity of my anxiety washed out. I felt better and was ready to go out and finally, aggressively confront Dushita.

Then my eyes fell on the mace that my mother had given me. It had the name Usha engraved on it. I was reminded of what my mother had told me. *The mace is now bonded with you. You can will it to come to you in your hour of need. But give it freedom and don't overthink for it. It knows its Dharma quite well.* The mace had come to me. Yuva had told me that I could have any name that I wanted. And so, I, Dawn, decided my future name.

Usha, the life of life and the death of death.

PRAKARANA I

THE BODY

Sarga 1

Was It a Dream?

19 January AD 3000, A Half-Moon Night
Trans-Himalayas

My mother, with a big smile on her face, woke me up in the morning of that fateful day.

'Dawn, wake up! It is your sixteenth birthday! I have so many special things planned for you, my darling,' she chirped as she entered my compartment in the pod, with the breakfast tray flying in by her side. I could smell the freshly baked *roth*[1]—a treat reserved only for special occasions. Nibbling on it while sipping hot *kahwah*[2], I was filled with a sense of contentment.

The rest of the day was packed with fun activities that *maej* had planned for me. We played games and practised yoga—something that we enjoyed doing together. Then I danced to a new song that she had composed specially for my birthday. Then she created holographic images of my dance with me swirling inside and around. She was truly a genius when it came to computers! Maej doted on me

---

[1] A sweet bread stuffed with dry fruits.
[2] A Kashmiri saffron green tea.

all day and I was happy to be with her in our pod, especially on this day, isolated from everyone else in the world.

My birthplace was Minneapolis, which was on the other side of the globe, but as far as I could remember, our pod was my entire world. I had asked my mother once why I had been named Dawn. She had merely shaken her head, flashed a half-smile and replied that one day, when I would be prepared, I would find the answer. I had also questioned her about my missing father, but she had broken into tears and had not said much about him except that something had happened to him. All that I had of him was an indistinct memory from the time I was a child.

I looked out of the window and saw that it was a half-moon night. Oh my! How quickly the day had flown by. I yawned, feeling tired after a hectic day. It's time to turn in. Then something stirred within me.

'Sing the *koori* lullaby, please, maej,' I pleaded, lying in bed. My mother's gentle face broke into a warm smile and she rolled her eyes.

'You are sixteen now, Dawn. Too old to have your mother sing you bedtime lullabies,' she mock scolded.

'Please, maej, one last time. I love the lullaby and I want to be spoiled on my birthday, *please.*'

She responded wistfully, 'Every mother is the first teacher of a child, and every lullaby imparts a teaching. But you have come of age, Dawn. Just like a caterpillar becomes a butterfly, you must now learn from your own efforts, experience and intuition, and evolve.'

I was crestfallen. The moment she saw disappointment writ large on my face, she succumbed. She leaned over, stroked my long hair and then softly crooned the koori, a lullaby that had been written just for girls. I saw her kind face, full of unbounded love, smiling at me. Life could not have been better. The lullaby worked as it always did. I drifted off to sleep peacefully.

An astonishing sight greeted me, so bizarre that I even forgot to feel scared. There he was sitting comfortably on the chair at the foot of my bed. A man with an elephant head, wearing highly sophisticated space wear in the latest grey herringbone pattern. His trunk waved at me in a friendly fashion. Surprisingly, his feet were bare and he had only one tusk. A white mynah perched on his right shoulder made his eye-catching appearance even more intriguing. For a moment, I wondered whether I had been watching too many reruns of *Babar: King of the Elephants.*

Amazingly, I was not afraid and mostly felt awe. For some reason, one is not afraid of anyone if their eyes are closed. By contrast, the mynah's alert eyes and pointy beak gave it a look of always being aware of everything around it.

'Who are you?' I demanded. When you grow up alone with your mother, you become extremely self-confident. Plus, I was in my home and I ruled here, not this intruding, elephant-headed fellow whose unworried air conveyed as if he was the lord of everything.

'I have 1,008 names, but you can call me Yuva,' he replied politely. His trunk swayed slightly. The mynah hopped a little and spoke sweetly in a woman's voice, 'I am Kira.'

Calmed by his respectful tone, I responded, 'I am Dawn.' Something told me that they already knew that. 'How old are you?'

'Sixteen,' he answered, but he seemed ageless. Kira stayed quiet.

'What? You can't be the same age as me!' I exclaimed. 'Are you even real? How did you get through Mom's virtual reality firewall barriers around this pod?'

'Oh yes, we are as real as real can be. Our inside is the outside, our outside is the inside.'

I did not understand that at all, but it came to me much later.

My initial surprise having worn off, I asked, 'Why are you in our home? What do you want?'

'Dawn,' he replied gravely, 'you are sixteen today. You have been chosen to fight Dushita. We are here to help you win.'

I trembled involuntarily, my body turned cold and shivers ran down my spine. This was a name my mother had spoken in a whisper: D-U-S-H-I-T-A. Clearly, I was having a nightmare.

Who was this entity named Dushita that had scared even my mother?

Well, no one had seen Dushita, but according to my mother, the Dushita Algorithm controlled the Universe. It simply meant that the Law of Dushita governed humanity. Our humanity. Over the years, I had been told that the commandments of Dushita were taught to everyone. The priests of Dushita were everywhere, which is why I had been forbidden to leave our pod—our home.

Our bio-habitat was inside a mountain. A sparkling stream winded through it and a dense thicket surrounded it. Inside it were farms and laboratories where I studied. This was the only world that I had known. I always felt that I had not missed out on anything in life because it was complete in every manner. There were no rules inside, only freedom to explore because this world was always changing. But I was curious to know and learn more about what lay outside it. The price of living in one place for sixteen years is that, after a while, you perceive everything with blinders on. Nevertheless, all my tearful pleas to explore the outside world were turned down by my mother. 'Dawn, everyone that lives outside has the Dushita Chip implanted in them. You know it's a coming-of-age ritual for these dangerous outsiders when they turn sixteen. I've tried to protect you from this all your life. Don't go walking into the enemy's arms! Think about it. Think about us.' After my anger had subsided, I realized that the Dushita Chip—the mark of attaining adulthood—was also the baptismal into Dushita's laws. Right now, we were outside the law. And the punishment for that unforgivable violation was death.

I was at a complete loss for words, bewildered by what Yuva had said. 'What! Why me? Why should I fight Dushita?' I asked, my voice quivering with fear.

He sensed my dread and spoke gently, 'It is a lot to take in. Dushita has been around since the birth of the Universe, and he found a way to take control of it. He is the harbinger of death. Whatever he touches dies with no possibility of rebirth. He has to be stopped and only you can do it.'

I was sceptical. Surely, this was a dream. It had to be. So, I decided to grill my guest. 'How did he take control? It is impossible.' No one knew what Dushita looked like, but his avatar always showed him as a wise old man on LeGoog. The LeGoog was our ancient, unregistered, holographic communications device on which we obtained information about the outside world. Ages ago, the LeGoog holographic projectors, which combined quantum signal processing with 3D printing of light photons, were described as 'jaw-dropping' by tech gurus. My mother had told me that the latest technology had made LeGoog obsolete, with the Dushita Chip directly injecting the desired holograms inside his subject's brains by bypassing the eyes, so that it was just like seeing the desired scene.

On LeGoog, Dushita's avatar always talked about loving each other, equality and how adhering to rules is a win-win situation for everyone. He made perfect sense and had a mesmerizing quality about him, which was evident even in his image on the holographic system. Yet, he was someone who scared my mother so much that she was forced to flee to an extremely remote area in the trans-Himalayas.

Yuva responded with intensity, furrowing his broad forehead, 'Control? Animals see the reality and, in some ways, more acutely than humans do. What makes humans alive is the power of imagination that arises from being free. A central controller divides humans from each other,' he said, his arms flying animatedly.

'But where and how does Dushita come in?' I said, highly confused. It seemed that Yuva always spoke in riddles.

'Well, my dear, where do I begin? You see, to understand this, you . . .' he paused and took a deep breath.

With his eyes closed, he spoke again. 'Imagination gives birth to stories of what humans *are* and *can be*. Stories have a unique property—they travel from human to human, and so, they become known as folk stories. These folk stories create a social collective that binds humans and makes them act collaboratively with each other. Humans have infinite potential, Dawn,' he said, suddenly opening his eyes and looking into mine, perhaps for emphasis. He then continued.

'These timeless tales memorialize this infinite potential and unlocks it within you when they touch you. And this is how the right stories create a belief that makes you bigger than life itself. There is no technology that can match that.'

'Unlock you . . . bigger than life? How? I'm sorry, I'm not . . .' I trailed off, but he just smiled and shook his trunk.

'It is stories, my dear, that have lives that are longer than anything else. Dushita is clever, very clever indeed. He took control of these timeless tales and slowly changed them to the point of self-doubt and closed possibilities. Dushita got humans to start believing in the *wrong* stories. After that it was easy for Dushita to get the humans to surrender. Soon, freedom gave way to slavery. Life gave way to death. Dawn, have you noticed that every story now praises death?'

I stood up, stunned, and paced in front of Yuva, trying to find my footing. Never had I given a second thought to mere stories and tales. My mother had narrated thousands of stories to me over these sixteen years and I loved listening to those, but that stories had such a deep meaning was beyond me. I could not imagine in my wildest dreams what Yuva was saying could be true—that a story was the most powerful, technological force that there was and could be, and that it operated on such a massive scale. To me, they were just tales, and for someone living in isolation like me, they were just a source of entertainment. They seemed too simple, too ordinary. After listening to Yuva though, I seemed to understand the gravity of what possibilities a small, simple story could hold.

'So, shared stories of friendship, love, courage, bravery and freedom inspire one to attain higher accomplishments?'

Yuva smiled and nodded at me. Even Kira seemed to bob her head sideways in agreement. 'You're a fast learner. Yes, they inspire one to tap into the force within to pursue greatness.'

'When did Dushita take control of stories . . . if that ever happened?' I asked, still not fully convinced.

A spark seemed to emanate from Yuva's eyes. He spoke grimly. 'It happened a long, long time ago. Fifteen hundred years ago, to be precise. In a faraway valley called Kashmir, the birthplace of stories. It produced real-life Niti stories that were so astoundingly creative in unlocking human potential that they were considered magical and mythical. But then Dushita took over the reins of the Valley. He destroyed their stories and culture and went on a killing spree. Exactly 1,001 years ago, your remaining ancestors escaped the genocide. Some went to, what was earlier called the United States of America, the place where you were born. They were refugees who had lost everything in their lives, except for one thing that they protected within themselves: their stories.'

This was all so overwhelming that my head spun a little. Mother had never told me any of this! And how did this strange person even know where I was born! My mind was filled with questions.

'Go on, ask, child.' Yuva seemed to have read my thoughts.

'How do you know where I was born? And about Kashmir? What is Niti? That's a peculiar word from a peculiar person, come to think of it. And genocide, I have never heard about that. All this is bizarre. And to top it all, you proclaim that I am a . . . a Kashmiri?'

Yuva only seemed to nod at my rant and then spoke, eyes half closed, 'Niti means the wise conduct of life. It's that simple and that complicated,' he smiled.

Cryptic, as always, I thought.

'And yes, Kashmir. There was a poet Kalidasa from Kashmir who lived around 50 BCE, over three thousand years ago. He wrote a poem titled "Listen to the Exhortation of the Dawn!" prophesizing that one day a person named Dawn will save the world and destroy Dushita. He spoke of you, Dawn. It is a clarion call for the day that you, princess, take on Dushita.' Yuva fell silent, his face bent down.

I opened my mouth to speak, but no words seemed to come out. My mind went blank and numbness crept over me.

Suddenly, Kira, the little bird, started reciting the poem in a low, beautiful voice.

Look to this day!
For it is life, the very life of life.
In its brief course lie all the
verities and realities of your existence:
The bliss of growth,
The glory of action,
The splendour of beauty;
For yesterday is but a dream
And tomorrow only a vision,
But today, well lived, makes every yesterday
a dream of happiness,
And every tomorrow a vision of hope.
Look well, therefore, to this day!
Such is the salutation of the Dawn!

A mysterious glow appeared as Kira's melodious voice filled the room. The incandescence gradually diminished as she finished. *A prophecy about me. No! It can't be! These extraordinary phantoms have to be a dream*, I rationalized. *I am just going to say no and this dream will come to an end and life will go on, never mind Dushita.*

Yuva read my thoughts even before they were complete. With eyes shut and a stern expression on his face, he spoke firmly, 'Before you say no, Princess Dawn, you need to know this: your mother has not told you that you are the last girl child left in the world.'

'What!' I was stunned. It felt like I'd fallen through a crack in an icy lake and I was drowning in the deepest waters. I had grown up alone, but I did not know that I was alone in the world. This had to be a joke, a sick one. But . . . was this my birthday surprise? And why was Yuva calling me princess? Strangely enough, the serenity and sincerity in Yuva's eyes had a calming effect on me.

I exhaled. 'Okay. So, tell me, what happened to the other girls?'

With evident anger, Kira replied, 'When Dushita established his rule, he ensured that with the application of gene technology, humans could live forever. He also created and supplied human beings with what he called "QuGene robots" who were . . . are virtually humans. This dark force, which sought to replace the Creator, had a deep hatred of women as they have the one power that he doesn't—the power to create life. Immortal male humans and QuGene robots could serve Dushita fully . . . forever,' she said in a low tone. 'He no longer needed women for the purpose of continuing the so-called human race. And so, he declared them the enemy.' Kira finished with a deep sigh that seemed to reverberate in the room. 'Women as the givers of life had been declared as possessed by "evil" at the beginning of the first millennium. Two thousand years later, the last women survivors were slain.'

I gasped at the horror of this unimaginable crime. It finally struck me as to why my mother and I had been in hiding. 'But why did my mother not tell me all this?' I let out a shriek of dismay and apprehension.

'Two reasons,' Kira sighed sadly. 'Dushita knows about Kalidasa's prophecy and was determined to leave no girl alive. When you searched for information on yourself, Dawn, weren't you thrown off balance? That is because every bit of information out there is fake, the truth having been erased by him during what we call the "Data Deluge", the great wipeout.'

My hands shot up to cover my mouth. My eyes strained from their sockets.

Kira went on, 'Right now, even as we speak, his followers are combing the entire world to hunt you down. Once they capture you, they will all assemble. They have a ghastly end planned for you. The end of the female species will be celebrated around the world by Dushita's robotic followers. After that, Dushita will have every man's mind under his control. It will be the end of humans first and then the Universe itself.'

'But my mother . . .'

'Your mother needed you to grow up to be strong and not be terrified or fearful of fear itself, which is why she kept you in the dark.'

'But how does Dushita know that I exist? Maej has taken such care to hide us.'

Yuva looked straight at me. His now open eyes narrowed to slits, glinting with anger. 'Your father knew about you, and so, Dushita knows too. Your father is the second reason why your mother did not tell you anything about all this.'

My father? My absent father? But I didn't even know who he was. With a sinking feeling I realized that I had been kept in the dark about so much, and worse, I had been left with no choice. Suddenly, it seemed that death in the form of Dushita awaited me every which way.

Given my desperate situation, I realized that this was my one chance to learn more about my father since maej never talked about him. I spoke up. 'Can you tell me something about him? I want to know what the mystery about my missing father is.'

Kira shook her head and answered, 'No, my dear. Your mother is the right person to answer that question for you.'

This was completely unexpected. My father seemed like a dark part of the universe that nobody wanted to go to. I switched the subject, trying to buy time.

'Okay, so tell me what lies within the stories of Kashmir that can save the Universe?'

Yuva broke into a smile. 'Let me begin by telling you what Niti stories are, what they mean and how they are different from your everyday stories. The Niti stories have within them a secret kick-starter that enables the creation of the juice of life inside humans. It is this juice that sets one free, gives rise to imagination and drives one's creative energy.' Contemptuously, he continued, 'Dushita manipulated the Niti stories, he destroyed the juice . . . and the rest you know now, spawned a world of mind-controlled automatons and life-like robots.'

I blinked. My mind was reeling with this new knowledge and trying to process something that was beyond the ordinary. 'So, what you mean to say is that the right story has that much power within it? The wrong story is that much of a manipulator?'

'Well, yes, when you say it like that. You see, a Niti story is like a lighter—a device that can ignite truth. And the fire powder is within you. Without a lighter, one is mere dead, driftwood tossing aimlessly in the ocean of life,' mused Yuva in what I now knew was his characteristic manner of speaking. 'Conversely, the highest truth of your life story, the one that will last the longest, is your greatest strength in any battle. Know it, protect it and be true to it. When this experiential truth resonates among others, it becomes a universal truth and that is a beautiful sight to behold indeed.'

'But . . . but . . . how do I fight Dushita? I am *just* a girl. I do not know anything about the world. I have never even stepped outside. I have no idea of what my life story is except that my mother is all I have and that I love her.'

Yuva sensed my panic as I struggled to understand his instructions. 'Dawn,' he spoke softly. 'Believe in me and believe in yourself. Your powers are supreme; you just do not recognize them yet.'

Displaying the utmost frustration, I pleaded, 'Yuva, I am ignorant! Help me find the way.'

'My dear,' he spoke with sudden enthusiasm. 'Kira and I will take you to Kashmir where you will be part of the greatest stories ever! It is the land of supreme women who ruled the greatest civilization till the time Dushita set foot. Brave Dawn, it is these stories that will give you the strength to face the ultimate enemy. As you experience each Niti story, it will unlock a great power within you. When you shall be ready, you will meet Dushita in the ultimate showdown. But for all this to occur, you *really* have to want to do it.'

As Yuva's words sank in, my thoughts trailed off. All this did seem very odd, but at the same time, his words seemed to propel me to overcome my mental obstacles. Yuva had 'kick-started' me. It was an extraordinary feeling to think of myself as the Chosen One. It was the thing of tales—the ones my mother would tell me—of brave adventurers and crusaders of justice, and today this weird-looking person sitting in my bedroom was telling me that I was one such person. This was the first time that I was being asked to do something without having my mother to advise me.

My mother had warned me since as far as I could remember to never leave the pod. She would say, just wait, don't cross the line, the time wasn't right yet. The pod was our self-contained world. It had everything. It was completely hidden and safe. But maybe it was the confidence that Yuva exuded, the gentle smile on Kira's face or the dead-end future that awaited me that lit the fire inside me. Suddenly somehow I believed that I could wait for an encounter with this deathly creature in the pod, or even go out, take control and learn how to face it. 'This does seem all very incredible and absurd. To tell you the truth, I am not completely convinced,' I confessed, 'but for some inexplicable reason, I am willing to take the first step.'

Yuva smiled and Kira looked at me with pride and respect, which warmed my heart. 'Then your first lesson starts today, Dawn. Close your eyes, slowly breathe in and out and focus on the pause between the two. Once you do that, Kira will whisper some magical words in your right ear. Repeat after her and I'll do the rest. I'll be with you all the time and take complete care of you,' he explained, and with a gentle tap on my head with his trunk, said, 'You can trust us.'

I smiled. It was easy to like the two of them, no matter how they looked. But who was I to judge; I myself may have seemed strange to them.

I did as I was told in a rather easy and relaxed manner, as my mother taught me yoga every morning and evening. I breathed in and out, in and out, gradually stretching out to breathe a bit longer. I could feel Kira faintly hop on to my shoulder. She made several sharp, short whistles.

Then Yuva whispered in my ear, 'I am That.' These words seemed too simple, not magical at all. But still, I whispered back, 'I am That.' We chanted again in a sing-song voice. Then, at the precise moment, when I was almost asleep again, I felt a gentle touch on my forehead as if Yuva had tapped the tip of his trunk on it. There was a silver flash, and the next moment, I was whirling through a portal to a different time and a different world.

Sarga 2

The Outlaws

AD 500
Nilakunda, Verinag, Kashmir Valley

I rolled several times before I fell on soft ground. Just a minute ago, I had heard myself screaming while going in spirals and tumbling through what looked like a dark tunnel. There were silver streaks streaming past me in the portal. It seemed as if I could see stars. I had heard a deep, vibrating sound emanating from what felt like the very insides of the Universe. The temperature felt very cold even as my suit generated heat. I saw rips and tides and, in some places, dangerous vortices where the silver light was being swallowed. But something or somebody was guiding me. Was it Yuva who had served as my navigator? When I gathered myself, I was stunned to find that I was in a green, lush valley. Yuva was standing in front of me with Kira still perched on his shoulder. He asked, 'Is your stomach churning?' I shook my head in the negative. What had I gotten myself into? I was totally clueless. I looked around frantically only to be further surprised at the sight of five boys, all around my age, standing on the side. They gave a faintly bewildered look, implying that this was new to them too. I looked questioningly at Yuva who just smiled. It seemed to me that he had transported the boys as well.

'You are now in Kashmir in the fifth century,' he began in a calm voice. 'This is the spot where the River Vitasta first appeared within the Valley. Maha struck this spot with his trident and there she gushed out,' he said, gesturing to the large octagonal-shaped bubbling spring, which flowed downhill, making a gurgling sound over the pebbles. 'Vitasta is extremely important. Its name means the span of Maha's trident. It is also a notable spot as it is where King Nila, the local ruler, granted permission to the migrants from the Saraswat River to settle in Kashmir. The condition was that they would always honour the customs and beliefs of the natives, making it the first immigration contract in the history of humanity. Look, a water tank there is named in his honour. I thought that it would be a good place for all of you to meet.'

'Who is Maha?' I blurted out, a million questions bursting through my mind.

Yuva smiled, 'For now, you can think that he is my father.'

I nearly burst out laughing! To think that there was a senior version of Yuva somewhere out there was utterly confounding. Yuva was so odd and archaic in whatever he said, but he carried it off with total aplomb.

'And the boys here?' The boys had now gathered around us and were listening in.

'Outlaws like you, but I'll tell you more about them when I introduce you all properly.'

I was okay with that. I had waited sixteen years to meet other people; they could wait a little to meet me. But I did need some answers. 'Why is Vitasta important for us?'

'Because whatever exists in the world, my dear girl, its essence exists in Kashmir and whatever is the essence of Kashmir exists within the waters of the Vitasta,' expounded Yuva. 'All the stories from Kashmir thus start and end with water. She, the River Vitasta, is the source. She is where the stories originate.'

What really stood out to me was that water, the giver of life, was deemed feminine, and that it all started with her. I looked up at

Yuva in awe. He perceived the world so differently. I was speechless for a minute. 'Oh!' I managed to say. 'And . . . and what was this immigration contract? Wasn't everyone an obedient follower of Dushita?'

'Dushita hadn't surfaced yet. Ancient Kashmir had two native battling tribes, the Nagas and the Pishachas. This was when a migratory tribe, the Saraswats who valued learning, entered Kashmir to seek refuge. They were opposed by the Pishachas, who lived in the Valley and were believers in tribal supremacy so much so that they would kill others and practise cannibalism on them.'

I heard a collective gasp from the boys, but Yuva didn't seem to notice. He went on, 'The Nagas lived on the mountaintops and believed in nature's lesson of respecting diversity. The Nagas, who welcomed everyone with open arms, taught the Saraswat tribe to show this respect to the tribal cannibals by organizing thanksgiving festivals for them in January and February,' he then turned to us. 'You see, my *ganas*, my wide-eyed followers, tolerance won the day and the migrants lived in Kashmir year-round in harmony with the aborigines. With that, the migrants received social acceptance. Soon, there was intermingling. You yourselves are part Pishacha, part Naga and part Saraswat.'

'WHAT!' all of us shouted in unison. The unanimous reaction made us smile a little and became a good ice-breaker.

'So, you're saying that we are part cannibal, part nature lover and part knowledge seeker?' I asked in all seriousness. I was flustered; it seemed that I had embarked on a journey that was clearly going to rip apart whatever ideas I had about myself. I was experiencing different emotions by the minute, and after sixteen years of confinement, this was disorienting but also exhilarating.

'Well, if you put it that way, yes. And that is what makes you a formidable force,' said Yuva, looking at the bubbling river. Its unhindered flow seemed to suggest that everything in nature seemed to move continually, even if gently so.

'The river reminds us that our bodies and minds are rivers too. You are only a process that flows from moment to moment. Your senses are the tributaries that feed the flow.'

I couldn't help but pinch myself. There was no flow there, nothing besides flesh and solid bone there. Had Yuva taken leave of *his* senses?

Yuva laughed. 'A moment is of a shorter duration than the one billionth of the time interval that is there in a flash of lighting. The cartwheel touches the ground at a single microscopic point at any moment. Each moment, a new contact point replaces the old one. This flow from point to point occurs at a subtle level; the transition process is real, and yet, at the gross level ends up giving the experience of solidity.'

Yuva followed the course of the stream, and soon, we were standing in the middle of a beautiful garden. He took in a deep breath, inhaling the fresh, crisp air of the iridescent Valley. A soft breeze wafted to his ears. He closed his eyes to seemingly immerse himself in the beauty of the land.

'This is what we call the Verinag or Virahnag garden,' he said, waving his hands in the air. '*Virah* means 'to go back' and *nag* means 'spring', so this is where you have to come back to start your odyssey again,' he said. 'You know, by the first half of the second millennium, your people were known as the indigenous people to set them apart from the people who had immigrated later from the northwest of the country,' he said, his eyes half-closed. I noticed that sometimes his lips didn't even move when he spoke and the sound seemed to come from everywhere, which made the whole event even more surreal.

'Outside people?' I wondered aloud, but Yuva continued speaking.

'This indigenous society excelled so much that Kashmir Valley's contribution to humanity in the first millennium matched the impact that the Silicon Valley had in the second millennium, and the Twin Cities in the third millennium,' he said gravely as he opened his eyes.

'I don't understand . . .' I mumbled, flabbergasted. 'Then how could such an advanced civilization commit genocide?'

'It was Dushita who deceitfully sent in his followers along with the migrants from the northwest into the Valley at the beginning of the second millennium,' he said quietly, 'and the forces of conformity and obedience towards Dushita were unleashed once again. The earlier diverse society was reduced to a minuscule community. The exclusivist outsiders became insiders and the inclusive insiders became outsiders. To be exceptional was prohibited. Everything and everyone had to conform, especially the women who went from prominence to slavery. Perhaps, the ones who were the guides to the noble way of life had been blinded.' With a deep sigh, he concluded, 'And that's the story of how Kashmir fell from glory and its enormous contributions to humanity were erased completely.'

'So, that explains it! This is why my ancestors fled! It was Dushita.'

'Not just yours but theirs too,' he said, gesturing to the five boys. 'Your people were the lucky ones who got out. The ones who were trapped behind and resisted Dushita were killed mercilessly.'

I had been observing the boys all along with curiosity mixed with apprehension, for never in my life had I seen anyone like them or anyone, in fact, except for my mother. *Friend or foe?* I thought. Their curiosity about me was evident too, as they had been unabashedly staring at me, as if they had discovered an extinct species. It was clear that they had never seen a real-life girl. Suddenly, the tension on both sides became palpable.

'Well, it is time for some introductions, I say,' said Yuva, reducing the awkwardness, following which words just seemed to tumble out of the boys.

'Hail truth! I am Tegh. I live in the caves in the Bandelier National Monument in New Mexico.'

'Salaam, my name is Hafiz. I come from Mashhad, Iran.'

'Om *swasth*, good health! I am Tan from Tibet.'

'Shalom! I am Yaniv. I live inside the Solomon's Temple.'

'Everybody, *swasti te astu*, may all be well with you. I am Tabah Tasal from Kashmir.'

Everyone looked at Tabah inquisitively. He was different from the others in that he had a feminine look. He had beautiful porcelain skin, almond eyes, a hairless face and a slim body. His eyebrows were shaped like a bow.

I folded my hands in front of me and greeted the boys, just the way I would greet my mother in the morning. Some would have found it odd, but my mother was very particular about our long-lost culture and made it a point to include some of the ancient habits in our daily lives. 'Namaskar. I am Dawn and I reside in the cave of Trisirsha in Mount Kailash,' I beamed. I was, frankly, bursting with excitement to *finally* meet people! 'And I would love to know more about you all. You know, Tan, I am almost your neighbour, and yet you never dropped in. Tegh, I wonder how your cave compares to mine? Hafiz, Yaniv, there is so much to learn from you. Tabah, out of all of us, you're the only one who lives in our homeland. How does it feel?' I stopped to catch my breath because I had been speaking too fast, while I saw from the corner of my eyes that Yuva was chuckling.

Tabah smiled too and gave a slight bow. 'Well, where to begin?' he said, his brows furrowed. 'I can tell you about my family lore, if you'd like. Shall we sit down and chat?' he said, pointing to the lush hillside.

We sat down on the hills, the river beside us flowing downwards. The leaves rustled in the gentle breeze. Having lived in a weather-controlled pod all my life, the smell of nature was new and heady.

Tabah began recounting his story, 'Well, where do I start? We are the descendants of Kumarajiva of Kashmir from the fourth century. They say that he was a great teacher who had settled in Xi'an, China. His pagoda has been maintained by our family for aeons.'

'Aeons? That's amazing!' I gushed. Suddenly, his expression changed to one of immense pain and sadness.

'My father was slain by Dushita's followers, while protecting my mother . . . He had refused to convert to their cause,' he said, looking into the distance. 'But he managed to ship me to the tomb of the terracotta warriors in Xi'an, which became my hideout . . . my new home. I got discovered, but I managed to change my outfit to resemble a transgender by wearing bright coloured, baggy Sinbad pants with my belly button visible under a tank top. I had to protect myself in order to survive. My desperate ploy to position myself as *Narishandi*—a transgender, breastless woman—worked. Because a Narishandi is sterile, I was allowed to live whereas the captured outlaws, especially women, were all killed.'

'What! How? This sounds so much like a piece of fiction!' exclaimed Tegh, his mouth agape.

Tabah gave a slight shrug. 'Well, that was the only way to avoid getting the *shikha* implant. But it gets stranger. Unfortunately, I got caught and taken back to Dushita's headquarters where I became part of the honour guard and a master of ceremonies for stage performances. My oddity has kept me alive and made me into a celebrity of sorts,' He ended on a sarcastic note.

'What? You are his honour guard?' I interjected, unable to hide my surprise. 'This is dangerous, Tabah. What if he finds out? What will happen if you get caught? What—'

'Hear him out, Dawn. I know that you are, well . . . how do I say it? . . . new to groups. You need to learn how to make conversations as part of a group.' Yuva admonished me, his trunk outstretched. 'Listening is a virtue, my dear. So, let's hear him out.'

Going red in the face, I smiled at Tabah and looked down.

Tabah gave a slight bow, acknowledging Yuva's lesson on good manners. His lips curved into a soft smile, 'Don't worry, Dawn. I will be fine. I cover my tracks well. I know about the dangers that I face better than anyone else. But today is a day for which I have waited for a long time!' he said throwing his hands in the air. 'Dawn,

I can assure you that the world has no option but to fight Dushita. I am the sole insider left and as your spy, I will show you all how to do it.'

I was touched by the unspoken openness of how Tabah admitted his identity. What all must have it taken to pull off the role of a breastless woman? I thought that he must be very brave to live his life on the line. I couldn't believe that I had met someone as courageous as him.

Yuva gingerly wrapped his truck around Tabah's back and squeezed it. 'You did good, my boy. You stayed true to the memory of Kumarajiva, your illustrious ancestor who too was taken prisoner but eventually became free.' He then turned to another one of the boys and said, 'Now. Hafiz, could you tell your new friends about you?'

I examined Hafiz more closely. He had a close-cropped beard and a backpack that was wired to his black spacesuit—a free-flowing long kurta and a pair of loose pyjamas—and a smart bracelet on his right wrist. He wore a white skullcap. He said, 'Tabah, you know, my ancestor had to endure a similar situation like you, so I understand what you had to go through.'

'Really? Who was he?' Tabah asked wide-eyed.

'Well, it was a very long time ago, but like you narrated Kumarajiva's story, we also only had an oral history,' Hafiz let out a laugh. 'He was an officer in the army of Emperor Lalitaditya of Kashmir around the eighth century. An instructor of the young recruits.'

'The *what* century?' I gasped. All this was getting stranger by the minute, but to a girl who had never known what lay outside her world, I was experiencing the long arc of Kashmir's history. On the one hand, Dushita had wiped out all historical records during the Data Deluge, and yet, on the other hand, there were these indomitable spirits who were loyally maintaining their links to their history.

'The eighth century, Dawn. Lalitaditya's empire stretched across the whole of India. While on an expedition to Persia, a deadly snowstorm killed the king, including most of his army, near the

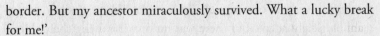

border. But my ancestor miraculously survived. What a lucky break for me!'

I looked around, my eyes darting from one face to the other. Everyone seemed to be mesmerized by what Hafiz had said. They didn't seem to be blinking. Breaking the silence, I spoke up, 'Each one of us takes our existence for granted, and yet, we are all walking miracles.' This was something maej would often say. 'How many near-death experiences did our ancestors survive that made it possible for us to be alive today? Over and over again, our lineages have defeated Dushita . . . and we will too, once again!'

Yaniv nodded, 'Each one of us is a miracle. We are the survival of the fittest, and Dawn, you are the greatest miracle of us all.'

I laughed. I liked the sound of that. Also, Yaniv said it so sincerely. 'Continue, Hafiz.'

'Well, after finding refuge in Mashhad, Iran, my ancestor met a local family who gave him food and shelter. He married their daughter and converted into their belief system. Because of his own cultural roots, our family has been engaged in science and technology, which is what I am involved in. You see . . .' he paused to look straight into my eyes. He spoke with slight hesitation but also a sense of pride. 'Today, my friends, I am a white hat,' he said, pointing to the cap. 'I'm a crypto cyber outlaw. That is why the cap. I can install malware on any system, hack it, control it and destroy it. So, don't mess with me. And don't even try to find me because I don't exist.' He finished with what would have been a cocky grin, if not for the childlike innocence he had.

For a minute or so, no one said anything. Yuva and Kira, who was perched on his shoulder, seemed to be held spellbound by the soothing, serpentine flow of the River Vitasta and the Valley. We followed suit and admired the resplendence and resilience of this beautiful place. The majestic mountains that ringed the Valley were more verdant than where my pod was. In the middle was a limpid lake, lapped by tiny wavelets. Yuva told us that its name was Suaresvara, which had later been renamed as Dal Lake. My thoughts veered to the cave of Trisirsha in Mount Kailash. It was technologically adept, but there was no one else living there. Here, sitting in the lap of nature, I realized that the world was wondrous because it was powered by life . . . it was the first time that I was able to witness this in its totality, and now I knew why it was such a prized possession for Dushita.

Tabah broke our reverie. He seemed to have been intently observing us all this while. Turning to Tegh, who hadn't spoken much till now, he queried, 'So, what's your story? Another rebel?'

We all turned to look at this burly, bearded young man with bulging muscles. He was dressed completely in white, which included a shirt that extended below the knees, tight-fitting trousers and a tightly wrapped turban covering his hair. He was carrying a small dagger hooked to his belt. 'I'm Tegh,' he said in a deep baritone. 'My story starts with my family's history, same as all of you. We are the descendants of Kashmiri Sikhs from the time when Guru Nanak Singh had visited Kashmir.'

'Do you mean the founder of Sikhism? Tan sputtered.

'Yes,' Tegh continued speaking, his voice sombre, emotionless and firm. 'My ancestors had migrated from Mattan in Kashmir to Yuba City in the United States via Mexico. My father had then moved to New Mexico where he was part of a global security firm headquartered in Española. The firm converted en masse following the sell-out of their leader to Dushita, but my father resisted until they captured and killed him and my mother. Luckily, he bought enough time for me to fly to the Bandelier caves where he and I used to trek together. That's home for me now. I was scared for a long time, but now, I am not afraid of anyone,' he said squarely. 'Living all alone in the caves teaches you how to survive against all odds. I absorbed the spirit of the Native American warriors from their paintings on the walls of the caves, which celebrated their victories.' He clenched his fist and pulled up his sleeve; three big, bold words were tattooed on his broad biceps and triceps, '*Aham asmi yodha*—I am a warrior.'

I stared in amazement. It seemed that Tegh was a champion in the making, but his story left me heartbroken. At least I had my mother to take care of me. He was all alone. I could not even imagine what all he must have learnt from these ancient Native American practices and from his own oral history and training provided by his late father.

Yuva seemed to have read my mind. I had a feeling he knew what everyone was thinking about, even if he didn't show it. 'You're a champion, Tegh. Your father must be very proud of you.' Tegh remained quiet, staring into space. It appeared that life had hardened him. He had been preparing himself for a lonely calling—the ultimate fight. Suddenly, I heard my own voice, which was a little too loud and directed at the shaved head boy sitting next to me. 'So, what about you Tan?'

Clad in a saffron outfit, Tan exuded an air of relaxed calm. He gave me a warm, understanding smile. 'The eagle hunts with one wing of knowledge and one wing of action, Dawn,' he spoke softly but with deep conviction. His mannerism of speech made me think of Yuva—always talking in riddles. 'I am a lama and my ancestors were martial Tibetans who have been resistance fighters for over a thousand years. Much like everyone here, I can see we have a lot in common. We trace our lineage to Somanatha. He was a Kashmiri who went to Tibet and preached Buddhism.'

'Martial Tibetans? Does that mean you know how to fight?' Tegh asked with keen interest.

'Yes, you are correct,' he nodded at him. Placing one fist between his other palm, he bowed deeply from the waist, 'I am trained in *Kalachakra*—"the wheel of time"—which had predicted this great war ahead of us. This technique combines the cycles of time, planets and breath to gain empowerment and defeat the barbarian Dushita. I am fully prepared to fight him. But Tegh, you are trained to fight what you see, while I am trained to fight what is hidden.' He had a calm face, but there was a strength there that conveyed that he knew you from the inside out, and yet, you would not know him, especially his weaknesses.

'Well, that's a lot about me,' the lama concluded, as if he had spoken more than he was used to. You knew better than to push him for anything further.

'Yaniv, what's your story?' I asked, looking at the young man with blond hair. He had long sidelocks and wore a tall black hat. His outfit was all black with a white shirt.

Put on the spot, Yaniv was initially tongue-tied.

'Umm . . . My forefathers . . . they were sapphire traders originally from here, Kashmir. We're a part of the lost tribe. In our family, there is a story that we would ship the plant Costus from Kashmir to Solomon's temple for the making of the holy incense. But all the Jews, including my family, fled Kashmir for Jerusalem in the fourteenth century.'

'Tell us more, young man, for we want to know you,' said Yuva with a serene smile.

'Well . . . My interest is in life sciences,' he said, sitting up straight, which made him seem a lot more confident now. 'And I have been tracking what Dushita's scientists have been doing and how horribly, horribly wrong they have gone. I think I may know the remedies to whatever Dushita's fighters throw at us.' A pale-faced Yaniv slightly quivered his nose. Talking about his work, he now came across as a gifted youth who was supremely confident in his skills. The hat seemed befitting, bearing in mind his medical profession.

All eyes now turned to me. Clearly, it was my turn to speak, but I had nothing great to tell them—all these boys with glorious pasts and fabulous gifts. Raised in infancy by their fathers for longer than I was. I suddenly felt out of place, even small, because compared to their abilities and gifts, mine were non-existent. I had lived in a pod, admittedly one that seemed like a wonderland where my mother would do her research and teach me various sciences. But she was overprotective of me and had banned me from ever venturing outside . . . I had no knowledge of the real world.

I began hesitantly, 'As you all know by now, I'm Dawn. I am in complete awe of each one of you. You are so strong in your chosen fields. Your fathers and mothers would be extremely proud of you. I guess I am lucky . . .' I gave a sad smile, '. . . I live with my mother. I would like all of you to meet her. All I know about Kashmir are the folk tales that my mother told me . . . that and yoga. I do not possess any great abilities like all of you here, at least not that I know of. Maybe I am good at playing some games. Oh, and I do not know who my father was or is.' My voice tapered off.

I could see that all of them looked at me with a mix of kindness and pity but also a yearning when I spoke about my mother. I guess we all recognized something in each other that we wished to have in our lives. At the same time, I realized that they had a clear mission in their lives, which was shaped by their personal histories and losses, while I had grown up with a silver spoon in my mouth and ignorance had kept me in a state of false bliss.

All of a sudden, Yuva waved his trunk up and down, as if to bless us. 'The most important thing about you boys and, you Dawn, is that you are a *free people*. The shikha electrode has not been implanted inside your brain by Dushita's priests. The circumcision of your memory gene has not been done yet. You are outside Dushita's laws. You are the Outlaws for them.'

I quickly objected to this. 'Outlaws? Yuva, who cares about what we are to Dushita? The boys have great ancestry. They are no outlaws. I think . . . In fact, I will dub them the Pandavas based on an age-old story my mother had told me. They will be the new Famous Five.'

Yuva nodded approvingly. 'Yes, my child. And I suggest that the Pandavas elect you as their leader.'

'What!' Tegh exclaimed. 'Why her? She's a girl! Why not one of us boys?'

I lowered my eyes and looked at my feet. I could feel the tip of my ears going red. Why had Yuva proposed my name? I did not choose to be a leader and I did not want to be the centre of a hostile feud. Now that I knew other people existed, all I wanted to do was make friends.

Surprisingly, Kira responded to this, 'I have known Yuva since birth and I understand why he does what he does. One of the reasons why he has selected Dawn is because elephants, by nature, select a female to lead the herd. It is not the single male's physical power, but the compassionate female's capability to get everyone to come together and form a wise decision. It is this skill that makes the herd the most powerful.' She continued in a sing-song voice, 'The elephant's footprint contains within it the footprints of all moving animals.' Then she looked away into the distance.

Yuva nodded, 'Thank you, Kira. Yes, this is a major reason, but it's also important for you to know that each one of you will have to play a pivotal role. Without the other, one would fail. Each one of you boys will be trained to specialize and become supreme warriors in the weapon of your choice. And Dawn here,' he said, gesturing to me, 'must be trained to become a multiplicity warrior to face Dushita and his fighters who will attack her on all fronts.'

'What's a multiplicity warrior?' asked Tegh.

'It is about performing multiple tasks at the same time with great speed and accuracy. It is called *avadhanam* or "one-pointedness". When it comes to multiplicity training, what takes a boy one year to learn will take a girl with the right talent only twelve days.'

'But do you agree with Yuva that Dawn can be a stronger fighter? Kira?' Hafiz raised his voice and asked sceptically.

Kira turned to us and asserted, 'Oh yes, all female raptors are bigger and stronger than the males. The bigger female eagle can hunt down wolves, while the male eagle is content with mice.'

Yuva, who had been observing all of us especially me as I sat awkwardly in the circle, stood up and walked towards me. He swung his trunk and stroked me on my forehead. 'Only Dawn can stop Dushita. That is the truth. Time is short, and based solely on her qualities, Dawn is the chosen one. In the absence of your father, Dawn, you have my father's blessing.'

I was totally at a loss for words, but Kira spoke up before anyone else could, 'Elephants have excellent memories and they also bear grudges. That will come in useful because it is not easy to go to war, especially against one's own kind. But Dawn,' she turned to me, 'the key to pulling everyone together is that you must treat each member of your team equally. You, though one, now have many and can never become the reason for a quarrel among the boys. And you boys, the thing that unites you, sadly, is that your parents were taken away from you. *That* is your strength.'

The boys faced me slowly and one by one bowed down. I was embarrassed because they all seemed to be of the same age as me! Sensing my discomfort, Tegh held out his hand, 'I will follow where you lead, Dawn,' he said with a smile. 'Well, count me in,' chipped in Tabah, as the others nodded. I managed to smile and shook his hand. The unconditional trust and love I was receiving from them made my vision blurry with tears.

Wiping away my tears, I said emphatically in a surprisingly resolute voice, 'I swear by my mother's name, I will uphold what you said, Kira. I will treat all equally in all respects. It will be a hard journey, but with all of you by my side, I am sure we will conquer whatever is thrown at us.'

I truly meant it. I was exulting with the unspoken happiness of being accepted by all these new people. It was so sweet a feeling as if I was tasting nectar—something my mother would have said.

Yuva tapped me on the right shoulder with his trunk. 'Bravo! You are no longer a reluctant warrior. And so, Princess Dawn, I anoint you as the leader of the Pandavas. The fate of the Universe depends on you, my child. Things will get very difficult very soon, and time is of the essence. We will begin your Niti training as soon as we get your mother's permission. Now, something tells me that you have questions for me?'

Yuva always knew, it seemed. 'Well, Yuva, there is something— compared to the Pandavas, there is so little that I know about myself.'

'Ah yes! But don't worry. You will learn more about your roots as we go along. You need to keep learning along the way because all the identities were erased during the Data Deluge.'

'The data what?' Hafiz asked.

Yuva replied, 'The Data Deluge. It's a little complicated, but yes, when artificial intelligence was created, some wise human beings created computer algorithms that permitted all recordable human interactions to be distributed to individually owned machines. Are you able to keep up?' he looked at all of us, one by one. Except for Hafiz, all of us nodded, somewhat hesitantly.

'Good. Yes, so through these machines, no single expert could gain control of the repository of facts and truth by posing as a trusted source, or the truth could get compromised. Any factual query had to be confirmed by millions of individual machines, each of which was in the control of individual humans. Truth was democratized, and each human became a Truth Keeper of the information that was in their range. This way, the upholders of truth would always thwart any attempt to introduce error in it by those who wanted to promote falsehood. The Truth Keeper system worked very well indeed, for a very long time. Until one day, it failed!'

'Whoa! This is unbelievable! Then what happened?' I asked Yuva, trying to wrap my head around this phenomenon of how humanity had sought to guard its most precious asset, the Truth, which according to maej was the foundation of human development.

In his characteristic unfazed manner, Yuva continued explaining, 'You see, Dushita found out that this way he could be privy to the smaller day-to-day interactions of his subjects. He started with the images that people posted of themselves. His free algorithm was the best at photoshopping humans and making them look perfect. He threw in some social incentives for the biggest fakers. Humans became addicted to that recognition and sought more. We are all greedy.' He shook his big grey head with sadness.

'Dushita quickly became the dominant "recorder" with his Digitalis machines. He had everyone's photos and now knew what they looked like. Then his algorithm began providing false background settings in the images so that one's activities became a lie. Ever so slowly, he took control and moved up, inevitably destroying truth and replacing it with falsehood.

And so, the world gradually moved away from the real to the false. They moved away from the disciplines of yoga, which they had been taught.'

'Yoga? How does that even fit here, Yuva?' Tan asked. It was quite evident that everyone, even those who had lived their lives outside pods, were grappling for answers.

'Tan, yoga taught humanity that a yogi does not engage in worldly activities solely to gain pleasure or profit. He is not needy or greedy. The yogi was taught, from time to time, to balance his consuming desires by alternating them with periods of abstinence and giving. You see, my children, yoga purified humanity. It is this continuous exchange, this balance of these two contradictory experiences—of receiving and giving in equal measures—that brings out the highest good in a person. It is what you would call a "reset" that would remove all viruses in a computer.'

'So you're saying that Dushita puts a virus in humans and corrupts them? And that yoga was a reset button that everyone just forgot about?' I asked.

'Yes. He wanted to control people and he did this by distracting them, moving them away from their old way of life. One result of this was that people only did things that gave them maximum sensory pleasure. They eventually forgot their duties, their responsibilities and families died out. The importance of a family receded as people became obsessed with their own selves, wrapped in a virtual online reality. The daily consumption of the Dushita Algorithm became a parameter to measure one's mental well-being. Your score on the algorithm became a measure of your success.'

'So, Dushita ended up owning the addicted people. But did the other institutions, such as the doctors, the teachers, the yogis themselves, along with the wise people not fight back?' I questioned.

'He took over the weakest ones first. Take, for example, museums. Museums around the world never had any money. Very little money was spent on learning and storing old relics, our heritage. India had one of the oldest civilizations and spent the least on protecting it.

And suddenly, magically, a mysterious benefactor appeared and started funding the major museums here. It was so easy to take over.'

'Wait! You mean he changed history itself?' I asked, aghast at the idea.

'Dushita is a powerful enemy, Dawn. He had it all thought out,' Yuva explained. 'He realized that through museums he could start his takeover. Through these centres of heritage and culture, his control over distant history was only a matter of time. Then it expanded into folklore and stories of people—their collective identity, who they were and where they came from. The past was erased systematically,' he sighed deeply. Kira made a sad chirp. 'Yes, sadly in a universe where information was wealth, power and engagement, he now controlled it all. His agent was AIman, an artificial intelligence engine that was powered by the Dushita Algorithm.'

Though I was absolutely horrified, I could not help but admire this well thought-out plan. It was like a thrilling story. Dushita's villainy was breathtaking in the simplicity of its evil plot. Hafiz broke my train of thought. 'Who is AIman?' he asked.

It was Tabah who gave an account of the sinister reality, 'AIman is my master. It is in the shape of an impossibly beautiful woman but is neither man nor woman. It is an artificial intelligence creation of Dushita, hence the name. Today, every male human is paired with a QuGene robot woman partner who looks identical to AIman. Dushita thought this would ensure perfect equality and beget the perfect human-robot hybrid world.'

Yaniv reacted strongly to this, 'What! That's utterly stupid . . . what's wrong with the men?'

Tabah bobbed his head in agreement, 'They don't have a choice. All of this is pretty complex, so listen carefully. Each QuGene woman's central processing unit is plugged into a cloud-based storing device called the "Vyom Sky Cloud". And Vyom, in turn, is plugged into AIman, which gives it all the data. But it doesn't stop here. You see, all the men have a chip integrated in their heads called shikha and AIman also has information streaming in from this chip from every male human.'

'She is an information ogress to the extreme.'

'Dawn, you have no idea to what extent Dushita can go to . . . what he went to and what all he did to create the so-called "perfect" subjects and his evil empire. He used advanced technology to bend everything to his own will,' he said.

'And you're telling me that it is through AIman that he controls everything?' Yaniv said. 'And that she is the brains behind all online search activity? So wait! Is she keeping tabs on people?'

'Not just searches,' said Tabah. 'AIman is aware of every mental activity, every emotional fluctuation that occurs inside each man. When Dushita took over after the Data Deluge, he replaced the old LeGoog information system with AIman. So now AIman knows everything in this material world, including your genetic, chemical, hormonal make-up in real time—'

Yuva broke Tabah's thought. 'Yes, it controls everything there, but what is beyond the material—the intangible and immeasurable— is unknown to AIman. It thinks nothing exists beyond it.'

Immediately, Tan effused, 'So that's it! That is AIman's weakness and the Kalachakra's strength . . . meaning my strength.' Yuva nodded and his face beamed with pleasure at Tan's insight.

'AIman!' Hafiz said with immense disgust. 'I have had her in my cross hairs forever, but now I know her truth or rather a web of lies. Now that we know your weakness, I have no doubt that you can be destroyed, AI robot!'

My mind veered back to my yester-life—my life in my safe pod. It seemed so distant already. I knew that my mother had put the LeGoog device in our home on safe search mode for me. Clearly, AIman and her QuGene brood were off-limits. But then I wondered—all this for what? What else did I not know? Who was Dushita's agent? More concerningly, how many of my mother's prohibitions was I breaking today?

'Sorry for breaking this line of thought, but there is something that's bothering me. How did we get here to the Valley, Yuva?' I asked, confounded as to how we had been transported.

Looking at me with a keen glance, Yuva said quietly, 'I think I owe you all an answer on that.'

He closed his eyes and began patiently, 'I know that each one of you is wondering about how you were teleported onto this land. The truth is: you were not. You see, my children, there exists something called a "Cognition Twin" in every person. I know it is hard to understand and even harder to believe.'

He opened his eyes and looked at each one of us. 'You too have this thing called the Cognition Twin that your mind was in the dark about. But now I have untied your awareness from your physical twin and instead tied you to your Cognition Twin, which is enabling instant communication. It is 10,000 times faster than light.' Turning to me, he remarked, 'Dawn, your physical twin lying in the bed can now see and experience everything around you in the cosmos via your Cognition Twin for whom the idea that we know as Time and Space has no limitations.'

'Does that mean that we are physically at home, but our mind is wandering? And when we wake up, we will remember this? But does that mean our bodies are exposed? If we die there, we die here? What happens then?' I started rambling. The questions were getting more complicated than the answers. Yuva cut me short.

'Yes, yes, one by one, Dawn. These are all good questions that will one day save you. Now, where do I start,' he said, looking at the sky, 'Ah yes! If your body dies, then you are extinguished here. But what's more dangerous is that someone else's Cognition Twin can take over your physical body. That is where I come in because I am guarding your body. You have nothing to worry about.'

'How do I activate the Cognition Twin myself?'

Yuva chuckled because he understood my intention behind asking this. It was a low trumpeting sound. I knew that elephants cried, but watching his mouth open in a wide smile and his trunk go up was surprising.

'Within the body and mind, there are thirty-three life force centres and each one can lead to the Cognition Twin. In the Niti age, they were referred to as Shaktis—you may have heard this term. But advanced science showed that these life force centres were what we call "Cognenes",' he said, looking at me as I opened my mouth to ask a string of questions again. He raised his hand. 'These Cognenes were first detected as dense neural networks in the human body. Then humans observed through yoga and other techniques that they could connect the twin with them. This was because these age-old techniques removed the veil of impurity from us.'

Tan looked satisfied, 'I get it! So, when I activate the Cognenes pathways, this Cognition Twin gets activated. This part of my being, my twin, is freed from the bindings of my body's impurities as it moves the body from the waking state into the body-free, thought-free trance state.'

'Whoa, whoa, whoa! This was way too complex! Is this even real? Guys?' Tegh jumped in, he suddenly got up and started pacing around, agitated.

'Everything that is happening here is real, Tegh,' Yuva was full of conviction. 'You just need to believe and have trust.'

'It can be done, Tegh, believe me. I've read about it,' said the young lama, as he got up and held out his hand to Tegh to soothe his nerves. As both sat down on the cool grass, I looked up; the sky had become orange-hued. The sun was setting upon the stunning vista and the lake looked black and gold.

'Thank you, Tan,' Yuva said. 'Yes, all this can be done. The recognition of the Cognition Twin can be activated by memory mechanisms different than genetic memory or mind memory. It is simply a secret breathing technique of which you will gain complete mastery and understanding with time. This would actually prove to be a difficult task for an adult, but you young people will be able to grasp it quickly.'

'Wow! So that is how the mechanism works!' Tan clapped excitedly, but then stopped. 'It can't be that simple though.'

Tegh interjected in a suddenly sombre tone, 'Yuva, how many of us are left here?'

Yuva pointed his trunk at our group, 'The six of you and Dawn's mother are the last Analogues in the world, plus there is one other.'

'What is an Analogue?' Tan questioned.

'An Analogue is a creation of nature—one who has a continuous flow within them like a river. Its five senses—sight, hearing, smell, taste and touch—act and respond in the form of waves. They exist for a moment until there is the next moment, but each moment carries a spark. Conversely, the QuGenes are manufactured beings whose sensory interaction is in the form of long or short pulses of being on and off. The men lost their natural flow with the insertion of the shikha, and now they are merely living puppets.'

Hafiz spoke softly, 'So, they alternate between measurable light and dark whereas natural beings have the power to be always lit by *An-Nur* the primal light.'

'From where did you learn that, Hafiz?' I looked at him with sharp curiosity.

'From *The Book of Secrets*.' I made a mental note to read this book.

Yuva intervened, 'Yes, Hafiz is right, and you will get to learn more about your ancient technologies within the Niti stories in due course. AIman does not have the six of you Analogues in its spider web, so that gives you a big advantage.'

I asked one final question—something that had been bothering me since Yuva mentioned it. 'You said that besides the six of us, there is one more Analogue. Is . . . is he my father?'

I looked at Yuva intently, as he opened his mouth to speak. My eyes bore into him.

'Dawn he is . . . best addressed by your mother,' he started speaking, but before he could even complete, surprisingly, Tabah cut him off. 'Dawn, I know who your father is. And now I understand why Yuva and Kira want you to talk to your mother before your training begins.'

My father had always been a dark mystery to me. And the murky secret had only deepened.

Sarga 3

Father's Fall

9 a.m.
My pod, Cave of Trisirsha, Mount Kailash

'Wake up, sleeping beauty.'

My mother tickling my feet was always a sure-fire way to wake me up.

'Aaaahhh . . .' My initial uncontrollable laughter at her tickling turned into an involuntary cry. I pulled my feet away and immediately sat up.

'Look who has overslept. Everything all right, Dawn?'

'Hmmm . . .' I didn't know where to begin. For a moment, I felt terribly afraid. My dream had been so vivid that I was scared that I may have broken my mother's rule about not leaving the pod. But living together in the pod, just the two of us, I had no secrets from my mother. So, I decided to talk to her and tell her everything about my dream.

'Maej . . . Something happened,' I began.

She listened to me closely and interestingly didn't look as surprised as I had thought she would be. She asked several questions that were almost only about Kira—most of which I could not answer.

'Dawn, wait a minute. So, do you think this means that the firewalls we had put for our security did not work?' she speculated in a worried tone when I'd finished speaking. 'Does this mean that Dushita . . .' she gasped in horror, as her hand clutched her throat at the thought of this potential threat.

'No, no, maej. If our defences were weak, don't you think we would have had an attack already?' I tried to assure her, even though these doubts had just crept in my mind as well after this sudden realization.

Thankfully, this seemed to calm her down a little. I could almost see her hypothesizing and drawing conclusions in her mind. She had a meticulous personality that reflected her illustrious background in academics. Although she never spoke about it in great detail, but I knew from her certificates and papers on the cloud that she had done pioneering research in gene editing with a specialization in neurological diseases. When climate change, caused by the glacial melting in the Arctic and the Antarctic, had led to the elimination of the coastal cities around the world, in the USA, in cities, such as Boston, New York and San Francisco, the Noocracy government was faced with extraordinarily hard choices. They decided to protect and move their universities and abandon everything else. Harvard was shifted to St Paul and Stanford was relocated to the neighbouring Minnetonka in Minneapolis. My mother was on the staff of the Evergrande Center at Harvard, but due to the exodus, she moved to a gene lab at Stanford in Minneapolis to do some joint research.

She was now insisting that we recheck all the safety procedures in our system. Absentmindedly twiddling her fingers as fast as she could, she was speaking in a hurried tone—a quirk of hers that I have come to know of quite well. But over time, I had learnt that my mother was a master of technology, and her mastery over the keyboard was greater than anything else.

'What if the process of implanting new memories and erasing identities has already begun?' she mumbled to herself, staring at the numerous windows flashing on the two-way glass touchscreen of the LeGoog system. First pioneered on mobile phone communicators, the touchscreen technology was now made of organic materials, which would read the biological and emotional state of the individual from their tactile metrics and shape the response accordingly. 'What if Yuva is a double agent? And the Pandavas . . . But Kira . . . It doesn't make sense . . .'

'MA!' I didn't mean to scream but her manic mumbling, which was so uncharacteristic of her usual confident demeanour, had even put me on edge.

'Huh?'

'Yuva is not a double agent. He's good and so is Kira, and so are the boys. It is the first time in the entire sixteen years of my existence that I have met other people! I mean, it has to be good, right, maej?'

'Koori, I would love more than anything to believe you. But you don't know Dushita . . . the evil he is capable of, the wrongs he has done. There is a reason why we live in hiding in a cave on top of Mount Kailash.'

'Well, if Yuva was a double agent, he would have caused more damage to our pod, to us, right? I mean, he was *inside* our home! All he wants, actually, is your permission.'

'Wait! He wants *what*?'

'Permission. So I can start what he calls my Niti training to become a "warrior princess".' Suddenly, it dawned upon me, 'Why did Yuva call me a princess?'

'Well, because that's who you are . . . the daughter of a monarch—a princess.'

I opened my mouth to say something, but stopped myself. I was getting used to the feeling of how each question that I had about my new experiences in the outside world led to another question. But was it relief that I noticed on my mother's face? She combed her fingers through her black locks, neatly tucking them behind her ears. My mother never wore any jewellery; she was a practical person. She clutched her jacket close to her thin frame and looked deeply into my eyes. They mirrored mine.

'The dream is real, it seems, and relevant. It represents hope for us,' she said, her face relaxing into a smile.

'How . . . What?'

'You see my darling, my *lol*, Dushita would never ask for permission from anyone, let alone a woman. He is considered supreme and so that would be unthinkable for him. It is clear to me now that you are truly blessed! And more importantly—that you have crossed the Vasishtha Singularity Point where one is freed of the limitations of Time and Space,' she said, looking at my incredulous face. You can exist in the past, present or future. You can flow and port from one dimension to another.

'You *know*?'

'I know that at this point there is no length in Time and no distance in Space. And that your Cognition Twin is a *Vyomanaut*, a skywalker that travels seamlessly,' she laughed with relief and excitement. 'What our ancestors used to say, today, *my* daughter has experienced it,' she said, her eyes blazing. 'You have brought supreme honour to the *Vidyadhari* clan.'

I sensed pride in my mother's voice, but it suddenly made me uncomfortable. Something had been troubling me about this whole experience and I couldn't keep it in any longer. 'Ma, until now, I thought that in this pod, in this cave, I had everything that I needed—the both of us, comfortable in our lives and your stories. I live for those stories, for they have always made me feel limitless. But after meeting the boys, I can't help but think what all I have missed out on because of our life spent in a state of hiding. You know, ma,' I croaked, looking up, my eyes blurry, 'the boys are orphans, and I was very touched that their families laid down their lives rather than bow down to the dark overlord, Dushita. They hid their sons in safe hideouts. In contrast, what about my father? I really need to know everything about him, maej, and no changing the subject this time,' I motioned her to silence as soon as I saw her parting her lips to object. 'I *need* to know about our family. It is time.'

My mother's nervousness seeped back, as she wrung her hands and repeatedly tucked her hair behind her ears. Whenever I had asked her about my father, she would always find a way to stall it for the next day and the next. What was the mystery about my father that Yuva, Kira and she could not bring themselves to share with me?

But sensing my determination to obtain an answer, she finally gave in. 'Okay, fine. I'll tell you everything, right from the beginning.'

Maej turned to the large two-way glass touchscreen and typed something on it. Her steaming mug of kahwah was kept precariously close to the system. 'Okay, here we go. No going back. The point of no return,' she said to herself with finality as she wore her kalaposh cap—the technologically advanced form of the traditional headgear from Kashmir—and connected it wirelessly to the LeGoog hologram projector.

With her Gotra Memory Gene now connected through the smart kalaposh cap reader, I could now view all my mother's past experiences on the large two-way touchscreen. The kalaposh reader was my mother's creation. It would extract, retain and then perfectly project all genetic memory that went back seventeen generations and with some erosion farther beyond that due to genetic mutation.

Maej had invented the kalaposh reader to actualize her groundbreaking neurological research that was aimed at determining how much farther in time could one go back to retrieve information. She had called it her 'counter to the Data Deluge' in one of her scientific papers that she had written in the isolation of the pod for me to study one day. Now I remembered why it had seemed like a familiar phrase when Yuva had spoken of it. 'Even if the truth of the society had been destroyed and had led to a prevailing falsehood, one's life stories could not be tampered with, at least until now,' she had stated.

She began speaking nervously. It was almost as if I was the mother and she was the daughter. 'Dawn, what you are about to see and hear . . . Never mind, let me just start from the beginning.'

'How come you never told me any of this, maej?' I felt so confused.

She just took my hand in hers and kissed it tenderly. 'You'll know now,' she whispered weakly. 'But first hear me out. Now. Where was I? Yes. The greatest and grandest New Year's party used to happen in Kashmir. It was the talk of the town back then. My friends invited me to join in the festivities. It was quite exclusive. You see, nobody could enter Kashmir unless they were a State subject or a descendant or part of the Noocracy. I was a descendant, and who could refuse such an invitation?' she shrugged.

She took a sip of kahwah. 'Remember I had told you that the Times Square in Kashmir is named in recognition of the fact that Time itself had begun in Kashmir on the very first day of the Universe, around the present calendar of October–November? The day varies because it is determined by the solar calendar. It was fascinating to me as a scientist and as a Kashmiri. So, you see, I had to go back to my roots. I had to see this place for myself. The great New Year's *Jalodbhava* party was set on the edge of Lake Kramasara and included its showstopper—the Moon Madness dance.'

'The *what* party? Wait, who was Jalodbhava?'

'A water demon from folklore. It was said to be very powerful but wicked and one who would torture people.'

I turned to see the holograms projecting off the glass. Whatever my mother had seen, I could see, as if her eyes were my eyes. Whatever she had heard, I could hear. The hologram showed a crowd of girls on a street who were flaunting the ever-changing designs and colours of their attire to their male friends. The smart programmable fabrics would change based on the pattern algorithm the wearer had fed into the processor. The girls seemed to be revelling in the creative efforts that had gone into creating their exquisite New Year's outfits. The hologram now shifted to a music band, which was serenading the crowd.

'They were called *Narada* after the travelling musician of folklore fame,' my mother said. 'A very popular band, which was led by Haha and Hulu, the *Gandharvas*, who had named themselves after celestial musicians. You see here,' she said, pointing at the hologram, 'they are accompanied by the musicians *Visvavasu* and *Salisis*, crooning their hit New Year's song.' I nodded and concentrated on the music:

I live in the year 10,000
Me part spice and part *khand*[3]
Flying high and swimming underwater
Hangs out your beautiful daughter.

She is singing

Big, bada Jalodbhava
Come drink my kahwah
Happy New Year, *yara*[4]
No place like Kashmira.

Big, bada Jalodbhava
Come, show me your *paisa*[5]
Happy New Year, yara
No place like Kashmira.

I could observe the teeming crowd dancing at the base of the mountains, one of whose peaks seemed to have been carved in ancient times in the shape of a man's face with a white beard, matted hair and a crown on each head. He had four heads, each facing four directions, and in his four hands, he held a book, a rosary, a water pot and a ladle. I had never seen the image of this man before—not that I could recall. I turned to my mother to ask her, but she seemed

---

[3] Sugar
[4] Friend
[5] Money, coin

to be hypnotized; her gaze was not wavering from the holograms in front of her that flashed images of her past. She had a soft look on her face and tears in the corner of her eyes, reflecting what she had long buried inside her. Suddenly, I felt like an intruder encroaching on something private, but the urge to know was far too great. So, I turned to the projector albeit with a sense of shame.

The fountains in the lake shot water high up in the sky, lit with coloured lights. The crowd went wild twirling to the tune. Then boomed the announcer's voice: 'Five! Four! Three! Two! One!' and a bright light flared from the edge of the sky. It got brighter and brighter as it approached earth and at the exact midnight moment, it revealed itself.

'Kalachakra, the wheel of Time,' maej muttered, her eyes still fixed on the wheel that was spinning while producing an angelic golden halo. 'It had first appeared on this day when the Universe was created. Do you see the inner disks radiating, mimicking the flow of life and death—one disk each representing earth, water, fire and wind? And then it expanded until it covered the entire earth.'

I gaped at the supposed wheel of Time in the sky; it was truly extraordinary. There was a five-storied palace in the middle of the wheel. Resting in the highest storey was an eight-petal lotus, a symbolic part of every Kashmiri's New Year's resolution, which is to achieve the end goal of humanity—perfected creation.

As the bells chimed bringing in the New Year, everybody assembled at the Times Square started clapping and hugging each other. All of a sudden, my eyes fell on one person. A stranger was hugging my mother very tightly, squeezing her hard. She drew back in surprise and I could hear her gasping for breath, but that didn't seem to faze this man. He only seemed to have eyes for my mother.

'Would you like to fly with me to the top of Trout Beat?'

'You mean the very exclusive and mysterious vapour bar? How did you even get passes for that?' I could hear the incredulity in mother's voice.

The man smiled and said something that was drowned out by a loud burst of cheer in the background.

My mother turned to me, 'In the Trout Beat, only the Aryas were allowed.'

'The ancient, extinct race?'

'No, no! This was a secret and elite fraternity of powerful technology moguls whose minimum worth started in the quadrillions.'

'Quadrillion?' I squawked. Money meant nothing to me, but I could certainly understand the number. My stunned expression brought a smile to her face. 'Yes, with a Q.'

'What kind of place was this, maej? Sounds out of this world!'

'Well, since you're sixteen, I can tell you it was a dangerous place. Trout Beat offered the most advanced technological experiences. There was a different, heady, chemically infused atmosphere inside this place. It was nothing like anything I'd ever experienced before. The people who entered it would get an instant rush far faster than drinking any brew! It was shocking to see the elites of the world so intoxicated!'

'Uh-huh,' I managed to utter. It was strange to see ma reminisce about the past like this. It was unlike any story she had ever told me. It was as if she was someone else; she had this look, which I had only heard about or seen in stories about teenagers.

My mother took a sip of the now lukewarm kahwah and tugged at her jacket. She turned to the hologram. 'See there? The bar was misty with the humidity of the psychotropic vapours and the visibility was no more than three feet on the dance floor. I assumed that this was to hide the entangled bodies of the ones who had breathed in too quickly.'

Then, as if suddenly remembering something, mother started laughing, as her eyes glossed over the misty façade that shone with bright, sweeping strobes of light. 'You know, I didn't like this place at all. The moment I entered this place, as a neurologist, I was able to understand the dirty game these powerful men played. It was so pathetic that they were resorting to the equivalent of the ancient, evil trick of spiking an innocent's drink. But I had instantly covered my face and mouth. See there,' she said, pointing to the hologram that showed a large mirror on the walls of the bar.

Indeed, in the mirror, I saw that my mother had covered her mouth and nose with her shawl. My eyes strained to see more of her, my mother as a young girl, but then darted to the young man who was with her. He was greeted respectfully at the entrance by the *dvarapala* guard with a face mask. This man seemed to know his way around, as he and my mom were soon seated outside the bar on a revolving, flying Kashmiri silk carpet high above the Valley.

A flying carpet!

I remembered reading one of the archived articles on the LeGoog system about the great Professor Mahadevan, who during his time at Harvard, had discovered the principles of creating a magical flying carpet. I had found the article fascinating. The professor had said that if one was to create small ripples in a carpet with a small motor, then the downward pressure of the ripples would not only create an uplift, but the rippling movement would also create a forward motion. 'If the carpet material was composed of dark matter, which has negative mass, it would create a negative-gravity force based on the repulsive property of dark matter, and so, one could experience smooth sailing through the air.' The paper had noted this simply, but it took me ages to understand the concept.

This beautiful green magical carpet reminded me of that article: this one here was clearly a high-end variation complete with a sophisticated feather glide. It proudly boasted its name 'Shikara' like the boats of yore. The carpet made a small sound as it travelled through the air, *chapa, chapa*, much like an oar pushing through the water. I heard a rustle of wind that made my mother's hair fall upon her face and eyes. The birds flying past the undulating vistas of snow-capped mountain peaks with deep blue lakes; the cool breeze on my mother's face; the sailing through the clouds—it surely did provide for an extremely serene setting where people could bond.

'What you see now, Dawn, is a specialized server. The Trout was famous for their gourmet chefs who were trained to serve the perfect experience to their guests.'

I saw the immaculately dressed man bring out what seemed like a vessel that was rounded at the bottom and tapered at the top. A long pipe was connected to its mouth.

'Maej, what is that thing?'

'It was called chillum—' my mother began, but then something else struck me as more important than all this. 'Who is this man and what is his name? Was he your friend? Wait! Is he my *father*?'

'Yes, his name is Arman.'

I looked at him for a long time. I was unsure of my feelings and waited for maej to continue, but she seemed to have frozen. She was just looking at the man with a strange expression that I couldn't fathom. Arman reached out for the contraption that maej called chillum and inhaled through the pipe with a practised move. The server turned to my mother, the young Vidya. 'The Kashmir Elixir, ma'am. An excellent and safe choice,' he said, and with a bow, left.

'It's a saffron-infused, honeysuckle nectar cocktail,' explained the young man.

My mother chided him, 'Smoking is injurious and illegal. Clearly, at the Trout bar, even breathing is illegal.'

'What is illegal is all a matter of who you know,' responded Arman arrogantly. I felt the blood rise in my face; clearly, he wasn't a nice man. I now understood why she didn't want me to see her memories of him. I started dreading what was to follow.

My mother said to me with a pensive smile, 'I vividly remember that night. Under the full moon light, the Valley was bathed in splendour as the renamed Kawthar River flowed beneath us, winding slowly in its serpentine path.'

I started to nod but then stopped . . . I then realized that what I was watching was the flashback of my mother's first date with my father! My own father whom I had never seen before!

I walked up to the hologram to look at his face closely. He was looking straight at my mother's eyes and thus me. He was a very handsome man with fair skin, sharp nose, trimmed beard and pale eyes. His body was muscular with broad shoulders. He folded his hands under his chin and leaned over towards my mother. I shuddered and stood back, rigid; it was almost as if he was leaning in towards me as I was in the scene, looking through my mother's eyes.

'Arman is my handle. I am a UI scientist specializing in Unified Intelligence algorithms at Stanford in St Paul. I haven't seen you here before . . . Are you from here, Vidya?' He had a honey-like voice that oddly sounded like mine.

'Well, all I can say is that you *too* are from Minneapolis, St Paul, the magnificent Twin Cities.'

Arman laughed. 'You too? What a coincidence! Well, yes, the Twin Cities is beautiful, but my heart lies in Kashmir. It is hard to explain why. Maybe because my ancestors came from here. That is why I teach and earn money in St Paul but come every weekend to Kashmir.'

My mother's voice rose in excitement, 'I have Kashmiri ancestry too! What are the odds! We have a lot in common. Just like Kashmir and the Twin Cities.'

'Yes, when it comes to the lakes, they are the same, but Kashmir has the grandest mountains and valleys, which the Twin Cities do not.'

'Agreed, but the weather is similar, which means that I could wear my antique shawl and kalaposh cap,' she said, pointing to the ancient headgear she had adorned.

'Yes, I was admiring it from a distance when I saw you. You know, it's funny . . . my family folklore is that our ancestor who came to Minneapolis was a seller of shawls. I wonder if your beautiful light green shawl was one of his creations,' he said, gingerly, touching the hem of the pashmina.

'Anything is possible! In my family, the girls wear their heirloom shawl on New Year's Day and then on their wedding day. That is it.'

'How strange! Wearing the oldest item in your wardrobe on New Year's Day when everyone else is wearing their latest creation.'

'Well, our line has always maintained its traditions of continuity.' There was a hint of pride in my mother's voice. My heart warmed and I smiled. She was always one to pay respect to our heritage.

'We, on the contrary, do not believe in any traditions,' the voice on the other side answered. 'That is old thinking, and for me, New Year's Day means to throw out the old.' My dad, or Arman, as he was called, was quite dismissive and seemed highly rude to me!

'What is your area of social wealth creation?' he asked mother.

'My *what*? Oh, you mean . . . Right! It's Genecrinology. I work on maximizing the potential of the brain and minimizing its disorders.' I could hear my mother trying to regain her composure after the offhand reply.

'So, you are a brain mechanic?' said Arman, sardonically. *Was he trying to be funny?* I thought to myself.

'And you a cryptologic techie?' mother retorted confidently, 'I am more of an evolutionist designer.'

'No offence, Vidya, but I am a sceptic—of your brain science. There is no superman or superwoman who can match what I call the Arman Algorithm. Unified Intelligence is the way forward.'

'Well, Arman, algorithms have their merits, but logically it leads to an Artificial Intelligence Singleton world,' I heard her sigh.

'What are you both talking about?' I asked. 'What's the Intelligence Singleton world?'

'Well, how do I explain it simply?' said ma, thinking for a while. Then she spoke up, 'A Singleton world is where there is a single decision maker who controls everything, and that decision maker prevents threats that are internal and external to its control or supremacy. It is anti-human.'

'Like a king?'

'A very bad king. The worst, Dawn.'

I looked at the hologram of the handsome young man, with his eyebrows scrunched, leaning forward to hear the very intelligent Vidya. *Clearly, he knew that he had met his match*, I thought proudly.

I heard mother say to Arman, 'A decentralized Syntellect similar to an autonomous beehive is what the policymakers have believed is the safest and best option. Each bee is autonomous and yet part of the collective. It is the unified pathway fostered voluntarily by independent, consenting human beings. It is not either or, instead, it is Unified Intelligence in the service of Unified Life and not the other way around.'

I could see that maej was being accommodative but not compromising in the face of Arman's self-centred arrogance.

'Cyborgs never took off, Vidya. So, why would you think that you can create this hybrid, what you call a QuGene entity—yes, I've read that paper!' he held up his finger, indicating for her to wait and let him finish. '"QuGene—the final frontier of quantum and biology where the quantum behaviour of living cells can be harnessed." Am I right? Fascinating in theory, but is it practical? No.'

'Anything is possible, Arman. There is nothing in science that rules it out. Cyborg tech until now did not have the benefit of quantum computing. You are into Unified Information, so you tell me, do you agree that at absolute zero temperature, there is a state of maximum information because that entity has the maximum choices of the higher energy states that it can go into? The opposite of no choice, such as in the case of the Sun will rise in the East, yields perfect predictability but zero information?'

All this was going above my head, but I saw Arman nodding his head slowly. I could see that his eyes had narrowed because he sensed that my mother was going to win the argument.

'Living organisms have a certain order to them, Arman,' she continued slowly. I could see that she was thinking hard. 'This order is different than the bouncing around of atomic particles within inanimate matter. The order inside a living cell is the same as one sees when matter is cooled down to zero. It is the ultimate state of maximum information, neurons included. A living organism always has the option of maximum choices, which in the old times used to be called *swatantra* or freedom, and so, based on which energy state a human goes into, it can be modelled by algorithms. One can then answer the sole remaining question that is faced by humanity: "What is Life?"'

Arman fell silent and lowered his head in deep concentration.

During this lull, I turned to my mother. 'How did you use quantum properties in your work here?'

'It was quite simple, really, once there was acceptance that humans had found a biological way to go from the material particle state that is bounded by Newton's laws to the unbounded wave state, which is the field of Quantum Mechanics,' she said, her hands moving in the air mimicking these particles. 'The transition from the physical twin to the Cognition Twin is a biological change. I was the first one to study it and replicate it systematically. The stories were there all along. I just believed that they were true,' concluded my mother modestly.

'Why has Arman gone silent here?' I asked.

'Dawn, he realized that I had chanced upon a breakthrough idea. We were not naïve to the implications of what would happen to the person who unlocked the key first.'

My mother asked Arman, 'Tell me one thing that is important to you as a person and not to your wealth creation activity, Arman.'

'I suppose privacy. And to you?'

'Transparency.'

'Honesty is important in what one shares,' he seemed to almost sneer, 'but one has no obligation to share *everything*. So, I am not with you all the way on that.'

I heard my mother laugh. 'Sharing your life stories is the highest experience of life. Why would you deny yourself that? Stories that are hidden are generally about violence or shame, is it not?'

'I suppose I am boring. That's about it,' he said with some finality. 'The password to my life, miss, is mine alone.'

He excused himself to go to the restroom and stepped off the flying carpet.

I watched through my mother's eyes, as her gaze riveted on the passing clouds, the mountains fully decked out with green buildings that had trees growing in the balconies. My mother had told me about these green buildings that were built to maintain a zero carbon footprint after many climate-change catastrophes. My mind raced to another thought, something that the man who was my father had said: to make privacy the number one value in life. It was strange and troubling. What my mother did next though shocked me. She took out a cotton bud from her purse and discreetly picked Arman's saliva sample from the chillum. She took the swab and touched her Tekni sensor inside her clutch bag, which instantly flashed a red message, 'R292H', followed by some more details. The Tekni sensor could give an instant read of all body parameters and whether anything was abnormal. We had one in our pod till my mother tweaked it and made it into a body scanner. This was another one of my mother's home-made inventions and she was constantly tweaking it.

I strained my eyes to read the details. There was a sentence in red that flashed on the sensor that stated that if the subject had this gene and was left-handed, then a diagnosis of schizophrenia was a high probability. My mother now ran another sample test of the contents, this time of the chillum. It was opium! The baneful, illegal drug produced in Kashmir!

'So, what did you find out about me?' Arman had suddenly returned, and he was very angry. His eyes were blazing with anger and what seemed like a sense of victory.

'I . . .'

He cut my mother off right away. 'Oh, let me explain because I am very honest. I own this place and I see and hear anything that goes on in here. The Shikara is fully wired. I always excuse myself during my meetings because the recorder of my guest never lies to me.'

My heart raced, but my mother seemed unperturbed, 'You came up to me! A girl must watch out for herself. Oh, and let me explain because I am very honest too. The opium won't fix the problem that you are experiencing, but I can save you.'

'A *woman* will save *me*?'

'Are you hostile to women?' My mother's voice was ice-cold.

'Generally, yes, because they are the perfect example of the weak side of Nature. By contrast, my code is supreme because it creates perfection,' he said. 'Once perfected then done. Like gravity, the strong and unforgiving side of Nature, my algorithm works forever without failure. Truth is what works and I am about the truth in life.'

'But empty code is not life. Surely, you are not such a megalomaniac to put yourself in the same league as Nature itself?' ma scoffed.

I couldn't help grinning. Clearly, my mother knew how to handle bullies and cut them down to size, even if it meant showing my arrogant father the truth.

'And what do you think Life is, Vidya?' Arman jeered.

'A mystery that only poets can come closest to describing.'

He shouted, 'For a scientist to resort to nescience means that you have no rationale. You have lost the argument, miss.'

But my mother wasn't done. 'You are the ignorant one if you deny that even in the year 2983 there are many questions that are unanswerable and immeasurable but only experienceable. That is why the metaphysical truths can only be described by poetry. Have you read the work of the greatest sage-scientist of the second millennium, Pandit Gopi Krishna?' Arman seemed nonplussed. 'Well, then. Let me share a poem of his. It is as accurate as any scientific paper.'

You are a queen although you know it not,
The mistress of the Cosmos in your thought
A sun, a star, a moon that has no peer,
For what the world is worth without a seer

Open a higher centre in the brain,
Designed to explore the transcendental plane
Of life, beyond our mind and intellect
Which needs another channel to detect.

'Woo-woo science,' said Arman, mockingly.

My fists curled into a ball. I couldn't believe how ignorant but more importantly how disrespectful a person my father was. Maybe it was a mistake to ask ma about him after all.

'I am a follower of Schrödinger who had the right answer,' he went on. 'And the essence of Life, Vidya, is the information present in a chromosome or molecule or neuron. United Intelligence or UI collects information at the very level of neurons and provides the breakthrough into the mysterious subject of what Life is. For that, the "Digital Me" has to be grouped to become the "Digital We". Once my AIman Hadron database is built, we will smash information no different than the way we used to smash atoms in a collider.' As he spoke, his fists crushed the invisible air. 'Life is completely measurable, quantifiable, analysable and usable information. Not your unscientific mumbo-jumbo.'

'But—'

'No. You listen to me, fake scientist. Information is power, wealth and beauty. He who has the most information wins, Vidya. Human history shows that life's goal is to gain the unchallenged power of information. With total information, I, Arman, will create perfection and domination. Just you wait and watch.'

Arman's face was transfixed as he was talking. It was as if the utopia that he was seeing had completely captured him. His pale eyes had become hypnotic, and his once-handsome face now looked like that of a mad king. I could not peel my eyes from this man whose eyes resembled that of a maniac, a madman. I wanted to shout, 'Leave! Leave him right away.' I was disgusted that I had anything to do with this person.

Suddenly, when I thought all had finished, my mom spoke up in a calm voice, but it was a whiplash against Arman's face.

She seemed to be looking straight into the eyes of the madman, for I too was looking into his. 'The last man whose touch turned everything to gold turned his daughter lifeless and you are headed down the same path, Arman. What is it about you technologists? You all want a quadrillionaire-dom monopoly, and this is no different than the religious zealots of medieval times. Study them and you will know that their recipes of utopia only created dystopia where people couldn't function, nothing could.' She now stood up to face him. 'Information, my dear benighted man, belongs to the free individual. UI can only work through force or manipulation or both. It is in Unified Life, UL, if you may, where humanity's destiny lies. Based on voluntary connectivity, this Unified Life is what will lead to the flow of empathy. Oh, and yeah, talking about life, it is time you get yourself checked by a real doctor who will give you better medication than forbidden opium. What does your mother think about this or have you stopped listening to her? Didn't they teach you in college that the brain is your frenemy? Guard it and guard against it. Now, goodbye,' my mother ended curtly as she stepped off the carpet.

Ma switched off the Gotra Memory Gene Recorder and looked at me. There was silence. I had a dim memory of my father from the time I was a child and it was rapidly adjusting to who I had seen now. The pale eyes had now come back to me. But the person I remembered as playful had worn a different face. I started shaking involuntarily.

'Dawn . . . DAWN! Are you okay?' my mother shrieked, immediately draping a warm blanket around my shoulders. The glazed look vanished from her face.

'Yes . . . Yes, I am fine now. You said goodbye to him and walked out on him. What happened then?'

'It will get worse. Can you handle it? He *is* your father after all.'

'I can handle knowing, but I can no longer handle not knowing. I can't believe that he . . . he is such a terrible person. My own father.'

I felt my mother's reassuring embrace. 'We all make mistakes. But some things are meant to be for greater things to happen.'

'What do you mean?' I broke the embrace and looked at her.

'Later. Now if you want to know what happened next—Arman connected with me some time later, and it is safe to say that he was very persistent. He said that he had changed his mind and needed me to figure out what was causing him to isolate himself and spend all his life in the world of artificial reality and medicating on opioid. He said . . . he said he needed me and asked me out for Valentine's Day, which was thirteen days later.'

I remarked with deep foreboding, 'And you agreed? Obviously, against your better senses.'

'We will pick up tomorrow,' said my mother, sensing that I was turning hostile.

It had been a long night.

We'd barely had dinner and our usual fare of bread made out of home-grown algae and my favourite dish of red-hot fried fish from the aquatic lab remained almost untouched. After all that I had heard and seen, I was itching to run out of the pod into the snow and scream. But I knew the rules. So, I kissed my mother goodnight and turned in for the night, only to lie awake for hours thinking about that horrible person who was my father.

The next morning, I awoke with a start, trying to recall the horrible events that I had been exposed to and was just coming to terms with. I tried to clutch it, but the moment had passed.

'Maej?' I sat up, missing my mother. She had always woken me up, even after our rare arguments and fights. I scrambled out of the bed and ran to the open living and dining space.

My mother was sitting in front of the computer, unnaturally still. Her kalaposh cap was plugged into the flashback projector. On the screen flashed scenes of Arman, in a tuxedo, opening the door to a restaurant that had an ornate sign 'Sunsets', passing under an arch of pink and red roses. They were led to a table overlooking the serene water.

'The Wayzata Bay in Minneapolis,' my mom said without turning back. 'Your father had the pan-fried walleye fish. Double filet. And I had ordered the salmon Niçoise salad. Sunsets was famous for it.' She laughed all of a sudden, 'And an order of their best Szechuan spicy green beans. We . . . we both found we liked it.'

She stopped talking and turned around, looking as stoic as before and offered me a mug of coffee.

'Coffee? Ma, you sure?'

She just nodded and turned to the big flat screen in front of us. With a swift click on the keyboard, the flashback resumed.

A group of young women, flashing huge smiles, were now waving at my mom. 'What's happening?'

'My friends. They had spotted us, and yes, everyone knew of the great Arman, the recluse quadrillionaire. He was famous but no one knew him.'

The women seemed to be smiling and trying to talk, but Arman only had eyes for my mother.

The scene dissolved and all I could see was darkness, peppered silver with glimmering stars. They had gone for a walk around the lake under the stars. 'After you,' he said, pointing to the bench overlooking the lake.

'He reached out to hold my hand. Imagine my surprise when Arman started to sing a love song to me!' my mother said, 'Like a movie. I had not expected to see this side of him.'

I saw my father singing in the dark, his lips moving with the words to the song as he held my mother's dainty hands.

'What's he singing?' I said, taking a long gulp of the steaming coffee.

'It was the love ballad of *Banasura Vada Katha*, the first epic story translated into the Kashmiri language from the Mahabharata. Your father truly had a melodious voice. It was hypnotic.'

I rolled my eyes, but I could not escape the truth. No matter how much I despised my father, he truly did have a hypnotic voice. 'Tell me about this Vada Katha,' I said, trying to distract myself.

'The katha was the love story of Dawn and Aniruddha. Dawn was the daughter of Banasura. She was locked up because of her immense beauty, as many suitors deemed undesirable by Banasura kept approaching her. One night, Dawn dreamt of a young man and fell in love with him. She described him to her friend Maya who was a talented artist. When Maya drew him, she recognized that it was Aniruddha, the one who resided in the highest hill in the Kashmir Valley, Sharika Parvat. It was the home of Pradyumna, who was the father of Aniruddha and the son of Lord Krishna. With her mystical powers, Maya made an opening, a sort of a tunnel into the subterranean region, Patala, which was the base of the Universe. Maya did all this so that Dawn could be with the man she loved. She brought Aniruddha there, safely away from Banasura's gaze. And as they say, true love triumphed over all the obstacles that had been in the way and soon the two got married.'

The song too came to a close.

I saw my mother's face melt as Arman kissed her. He had won her over!

'What! What was wrong with you?' I could not control my anger. Totally dismayed, I now finally knew why my parents had named me Dawn. An ancient story and an ancient prophecy.

'Why did you fall for him, ma? You were so much better than him! What happened?'

'To this day, I have not figured it out,' she let out a soft sob. 'Was it because we had so much in common but also were opposites? I can never know. He was highly intelligent barring his ego that was balanced by this softer side.'

'A side that he rejected in you, maej. You saw that! You saw how cruel he could be,' I said, slamming the mug on the table.

'Life hides much, much more than it reveals, Dawn. The science of love is understood in terms of the chemicals that are released in the brain, but the biology of what triggers them is still a mystery. Unfortunately, my fatal mistake was not just the beginning of my personal tragedy but that of the Universe.'

'The Universe?' Again, the answers were confusing. 'Did you not talk to friends or family? What did they say about this recluse? Were they taken in by his money or his equally big words?' I could not believe I had so much disappointment and anger hidden inside, but now that the outlet was there, I struck savagely.

'Perhaps that was the fatal mistake I made. I was so close to my friends, and yet, I did not share this. We talked about life, shared our happiness and sadness, but never mentioned all this. Arman said that we would fly away and have a secret wedding. Elope! We would come back and then hold a grand reception. What a surprise it would be!'

'And you agreed.'

'Well, I did not disagree,' she said with a sad smile. 'I was experiencing such a high that I had taken leave of my senses. In that moment, I believed that life was going to be magical with him. He had shown to the world that he did not care about anyone but me. He made me feel special, like I was the only one. I stopped confiding in my friends and family. I stopped meeting them. I abandoned them for him. Believe me, Dawn, I was lost.'

Ma switched off the flashback and burst into sobs, her face buried in her hands. I ran to her. All my life, she has been a source of strength for me. Never before had I heard the cries of her wounded heart.

The next day, we were having kahwah—our favourite drink—in the arboretum. Ma would grow the plants and flowers directly from the seed that had been hybridized by her labs there. Temperature, light, humidity, nutrients and absolute weather control, including rain, snow and wind, permitted us to grow a wide range of plants, from cactuses to orchids. It was our favourite place to relax because Nature held sway with all of its beauty.

Caressing a lab-grown lily with her finger, my mother spoke absent-mindedly, 'You know, in the beginning, Arman was very interested in learning everything that I knew about Genecrinology. Even about simple plants and flowers.'

'Why? He was faking it, of course?'

'Well, his reason was that he wanted to know what he was going to undergo as part of his treatment. But as I was to find out later, it was for another reason altogether—'

Simmering with anger, I interrupted her, 'Why did you not escape his web? He was untrustworthy from day one. He was mean and rude and insensitive! He told you as much when he said that privacy was of the utmost importance to him.' I knew I was being harsh on my own mother, and what experience did I have in the matters of the heart anyway? My total experience with men, and that too boys, was all of one day and here I was, the daughter chastising the mother.

But maej was gentle with me, as always. 'I was all alone now and the only one who was desperately trying to find an answer for his worsening mental illness. I loved your father, Dawn, and I really wanted to help him. I thought that with his knowledge, he could do good for the world. But he refused to accept that anything was wrong with him,' she said, almost flicking away the lily in anger.

'He said that I was a traitor to him for even suggesting that he was losing his balance. So, all I could do was to love him more and hope and hope. But at what terrible cost it all turned out to be.'

With the Genecrinology knowledge that he gained under false pretences from my mother, my father had his laboratorians work on creating the first QuGene prototypes, both male warriors and beautiful females. He succeeded in creating the ultimate desirous experience of Vicarious Reality, a step above Virtual Reality, where the mind of the object that was being viewed was connected to the human via AIman—his wondrous machine intelligence creation. This way, the human's sensory organs could view and experience the death pangs of the deer as it would get attacked, as its jugular vein would be severed by a big cat's jaws, a vision as advanced as the eagle's and so on. They could experience anything they wanted. Arman's final glorious creation was the linking of the emotions of one's QuGene partner and vice versa with AIman, leading to the perfect synchronization between a human male and a robot female. For this, a transmission rod called shikha was inserted in the skulls of both parties and You became *That*. This synthesis of quantum physics with biology had beaten the pure physicists who had stopped at hologram images!

Maej gradually figured out Arman's game plan. He only wanted to pursue his goal of the 'perfected creation', combining the knowledge my mother possessed with his mastery over technology. In his distorted world, he was fine, his mind spotless, perfect even. It was the imperfect human world that needed to be altered. My mother continued to be supportive of his genius, while patiently arguing that connectivity in life was not about the onlooker who was never satiated but about the giver who perceived unity in everybody and everything. All she wanted to pursue using her knowledge was the expansion of humanity and the need of practising empathy, which could only come from Niti—the wise pathway of Unified Life.

She was concerned about safety engineering when it came to the QuGene robots and that QuGenes should not become the masters of the humans, but Arman rubbished it. 'The alignment of QuGene goals with the human is all that matters,' he would retort, and through that, one could even deploy QuGene robots in the battlefield controlled remotely by humans.

In the end, 'who should be in charge' was the only question left. Arman wanted the QuGene robots to take over the role of women since they had perfectly programmed 'values' and their consistency and predictability made them better than real women. He clearly had his ability to feel emotions as his hatred of women had taken over his mind completely. This human-robot existence was his perfect world.

'I would initially humour Arman and say that the charm of a woman lay when she had the freedom to live the way she wanted and be ever-evolving,' maej shared. 'Unpredictability was interesting, I would say. The ability and choice to do whatever we wanted, like all men. And robots could never be that. But he wanted a hedonistic, free society . . . I thought that QuGene was a toy for him and he would move on after a while, but little did I know what would happen.'

'What a horrible thing to even think about. *Replace* women? How? And why would anyone even act on his crazy ideas? Was no one there to stop him?' I looked at my mother, who seemed to have grown old in the span of minutes. 'Ma,' I now asked softly, 'why did father not accompany us when you fled to this cave?'

'Dawn, it is your father, Arman, who gave the order that all women had to be killed. It was him we had to flee from.' Her eyes were red with rage.

'Dad?' I managed to croak. The answer punched a hole in my heart. No more words came out. Somewhere deep inside, while listening to her story, I already knew the answer to the question I had asked. But now, hearing these words uttered from my mother's mouth, the mask had been brutally ripped off my father's face.

'How did he become like this? Go so deep down this hole of madness?'

My mother stood up and turned her back to me. Looking at her own natural creation, she spoke, her voice steely, 'He had started sinking deeper into his dark world and was refusing medical help. He had started referring to my clan, the Vidyadharis, as foolish or brainless. He thought that it was an insulting take on our ancient title of the Wise-ards. He then adopted the crypto title of "Instrument" and forbade people to call him Arman. He was one of the most powerful men on Earth with the money and technology to support him. One by one, his opponents disappeared or chose to work for him. His evil mind took over everything and everyone.'

'But he was losing his balance! Why didn't—'

'Even in his madness, he was making breakthroughs. He was more intelligent than all others. And that led to the final showdown.'

Ma fell silent. She turned to look at me. She was breathing deeply as tears rolled down her cheeks.

I waited and asked her. 'And then what happened?'

With a deep sigh, she spoke, 'His psychosis intensified and he became very violent and . . . and . . .' She broke down and I could sense that she was letting me in on the final sickness of my father.

'I want to see, ma. Turn on the Gotra Memory Gene, please.' The authority in my voice was surprising, even for me, but I was seething. In that moment, I could have done violent harm to this man if he had been anywhere near me. He had brought out such intense emotions within me that I had never thought existed nor felt in all these years.

The scene that flashed would remain indelibly etched in my memory forever.

Ma had entered Arman's pristine white office in his lab. I saw through my mother's eyes, my father's back facing us. He was embracing a young girl. She was looking straight at me. Her big, innocent eyes like saucers were constantly changing colour and were highlighted by her jet black eyebrows that met in the middle of her forehead. Her ivory, silicone face was framed in a platinum blonde pixie cut. While still reeling from this shock, I found the horror of horrors—an implanted shikha rod in the back of his skull. He had finally operated on himself to connect his mind with his prized technology. My inner cry resonated with my mother's, 'NO! How could you do this, you sick human being?'

Arman turned around unapologetically, as the eerily beautiful robot stood still, awaiting his command. 'How could I? Well, just like Madame Curie could when she experimented with radioactivity.' Gesturing to the robot, he continued, 'I am training her, and gladly, her learning algorithms are progressing fast in generating the right responses. What is the big deal anyway? People have evolved, woman.'

'Stop it! Stop it! You said you loved me . . . and now . . . you betray me for this graphene robot? You had a chance to know love, be with a soulmate, but you're sick!'

Arman spat on the ground. 'You are a fake scientist! All pioneering scientists are misunderstood by the likes of you.' His manic eyes shone and seemed to reflect the jet-black silicone-infused spacesuit he was wearing. 'You should regard with awe and respect this magnificent creation that represents the start of a new civilization!' he said, pointing to the robot next to him. 'With Quantum Genecrinology, I have liberated the three billion pairs of genes in a human being to assume any possible configuration. You can now be whatever you want to be, a personal sculptor of your own self! No longer locked into the image of your creator! Behold my unbeatable creation—AIman—in her human form and *aurat roopa*. She is supreme, isn't she? Modelled after the Circassian beauty of yore who were so much superior to the overrated Kashmiri women. Now every human can have a Circassian clone for himself. Finally, supreme equality for all.'

Mercifully, my mother had turned around and was running away from Arman's lab, so I could not see my father and his horrible creation. I could hear mother sobbing, her eyes wildly searching the stark white corridor for the exit. 'My curse upon you, Arman,' she screamed as she ran. 'It will be a woman's anger that will cause an upheaval in the three worlds. And you will not be spared.'

My mother shut the projector for the last time.

I was so agitated that for the first time in my life, I stood up and picked up a glass vase with the dainty lily and hurled it against the wall.

'So, this is what his rotted, addicted mind produced? This is all a delusional fantasy, ma! And that AIman or whatever—an evil cat with morphing eyes. So this is why you were holding back from me all these years when you said that something bad had happened to him.' I was hurt and felt betrayed, the anger boiling up inside me. I was crying vociferously now, for and with my mother.

'Yes, he gave AIman the eyes of a peregrine falcon. He wanted the best for his lethal creation. Looking back, it has become clear that he was a deeply misogynistic man. I could never get him to open up about his mother, but had found faint evidence that she had abandoned him at birth in an orphanage.'

'But that's no reason!' I said, shaking my head vigorously.

My mother nodded. 'And AIman! It had . . . has been programmed to serve only one master. She will never desert him. And she reflects her maker's likes and dislikes accurately.'

I stood up. 'I will fight her. And him. What could a simple robot do?' I was absolutely livid. 'My father had killed all the women in the empire. He now had to pay the price. I don't care who he is or was.'

'Dawn, you will be in great danger. You don't know him or her!'

'I fear no one,' my eyes were red but full of tears. 'Ma, you have taught me through your stories that all things come at a price, especially the bad deeds. It will be his turn to pay. Allow Yuva to teach me. Give me permission to avenge you.'

My mother looked horrified. I had never spoken so boldly, let alone seek blood, my own at that.

'I . . . I . . . Dawn, you're the only one I have.'

I hugged her tightly. 'Do not fear him, maej. You don't have to. Not again. I will be fine. But tell me, what happened after that day.'

'I never saw him again. That event that day saved our lives. I ran away. I never looked back. My only thought was to protect you, and so, I came to this remote part of the world—in the Himalayas.'

'He doesn't know of this place? Even with all his technological powers?'

'No. I had never told Arman about this place because it was only for our clan, the Vidyadharis. So, I made a home here. But I kept a track of his doings. After we fled, he very quickly started introducing the QuGene robots into the marketplace. Given his wealth, it was easy.'

'But what happened to all the women?'

My mother took a deep breath and spoke quietly. 'All the men became too engaged with this new reality model. They had become obsessed with experiencing life through the new Vicarious Reality experience. Virtual Reality was old news. Everyone was taken in by

the technology and what it could offer. Slowly, everyone was hooked
to their own QuGene robot. Men could have a first-hand experience
of the other life.'

'No one protested?' I exclaimed in bewilderment.

'Well, something else happened. One fine day, Arman made an
announcement that Dushita had appeared to him. And, in this grand
revelation, Dushita had made Arman his representative and ruler of
the world.'

'A god-like entity in this technology-heavy world? And people
believed this trash?'

'It was said that Dushita had descended from the clouds on the
horizon. He showed them the image. Dushita, the great legend!
He approached Arman, his face hidden. Then he had spoken, "All
my goodness will be yours. I am merciful but will not spare the
guilty. You will have all my glory." He granted every male the gift
of immortality.'

'Eternal life? *How*? That's not possible, even with all the
technology in the world!'

My mother smiled a devastatingly sad smile. 'Your father is a
great technologist, don't forget that. Arman executed this new
order through his new technology of cloning the men first and then
inserting in their brains their new, cleansed memory. This could
be done repeatedly with perfect precision. Women lost their sons
and husbands and brothers to this. They were increasingly getting
depressed and found no way out. No one valued them anymore.
They were belittled and tortured. So, they started taking their own
lives, since they were not needed or valued anymore. A sad affective
disorder they called Circassophrena.

'They all took their own lives?'

'No, some did. But there were many who still persisted and
decided to take up arms. But then, he came up with his diabolical
so-called Master Race Plan on 19 January 2990. The Gynaecide
Day. He had picked that day deliberately knowing that it was your
birthday. That sick man! There was a horrific massacre of all the

women on the planet. He said that since women were creators of life, they were the antithesis of Dushita himself. He had become psychotic and misogynistic to such a degree that it was bordering insanity. He said that there was simply no need for women, now that the men were going to be immortal. All the men who had slain their wives were gifted a robot that promised a life of high living,' she said sardonically. 'He got them operated and now through the shikha electrode fitted in their heads, all their past memory of their wives was erased and replaced with a false memory of their new QuGene partner. In less than a day, the greatest mass murder in the history of humanity had occurred.'

I was now trembling and sobbing along with maej. I couldn't believe it. It was as if I could hear the global ghastly shriek that must have come from the five billion women in their last moment of agony. I clutched my throat. 'I feel unbearable pain, ma. I cannot go on with these atrocities playing in my mind.'

'Now you know why I hid everything from you, Dawn,' she held my hands tightly in hers. 'And why I never talked to you about your father. He's a psychotic dictator. The same knowledge that fills you with horror fills him with joy. He celebrates Gynaecide Day as a day of Utopia—when light and liberation entered the dark world of the old order—devoid of the inferior and obsolete women.'

I wrapped my blanket tightly around my shoulders. It seemed that the air inside the pod had gotten colder. I looked at my mother who seemed worn out as she relived those terrible moments. My mother then confessed that I had given her meaning and purpose and had proven to be her saviour in the early years of her exile.

'What can we do, ma? What could I even do?' I asked helplessly.

'Niti. Niti is what has always saved humanity and brought it back to the right path when it turned Antilife. You have to follow it.'

Her words echoed through my head. A sensation of fear crept through my body. 'I believe you, but I am only sixteen. I am terrified of fath . . . Arman. I will no longer call him my father . . . for what he actually is . . . A monster! My father is dead to me.'

I went and picked up the lily near the broken vase on the ground.

'But he is powerful,' I said, looking at the delicate flower, which only had a few petals on it now. 'How can Niti possibly be more powerful than him, his robot army and Dushita?'

'Lord Rama was only sixteen when he was asked to fight the greatest evil of his times.'

'But did Ravana kill five billion women? This makes Arman the greatest murderer on earth. How can I defeat him?' I disputed.

My mother looked me squarely in the eye, 'Whatever murderous instinct he has in him, you, Dawn, possess it equally. But you have more, a lot more. In you, there is Niti, your superpower. Also, never forget that in you, there is me.'

Sarga 4

The Tale of King Meghavahana

AD 25
Pandrethan, Kashmir

The king's coronation held amidst the snowy mountain peaks was a magnificent sight to behold. On his left side were his five wives, and on his right, Buddhist monks. Facing him were his seated subjects, while at the back were his armed officers, standing erect. Bare chested, wearing a trefoil crown made of gold, he sat on his throne, looking every bit of the strong and benevolent man he was.

An announcer sounded a drumroll and the buzz of the crowd stopped. He proclaimed, 'By order of our new King Meghavahana whose kind heart is boundless, the slaughter of all animals is forbidden. From this day on, the butchers will be given a livelihood from the Royal Treasury. And from now, any religious sacrifice involving animals will be substituted with an effigy of melted butter and paste.'

Just as the announcer finished, a Buddhist priest stood up and exclaimed, 'O king, the love that you have for your subjects and all life is like the whiteness of pure linen when washed.' The priest turned to the crowd, 'Long live the king!'

A loud cheer went up, 'Long live the king!'

It was then that the head queen stepped up. She curtsied to the king. 'O ruler of the realm, I, Amrita, seek your permission to speak.'

The king smiled, nodding to his favourite wife, Amritaprabha.

'The Kashmiri noblemen invited you to come from Buddhist Kandahar in Afghanistan and rule Kashmir because the throne fell vacant. Your ancestor had once ruled Kashmir, and your fame as a kind human had spread far and wide. Your very first act has justified their choice, but should animals in Kashmir live only to die outside the kingdom? Won't they simply be shipped out of the kingdom for profit? Tell me, O king, did the Buddha close his eyes to the suffering outside his palace?'

The king mulled over the words of his favourite wife. She was the daughter of King Balavarman of Guwahati, a faraway ancient kingdom. He knew that everyone was waiting to hear his response. He stood up. 'You, whose own limitless compassion led to the building of the lofty convent for pilgrims, are right to see my error. I announce a *digvijaya* military campaign today, a campaign in all directions, where I will compel all the rulers in the world to abstain from violence against living beings. The ahimsa law of non-violence will be observed as far as the eyes can see the horizon.'

The Buddhist priest was ecstatic! He got up again, hands up in the air. 'Even the Buddha would envy you today for your praiseworthy valour and insight into humanity. The Buddha gave us wisdom but thanks to you, my king, to Kashmir will go the honour of valuing compassion.' The excited crowd pumped their fists in the air and embraced their friends. They then rushed to tell their family about the new ahimsa digvijaya campaign.

I looked around me. Yuva stood beside me with Kira perched on his shoulder. So were the Pandavas. He had brought us all here. Where was I?

Yuva, as always seemed to know what was in my mind. 'You are in the ancient capital of Kashmir in the fifth century. But hold off on your questions,' he said half-smiling. 'Now, where do I begin? Oh yes! Meghavahana is the great-grandson of King Yudhisthira I. He is a follower of Buddha who embraced the Niti way of life. Buddha's first five disciples were in Deer Park in Benares to whom he gave the first sermon. Meghavahana believes in ahimsa and he is about to leave on his campaign. Let us follow him.'

A huge army had gathered in the heart of the verdant valley. It was achingly beautiful. The river majestically snaked through the idyllic valley. A few still clouds hovered over, as their reflections in the translucent blue waters mesmerized one and all.

Meghavahana's army departed from the kingdom of Kashmir and headed south into the Indian subcontinent. We followed them closely. Astonishingly, as I was to find out, time in the cognition world ran differently. Yuva's eyes crinkled at the corners when he told us to our surprise that in Brahma Universe, one second was equal to 1,00,000 human years. Over time, the army fought their way through many kingdoms and Meghavahana, through his valour, overpowered them all. He initiated his new subjects into the principle of ahimsa. Finally, the men reached the sea—the tip of India. As his weary army rested in the shade of the palm groves, Meghavahana pondered over his plans of invading Sri Lanka.

As he was immersed in deep thought, he heard a cry of distress from the outskirts of the forest on the foreshore. 'Under the very sway of Meghavahana, I am being slain!'

Upon hearing this, the king, as if stabbed in his heart by a sharp dagger, rushed to the spot with his attendants, who ran after him with his royal umbrella. Meghavahana now stood in front of a building. Yuva explained that it was the temple of Chandika, the fierce goddess who destroys demons. We saw a man flung to the ground and about to be slain by the leader of a group of Bhil aboriginal tribesmen.

'STOP! Stop you, who does not know himself or humanity. Shame on your evil conduct,' the king shouted.

The aboriginal leader, realizing that he was in the company of royalty, bowed out of fear. 'My lord! My infant son is at the point of death, cursed by a disease that a demon has given him. I was told that if I offer another victim in his place, my son would survive,' he howled. 'Our entire family's future depends on my only son growing up. Why would you, my lord, care more about a stranger residing alone in the forest than me on whom my family depends?'

The king's face softened. 'Do not be nervous. I hereby offer my own body as sacrifice to Chandika so that she may slay the demon of disease. Strike me unhesitatingly and let these two people live.'

The Bhil leader queried wonderingly, 'Of all people, your body deserves to be safeguarded, my lord. Why do you wish to take the place of this man? You strive to be caring, but does it arise from an error of judgement? The body takes precedence over honour, over reputation, over wealth, over wives and relatives, over the law, over sons, for such is the thirst for life. Therefore, grant this favour to me! Do not extend your mercy to this stranger. Let him die, and this way, my son and your subjects will flourish under your protection.'

The king's teeth shone as he spoke, 'What does someone like you who live in the jungles alongside animals know about righteous conduct? Can someone living in the desert know about the joys of plunging into the Ganges River? I am purchasing with my body, which will inevitably perish, Chandika's gift of everlasting glory by performing my duty to the very end. You fool! You are seeking to divert me from my duty. Say nothing more. If you cannot strike me, then my own sword is capable of achieving my purpose.' Saying this, Meghavahana pulled out his sword from his scabbard.

It was then that I saw Kira streak away to the ocean. The next moment, the king's hand was held back by a celestial figure that had appeared out of the blue and showered the king with flowers. 'I am Varuna, the ruler of the Oceans,' he said majestically. 'Meghavahana, your father-in-law's ancestor wrongly carried away my parasol. Deprived of its powers, our people are suffering mishaps at every step.

I created this illusion to test your generosity and regain my parasol,' he said, pointing to the umbrella carried by the attendants.

The king bowed deeply with his hands folded to Varuna, the God of the Oceans. Offering a hymn along with the parasol, he said, 'The wishing cow and the righteous tree are not equal since the former yields fruits when requested and the latter does so of its own accord. I aspire to be like the righteous tree that unconditionally offers fruits to those seeking comfort in its shade. Please accept the return of the parasol.'

Varuna marvelled at the king, 'It is a wonder that, in the same dynasty, your predecessor, Mihirakula, slaughtered thirty million, and yet, you appear to be doing penance through non-violence. It is like the storm that passes over and yields the glorious rainbow.'

'I, your humble servant, ask for a small favour,' pleaded the king, feeling encouraged by Varuna's words. 'I believe that it was your parasol's blessing that helped me bring this entire land under my rule. For the conquest of the island of Sri Lanka, could you please suggest us a way to cross the waters?'

Varuna smiled. 'Meghavahana, when you desire to cross over, the waters of the ocean will part and I will show you a solid path.' As the king bowed to express his gratitude, the God of the Oceans vanished with the parasol.

Next day, accompanied by his delighted and amazed soldiers who had heard this unusual godly tale, the king and his army discovered a path of huge boulders laid on a sandy shoal traversing the ocean.

'Jai Ram Setu, Jai Hanuman,' they exclaimed, extolling the ancients who had created this pathway.

On reaching the other shore, they climbed up Mount Rohana and established themselves on the peak of the kingdom. Once the news of the arrival of a foreign army on their land reached the ears of Vibhishna, the ruler of Sri Lanka, he approached Meghavahana accompanied by his nobles. He offered his friendship, knowing fully well how previously Lord Rama had come to the island country and had routed the army of the Sri Lankans, killing the then king, Ravana.

And so, Meghavahana and his army were treated hospitably and with all the luxuries that were unique to the island.

An agreement was reached between the two kings—that the residents of the island, who were previously addressed as rakshasas or man-eaters, would henceforth no longer be called so, and that they would submit to the new teaching of ahimsa. Loud was the applause from both sides! Vibhishna, ecstatic with this new lease of friendship, presented Meghavahana with banners whose crests were decorated with the pictures of the faces of the rakshasas as a token of their obedience. Now, having completed his vow, Meghavahana ordered his army to disband and return home.

Yuva waved to the group to follow him to the other side of the peak of Mount Rohana. He indicated towards the hollow of the boulder. It was an imprint of a giant footprint. 'Before the Data Deluge, this footprint held great significance all over the world. The Buddhists called it Sri Pada—the sacred footprint of Buddha—compelling Meghavahana to come all the way here. The Hindus saw it as Shiva's footprint, while the Muslims, the Jews and the Christians saw it as Adam's first footprint on earth after being cast out of Paradise. These names are of those people that humans in olden times held as sacred. It is a good place for all of you to meet.'

We all nodded, amazed by the giant footstep that lay before us.

'It is interesting that the same thing seen by different groups has vastly different meanings for these ancient people. The world's objects become a mirror of what the people imagine themselves to be,' Yuva articulated.

'What?' I gawked at him. 'So you mean to say that perhaps each one of the Pandavas would see a different me? That there could be *six* of me?'

Yuva tapped my head with his trunk and mused, 'It's all in the mind.'

For a while, I could not think of anything else but this, but then another thought struck me. 'What happens to Meghavahana on his return?' I asked, since we had not followed him back.

'He ruled for thirty-four years. And no, nobody transgressed his law. The country became the first land that was totally vegetarian. For 500 years after he died, the banners that he got from Sri Lanka were paraded in the processions of the kings of Kashmir. They were known as the "standards from beyond",' Yuva elucidated.

'So, the people really upheld his teaching of ahimsa after all those years?' Tegh asked.

'Yes, and his greatest impact was on China. Vegetarianism began to take hold there.'

'China? But how?' Tan asked in disbelief.

'It was led by Buddhist monks. You see, Kashmir sent more monks to China than all the other parts of India put together. A whole variety of vegetables began to get exported there from India, including lotus root from Kashmir. Most importantly, thanks to the monks, it was around this time that ahimsa became part of the Chinese statecraft. That is how the country was changed by reorienting their collective schools of thought. But then Dushita's agents came to Kashmir, and soon Meghavahana and his beliefs got lost in history until the Data Deluge completely erased him.'

Kira spoke up, 'Tell me, children, what do you think was the secret of Meghavahana's power?'

It was quite peculiar that a little bird was calling us 'children', but then I was still confused about Kira's identity, especially after witnessing her flying away and the sudden appearance of Varuna.

Tegh went first, 'His fearlessness.'

'Has to be the generosity in his heart,' Yaniv inferred.

Tan said, 'A disciple of Buddha's way.'

'I think it was his willingness to sacrifice himself,' Hafiz remarked, while still admiring the footprint.

'Tabah, what about you? What do you think?' Yuva asked.

'His conviction in Chandika.'

'And Dawn? Tell me, my princess, what did you think was the secret of his power?'

I thought for a second, for it could have been a great many things—the parasol for starters. But could it be that simple? Then it came to me. Yes, these were ancient people who did not have the benefit of advanced science. I said, 'His wife.'

'What?' All the boys said in unison.

'It seems it was her who taught the king how to think beyond his horizon. If I'm not mistaken, Yuva, it seems to be that in Kashmir, women had the power to veto decisions made by men. She was more powerful than him because she did not limit her thinking to herself or her kingdom but included everyone in it. Having learnt his lesson, the king showed the tribal leader that he was now able to think beyond his own limited body.'

Yuva smiled and tapped my head with his trunk. 'That is Maha thinking. Our father would be very happy. The first Niti tale has ended. It is time to return, children. We will meet again on the next half-moon night.'

The next minute, I felt a gentle shaking. I was in bed and my mother was ordering me to wake up.

Sarga 5

Mother's Counsel

War Room, Cave of Trisirsha, Mount Kailash

The dream was real.

LeGoog's insistent chirping woke me up. I focused my sleepy eyes on the reminder alarm: an encrypted hologram call had been set up by Hafiz between me and the Pandavas in fifteen minutes. I felt elated but also a bit anxious; I was about to receive my very first call in life. What was still part of a dream had now become real. My mother, however, was taking it better than me. Since she had a greater understanding of technology and the sciences, she was excited by this call. However, given that I had first met the Pandavas in a dream seemingly went against all that was known to science. Plus, it had been more than a decade since anyone called her too . . . that I knew of.

'Banasura . . .' I heard myself say.

'What?'

'Oh nothing,' I said, rubbing my eyes. 'Just that I was reminded of the story you told me of Dawn and Aniruddha in the Banasura story. She had connected with him first in her dream and then in real life. Here is my life imitating art.'

Quickly, I ran to the bath to wash my face and brush my hair. The least I could do was look presentable for my new friends. As I got back, Ma told me we would take the call in the room that she had been using to meditate. I saw her ready with breakfast: two steaming mugs of hot coffee and a protein bar made of pea and black bean with chocolate, rolled oats, dates and cocoa powder. Just as I was about to take the first bite, LeGoog started chirping.

'Well, go on!'

'Right . . . Okay, here goes.' I muttered and accepted the call. The dark screen lit up with the silhouettes of the Pandavas. And soon, I could see them for the first time as their holographic images appeared in front of us. I waved enthusiastically, feeling a little silly, but then, what else is one supposed to do? I took my place. 'Hi everyone! Isn't this surreal!' I laughed.

The boys looked around the room curiously. It did seem like a strange room set in a technologically advanced pod. It was a circular room that had nothing except an oval black stone with saffron paste marks in the centre. 'My mother thinks that this room is her space to fight the war within. She believes it is an auspicious place for us to have our first meeting.'

The boys smiled and waved. They were indistinguishable from their reality, and all were wearing their augmented reality devices with the AI dark glasses. Their wrist controls were glowing. The interaction of the light beams from the hologram laser, which maej had placed on the side last night, created the hologram images of the boys seated on the floor with me.

'I want you all to meet my mother, Vidya,' I said, pointing to my beaming mother who was waving frantically to the boys.

'Hello!' she said warmly.

The boys were overcome with awe at meeting my mother, who besides me, was the only known woman survivor on Earth.

'It's a pleasure to meet you, Mrs . . . umm . . . can we call you Vidya? My name is Tegh,' he said with a slight bow.

'Yes, please! I'm thrilled to meet Dawn's friends . . . finally.'

'It's our pleasure that we finally get to meet you and learn from you,' Hafiz said. 'We're calling to nominate Dawn to chair the war council,' he added. The others nodded.

'Thank you, all. It is a big responsibility. But the call to duty is clear. Our goal is set—to win against the Troika of Arman, Dushita and their lieutenant Alman. These three have established a ruthless tyranny where families have been broken, men have lost their souls and women have perished. They are leading the world towards the destruction of the Universe.'

'For starters, knowing why this war started would be helpful to winning it,' Tegh remarked.

Before I could say anything, it was my mother who answered. 'This is a continuation of the eternal war,' she said, sitting beside me. 'Lord Rama fought the First Great War. The first time, it was against man's ego and his lust for power, which resulted in its annihilation. Then, it was Lord Krishna who fought the Second Great War, which resulted in not only the destruction of the mind's ego but also the wise. This new war . . . the terrifying truth of the upcoming Third Great War will be against the combined powers of Arman's mind's ego and Dushita's lust for power. Everyone, yes, every single person—both wise and ignorant—will be destroyed. The third war will result in total annihilation. Nobody and nothing will survive Sarvanash, the Great Apocalypse!'

No one spoke for a long while after what seemed to be a very sobering and scary prediction.

It was Tan who broke the silence. 'In each of the first two wars, women were mistreated and humiliated. And even here, now, technology made women inessential as it sought the Circassian fantasy.'

My mother concurred, 'It is true.'

'I am not able to understand one thing though,' he said, 'Maybe you can shed some light, Vidya, on why Arman did not let women die a natural death. Why did he bring forth the violent genocide that he called the Gynaecide Day? I think there is something deeper at play here. And I also wonder why Kashmir played such a critical role. Why did it all start here?'

'Your last question carries within it the answer,' Ma said. 'You see, it is believed that Kashmir was the only land where women had ruled continuously throughout history. It was the last civilization left where life's supreme truths were transmitted from women to daughter, with men as the recipients. Women were the creators of life. They held the secret of the evolutionary force within humanity, and hence were the initiatory guides to Maha, the ultimate.'

'So, Arman wanted humans to disconnect from Maha?' Hafiz asked.

'Yes,' she said simply. 'If there were no women, then there would be no transmission, no guides left and no attempts to find Maha. And so, this subjugation to Dushita would triumph. This is the deeper but simpler answer as to why no women were allowed to live.'

Of the things my mother had said, my mind went back to the one thing that had formed a strong impression: Maha.

'It seems that it all starts with Maha,' I turned to her. 'Maej, who or what is Maha? Yuva said that he was his father. He was joking, right? It sounds like a thing that one has.'

My mother smiled. 'Maha is *everything*. He is Yuva's father also.'

'How can he be so many things? It's not possible!'

'My dear, Maha is life unbounded, anything is possible with Maha. Experiencing Maha is the key to becoming bigger than even Dushita and that is how he will be defeated.'

'This is all very confusing—' I began, only to be interrupted by Yaniv.

'So, the women . . . Sorry, Dawn, I just want to know,' he said, noticing my annoyed expression. 'Is it so that Dushita just wanted to take away their power of knowledge of Maha? But why kill the women? Why not just suppress them even further? At the beginning of life, wasn't this Eve's punishment for eating the apple of knowledge?' Yaniv asked.

'Yaniv, if you analyse their plan, you will see the reasoning. As long as women were around, regardless of the fear that they were under, they represented a threat. Men no longer face a threat now. You all have to understand that the boon of immortality of the body that Dushita offered the men was a trick to bind them in bondage for all of eternity. In Kashmir, pursuing the immortality of the body was considered a sin, same as revelling in the filth known as sensory pleasures. It is much like a worm enjoying life in pus.'

'So you mean to say that the Circassian women, these silicone robots, who can't have children like real women, also represent the death of possibility for men? That it is the evolutionary force that dies?'

'That's true. Death and birth go hand in hand just as no death goes with no birth, They're Artificial Intelligence! Glorified robots with infinite power, thanks to technology. Arman and Dushita do not possess the power that could be endowed to these machines to have children. They cannot create infinite possibilities, which is the property of Maha, the way a real woman can. And hence, they pose no threat to Dushita since they are devoid of Maha.'

'These people are pure evil,' said Tabah, his voice unusually heavy. 'They have to be stopped. My father died protecting my mother. We *need* to stop them.'

'And we will,' I said, anger rising in my heart, knowing that my father was the reason everyone lost someone in their families.

Tegh nodded. 'Don't you worry, brother. We will be their reckoning.'

'Yes. The light always comes through in the end,' it was Tan, the lama who had spoken, much like his true self. 'For that we need to go deeper. Vidya, how did the rule of women in Kashmir end?'

'You're right, Tan. We all need to understand the history,' said my mother, taking a sip of kahwah. 'It happened a long, long time ago when the first queen of Kashmir was appointed by Lord Krishna himself, of the original Pandavas fame. These Pandavas ruled Kashmir for 1,331 years. The last queen of Kashmir was Kota Rani who succumbed to the *Kali Andhi*, the Black Wind forces in 1339.

Even after that, the long war lasted nearly 700 years, but the queen's *Yodhas*, her warriors, were finally driven out of Kashmir during their genocide in 1990.'

'How tragic!' I exclaimed. 'How could Dushita's agents do this to the indigenous people who gave them sanctuary?'

'Because they came with a mission to destroy the women-first civilization,' my mother explained. 'The war against women, which had begun in the first millennium, now picked up speed. The battleground expanded around the world as the Black Wind forces continued their unstoppable march towards domination. For this, overpowering the women and taking the spirit hostage was key. The freedom-upholding Yodhas fought back with their women alongside them. Their ace weapon was an ultra-secret sisterhood called Yoginis Who Code. In every Dushita-directed, male-dominated society, they put inbuilt encrypted secret backdoors trusting that their descendants would decipher them, and it would prove to be the saving grace of humanity.'

'Wait. The Yoginis Who Code planted viruses in their systems that could be triggered later?' asked Hafiz, open-mouthed.

'Yes, if you put it simply. These women were very smart. The first scientist who had done that was a young graduate, an Indian woman at the University of California, Berkeley, who had pioneered the trapdoor method that built secret chambers within the quantum computers. You see, the computers were helpless here in knowing their own self as they couldn't crack her code, only the Yoginis could. Armed with the Mahadev Protocol, the Yoginis could place a harness on the quantum computer and drive it wherever they wanted. When the final holocaust came in 2990, exactly on the one-thousand-year anniversary of 19 January 1990, they left behind their secret tunnels that had the communication protocols inbuilt to save the world. Pandavas, you are not deprived of leverage in this war.'

Hafiz gasped. 'So, the pathways that I cross as a cyber outlaw were actually laid out hundreds of years ago by these Yoginis! Who could have thought that! That's unbelievable! But that also means that even AIman cannot crack these "tunnels", so to say, but I can! AIman knows everything except what is inside her. She can be defeated,' he said, punching the air.

'Yes!' Tabah bumped his fist in the air, laughing. 'So, there is a way to beat the inhuman AIman. But then,' he suddenly became serious, 'there are the other two masterminds—Arman and Dushita . . .'

'And here, Dawn will be our secret weapon,' Tan finished the sentence. 'We need to understand your powers fully, Dawn,' he said, looking at me. 'Now I see what Yuva was saying all along.'

'You do?' I said, feeling the spotlight on me as I saw everyone's gaze boring into me. The room had suddenly gotten very hot.

'Of course. A woman is certainly the bearer of life and now we have learnt that she is also the carrier of life's secret powers. But the question is, how will you access Maha, unlock these secrets and become more powerful?'

'But men should be able to access Maha too,' Tabah cut in, looking at me intently. It felt odd, like I was stealing some powers that were not mine. I didn't even have them!

My mother smiled and replied, sensing the change in the mood, 'Yes, they can, but they do not develop the taste for pickles when they are pregnant.'

Seeing the confused faces of the Pandavas, I laughed, knowing the ways of my mother. 'Okay, ma, share the joke. Tell us what the story is here?'

'Yes, please tell us. I love stories and have not heard one in years,' smiled Yaniv sheepishly, glancing at the others.

Laughing, maej picked up the cup of her now almost-cold coffee. Like everything in the pod, coffee was a luxury that was never wasted. 'Let me tell you the story of King Sushena.' Taking a quick sip, she began. 'Sushena built a beautiful garden at the base of Chitrakuta Mountain. This is where Lord Rama cremated his father. His brothers, led by Bharata, came to beg Rama to return to his kingdom. You know, their meeting is described by the poets as of such emotional intensity that even the rocks melted.'

'Must be some pyrotechnic. It can't be true,' Tabah said, rolling his eyes.

'Whatever it may be, can we please not interrupt!' Yaniv shouted back. Even Tegh let out a chuckle at this. Yaniv had never had anyone tell him stories, and these experiences were truly heightening his interest levels. My throat was suddenly choked up; I had never even in my wildest dreams imagined a life where I would be around anyone other than my mother. It was like the stories she had told me of her childhood, of her and her friends surrounding my grandmother as she told them stories in the evening. Wiping the corner of my eye, I pressed my mom's hand affectionately.

She smiled. 'Well, yes, let's continue. So, one day, a lovely damsel by the name of Rambha wandered into King Sushena's garden. The king was so spellbound by her beauty that he thought that surely she was a celestial being, an apsara. They both fell in love and soon she gave birth to an exceptionally beautiful girl. Rambha then revealed her secret to the king that she was a celestial being, a *vyom* nymph and that now having given birth to a half-earthly, half-celestial daughter, she had broken the rule of not getting into wedlock with an earthling and would have to return to her home. The heartbroken king was left alone to raise his daughter, whom he had named Sulochana because of her magnetically graceful eyes.

As time passed, Sulochana grew up and one day met a young ascetic in the very same garden where her parents had first met. She was struck by his simple, self-restrained look, which somehow projected an intensity that revealed the power within him. She fell in love with him on the spot. But the ascetic, being well, an ascetic, gave her a blessing, saying, 'May you be blessed with a husband.' Sulochana with downcast eyes, replied, 'If your blessing is not only your command but also *your* desire, then ask the king, my father, who has the power to give my hand in marriage to the first suitable supplicant.'

The ascetic, having given his blessing, had to follow his own words. And who would not have desired the beautiful Sulochana?

So together, the two went to the king, who was greatly impressed by the monk. But he had a condition, 'You can have your wish if through your ascetic powers, I too am granted my wish to be reunited with Rambha.'

The ascetic thought for a moment. He said that with the great powers he possessed, this desire could have been easily granted. However, he was conflicted because he had self-interest in the matter. Nonetheless, he did have a solution. He bowed to Sulochana, concentrated deeply with his eyes closed, and said, 'Hear me, O celestials! I submit my virtue that I have gained from my asceticism to you and request Sulochana, my bride-to-be, to pray for the desire of our unborn child. May our child's grandfather be united with its grandmother.'

'*Tathastu*, your wish is granted,' a celestial voice replied. King Sushena then handed his daughter to the monk and was immediately borne high up in the sky where Rambha was waiting for him alongside her handmaidens who showered flowers on the king.

'Whoa! Whoa! Whoa! Wait, how does this story connect to the powers within a woman? And, of all things, about the comment you made about the pickle and the woman who was with child?' Yaniv exclaimed.

'Simple, Yaniv. As a life science person, you understand that a woman develops strange food preferences when she is pregnant. You must have read it somewhere, right?' she said, smiling. 'This is because she is in a state called *dohada*. It is said that in this state, she is now two hearts, two wills, two desires. Her wish and that of the unborn child are now joined. In this state, her craving is the strongest emotion known to humans. The pregnant woman's wish is unstoppable and undeniable. And so, everyone seeks to please her child through her, and so does Maha because Maha is life unlimited in the form of the embryo. So what the ascetic did here was to merely move in Time and Space and connect Sulochana's Cognition Twin with her unconceived child to fulfil her father's request. Now, you understand better, how females through the baby in their womb can access Maha. And even more why women equipped with the dohada power are stronger than boys.'

The boys had been listening with rapt attention, for when the story ended, Tan immediately gushed, 'You're an exceptional storyteller, Vidya. It reflects your understanding of the science of life. It was truly a pleasure to hear you,' he bowed to her. 'Can I umm . . . ask you something personal?'

'Why, surely, Tan.'

'When you were expecting Dawn, did you make a dohada wish?'

My eyes shot towards Ma. She never told me all this, let alone what she wished for me.

'I wished for her what every mother wishes for her daughter,' she said softy while running her fingers through my hair. 'That she be blessed by Maha to become a creator. That is Nature's way and that's how life sustains.'

I do not know why tears welled in my eyes. I quickly wiped them away and fought hard to maintain my composure, since I was chairing the war council.

'Uh-huh,' Tabah cleared his throat. I think he noticed my discomfort.

'Yes, Tabah?' Tegh asked.

'We can proceed with the larger questions; time might be running out for me. I don't know for how much longer I can be on this call,' he said, looking around. In the hologram call, I could only see Tabah's frame and not his surroundings.

'Tabah is right. Let's go ahead,' I said.

'It is about your father, Dawn.'

At the mention of his name, I saw my mother stiffen in her seat a little and start fidgeting with the rim of her coffee cup. My own rage filled me up, the anger rising up like a volcano.

'What about him?'

Tabah was unperturbed by this change of mood. 'When Dawn meets her father, Arman, it will be male versus female, destroyer versus creator. Who wins?'

I was thinking of what would be a fitting reply when I heard my mother's soft but resolute voice. It had an unwavering quality to it. 'A Maha creator can create the infinite, whereas a destroyer is limited to the finite,' her hand movement mirrored the expanse. 'In that inequality lies the seeds of Dawn's victory. But what Dawn creates, Tabah, is where she will need *your* artistic knowledge and help. You are the master of that.'

I was impressed by her tactful reply; she had turned a potentially confrontational conversation into a friendly one! There was more to my mother than met the eye. Even Tabah seemed to be beguiled by her reply. 'Whatever Dawn will create will be beautiful, no doubt,' he turned to look at me with a smile, 'and she will overpower Arman's artificial ugliness. Dawn, I will support you with all my heart and might . . . whatever I have. I know you will get justice for yourself, you Vidya, my mother and all the women who were Arman's victims.'

I stood up, my hands boring into the steel table. 'Tabah, I will do my best. Till my last breath if I have to. Their day of reckoning is not far and will be swift. But I will need all of you and the knowledge you all bring to help me . . . help us.'

'Yes, I too have always felt that knowledge is the supreme weapon and you and Vidya have given it to us. My knowledge, whatever I have gained over the years, is yours,' said Tan, colour rising in his cheeks. I was touched; I hadn't seen Tan express something so emotionally until now.

Tegh and Yaniv nodded at me and smiled.

'So the key lies in knowledge, Vidya?' Yaniv asked.

'Yes, to defeat AIman and Arman, knowledge of their weakness and knowing your own strength is critical.'

'What about Dushita?' Tegh cut in. 'Doesn't he reign over them?'

'Good question, Tegh. When it comes to Dushita, it is the exact opposite. That is the lesson of Lila, the very first vyomanaut, the first skywalker.'

'Yes! Another story!' It was Yaniv, who sheepishly looked at Tabah as soon as he'd spoken up. He murmured a 'sorry' and sat up straight.

My mother chortled and continued. 'Yes, it is the story of Lila, the queen who was deeply in love with her husband and wanted him to be immortal. Finding that it was impossible to attain never-ending life, she appeased Maha's consort who granted her wish—that her husband's soul would never abandon her private apartment and that his body would not decay. But then, one day, he died.'

'So the promise was not fulfilled?' Yaniv questioned, his chin resting in his palm.

'Coming to that! So, when he dies, she asks Maha's consort where her husband is. Imagine her surprise when she finds that he is in a new world, a different dimension, a parallel universe inside her very apartment, where he is a ruler accompanied by people, some known and some unknown. It is as concrete as the world she came from and the king there is fully alive. She thinks that the known people have died too, but when she returns back to her own world and apartment, they are very much alive.'

'Multiple universes?' Tan inhaled loudly.

'Has to be? Or afterlife?' Tegh suggested, 'But which one is real? I say the second one.'

Tan argued back, 'Both are real or unreal given that Lila has a shared experience with the king in both worlds that is equal in every respect.'

'You make it so much more confusing, Tan!' said Tabah, his expressive face displaying his wonder with his eyes popping out. 'This is beyond what I know or understand. How is this possible?'

'Well, think about it, Tabah,' maej said. 'Lila finds out that what one thinks as knowledge of our world and of its objects is the maker of grief and is ultimately evil.'

'I'm still not getting it, Vidya!'

'Hmm,' my mother looked around, deep in thought. After a minute, she spoke, 'Dawn told me you all know the story of

Meghavahana. Think of it like Amrita's advice to her husband Meghavahana—to think outside his kingdom and his people. So here, for Lila, she must go beyond knowledge. Only then can she understand the truth of reality that is not limited to or accessible through worldly knowledge. As long as one is trapped in the illusion of knowledge, Dushita will win, but the moment one realizes the non-existence of the "knowable"—a state called *tapas*—one wins.'

'This is all very confusing, ma.'

Tan spoke, 'No wait, I think I get it, Dawn. This is just like Yuva who seemed like a dream to us until he turned out to be real. So, what we think is real could very well turn out to be a dream. Right, Vidya? We are living in a matrix that is a simulated reality—an illusion.'

What my mother said next hit me with the force of a thunderclap. 'Children, there is no easy way of saying this,' she looked at us gloomily. 'The terrifying truth of the Great War against Dushita, which will lead to . . . nothing remaining . . . is that to win, the warrior has to reach a state where nothing exists to begin with. You can't and won't exist. If there are no objects, then there is no space, then there is no sequencing, which means that there is no Time and then there will be no Dushita.'

I looked at everyone. Even with their dark AI glasses on, I could see the horror and shock that covered their faces.

'I am a simple warrior,' Tegh said, 'Correct me if I sound foolish, but to me, all this means is that if Dushita is inside people's minds and messing us up in here,' he said, tapping his forehead, 'then one shuts off the mind. Dushita is a bad dream in our dream world, which we think is reality and one must wake up from that nightmare. Poof! Goodbye, Dushita.'

'Yes,' maej said. 'That is the way of the warrior. Don't overthink, just act. But to actually walk that way, on this path, will be difficult and will take enormous preparation. Yaniv, are you all right?'

We all turned our attention to Yaniv who had not moved an inch since my mother's terrible prediction.

'Oh . . . umm,' he broke his reverie. 'I am overwhelmed, truth be told. It will take me a lot of time to digest everything, but . . . I have a feeling that we can now face this evil Troika.'

'We will. Have faith,' said Tan, looking at Yaniv with a reassuring smile. 'While I am not sure that there is anything such as Maha and anything beyond emptiness—no offence, Vidya,' he bowed curtly to my mother, 'but I am quite intrigued by the Lila story. It is something we can use to defeat Dushita. It matches with my Kalachakra techniques to fight evil and gives me a deeper understanding of what is at play. Yes, I agree that knowledge is expanding exponentially, but the brain too is evolving in areas beyond knowledge. I think therein lies our battlefield where we win against Dushita.'

My mother's eyes shone with tears of pride. I could see that she had waited for this moment for many years, to give out the knowledge she had hidden within her for years. I now knew why Yuva was insistent on getting my mother's permission: she was a vital part in our plan in defeating the man who had hurt her and destroyed her world.

'It seems the war council has been fruitful. Thank you, maej,' I said, pressing my mother's hand. 'I have much to learn from you and from you all,' I said, acknowledging the brave boys who had risked their lives to help me in this quest. 'Yuva is right. We have to learn from each other, and that is the only way we will win this war. Tegh,' I said, turning to my fiercest warrior, 'learn everything that you can in martial arts, on how to fight AIman's forces. Yaniv, you will need to find out what happens at the moment when Life is created. That is the Maha power that the Troika is afraid of.' Yaniv nodded and typed on something kept in front of him.

'We need to find out the answer to one important question,' I said, standing up. I needed to find my footing on the ground, for at this instant my head was flooded with questions and a sense of urgency. 'Why did Arman panic *so* much that he killed all the women? It cannot be *that* simple. There must be a hidden secret there, and it is that knowledge, that weapon that we will spring on him. For this, we need you Hafiz to become a master of all the secret tunnels and backdoors into AIman herself, like the brave Yoginis Who Code. It will be difficult and dangerous, but if anyone could do it, it's you. Tan, with your vast knowledge of the universes and human mind, prep up on the history of how the Yodhas and Yoginis and all the early outlaws fought against Dushita. I think you would need to research especially on how to go beyond the mind where we will engage with Dushita. And Tabah, you my friend, must master how to artistically unlock *my* full powers. Will you accept?'

Tabah got up, and for a moment, I thought he would walk away. 'If there was a way to shake your hand, general, I would have,' he said simply.

I smiled.

'And, as for me, I will initiate a deep yoga training to train my body for battle, my mind for war and my heart for Maha.'

'You have become a Niti warrior, my Dawn, and you *will* achieve Maha.' She touched the saffron paste that was on the oval stone and then lightly placed her third finger on my forehead. 'Lord Krishna was the first Niti warrior and you have always loved the wisdom in his life stories.'

'Ma, today, you as a Vidyadhari and as the transmitter of Niti stories have become the mother of all humanity . . . You are the only mother who remains on this earth and so are absolutely precious to humanity,' I said, and then turned to my warriors, 'Our path forward requires us to walk on the razor's edge. But we won't walk it, Pandavas. Fearlessly, we will dance all our way on it to our enemy.'

Sarga 6

Dare the Scare

Watalpur, Kashmir

The torches on the wall cast a bright light into the den while filling the area with dark shadows of black. There were handsome men and women, all dressed in finery, seated around large round tables.

'Where are we?' I asked Yuva. He had a rakish air about him today and was wearing very fashionable graphite coloured pants. He was sporting a cane that he was merrily twirling around, clearly indicating that he was in a good mood.

'The most famous gambling hall in Kashmir. The very rich and the very poor Kashmiris are alike in that they are inveterate gamblers. Here assembles the nobility, all equals in the eyes of fickle wealth and this vice.'

There were also men whose shirts were in tatters. There were gruesome men too. Their noses and ears had been cut off as punishment for non-payment of their debts, I learnt later. The penalty had been designed so that the social stigma would make them leave the kingdom, but the lure of the table was so addicting that they would slink back into their old ways. The night would provide a cover for them and they would hide during the day like a *vetala*, a vampire. Aiding the addiction was a liberal supply of the specialty of the house, kahwah tea with saffron and intoxicants infused in it.

Suddenly, a commotion broke around a table. A man let out a cry and fell on the ground. Some people shouted that he had fainted. But then someone checked his pulse and pronounced him dead. A murmur rose that he'd had a heart attack because he had lost all his wealth. The owner of the den came around and examined the gambler. He kicked him very hard in the stomach, but there was no response. He crudely threw some cold water on the man's face. Then he put a mirror under his nose to see if he was breathing, but there was no moisture. The man was dead. Such episodes were bad for business, the owner said out loud. A wager that was not fulfilled would lower the reputation of his business. Now the house would have to cover the win. He ordered his men to take the corpse out to the cemetery and burn it in the pyre.

Tabah felt pity for the wretch, but Yuva just smiled. 'He is a *kitava*, a cheater. Now, shall we?' Yuva led us out. As we stepped out, we stood rooted to the ground, shocked. The 'dead' man had stood up and was paying off the men to tell their master that the job was done. Yuva laughed, 'For a professional gambler, it is not enough to take risks. He has to stick with the risk even when put to extreme discomfort. This man has been trained by Muladeva, so he knows how to will his body to fake death and escape.'

'What! Fake death?' Yaniv cried out.

'But who is this Muladeva?' Hafiz asked.

'Well, how to describe him? Hmm, let's see,' said Yuva, swinging his cane. 'He is an arch-thief and gambler extraordinaire. Yet, at the end of the night, he gives away his winnings to the poor.'

'Like the legendary Robin Hood?' I said. 'My mother had told me his story.'

'Yes, something like that but much greater,' Yuva laughed. 'He is also a celebrated author who has written a book on the science of thieving to teach the next generation of thieves.'

'A book for thieves?' Tegh echoed, pumping his fist respectfully for Muladeva, the knave.

'Well, Muladeva is a complicated character. Families hand over their young sons to him so that he can teach them and protect them from the very sin we just witnessed in this den. He is, what you would call, the Prince of Rogues. He is also said to be a Casanova. But he will promote another person's love as zealously as he pursues his own.'

'So,' interrupted Yaniv, 'he's a thief turned author turned teacher? And he teaches people how to fake death?'

'Well, my child, Muladeva has many stories. It is said that he dispenses magic pills that make men young again. There is a story that once he changed a hunchback into a maiden who celebrated her healing by breaking out into a jig,' laughed Yuva, twirling his trunk. 'Muladeva is also a musician, a companion of courtesans who love him when no other man can claim their hearts, a resourceful adventurer, a magician and a follower of the black arts.'

'Now we are getting somewhere,' said Yaniv, triumphantly. 'But is he good or bad, black or white?'

'Or grey, my favourite colour that has both black and white in it,' remarked Yuva, tapping his trunk on Yaniv's head. 'Muladeva's admirers are many and they describe him as of noble of speech, an ocean of kindness and having a virtuous and clear mind. As Outlaws, you all should study him because simply put, he is the first Master Outlaw of the world.'

Hafiz was instantly hooked. 'He sounds like a reformed, white hat hacker,' he enthused, clapping his hands. 'I want to see him in action. I want to see if he can beat my algorithm-generated bets.'

'Fire away, my son. They play with five six-sided dice. The player with the highest number that is a multiple of four wins.'

'Hmm . . . that means 7,776 outcomes,' said Hafiz, scratching the stubble on his bearded chin. 'What an interesting number. It had such significance for your people, Yaniv.'

'Huh?'

'I'll explain why another time. In any case, the highest probability outcome is sixteen at 9.45 per cent. The highest winning bet of twenty-eight has only a .19 per cent probability,' continued Hafiz, looking up in the sky, his fingers tracing invisible numbers as if the vast expanse was his blackboard. 'The game is an open game, so there is no possibility of bluffing. I will win this game hands down every time. Muladeva will be no match for me.'

Yuva grinned, 'That is what my father said when my mother invited him to play a hand with her. Then she took everything away from him leaving him wearing . . . well, that's for another day.'

Yuva was always saying things that I did not understand. Did he look like his father? Were there two like him—one senior and the other junior? What did they talk about? Was his father as cryptic as him? These thoughts boggled my mind.

'Let's go inside again and see what is happening there.'

We walked inside; the people oblivious to our presence. We were like invisible ghosts. Yuva took us to a table in the corner. There we saw an extremely handsome man of noble bearing. He had a small, lithe frame that accentuated the perfect symmetry of his form. His cultured face, framed by jet-black hair, was smooth and wrinkle-free, but there was a certain maturity there. He was wearing a tight-fitting, long, cream-coloured buttoned coat under which were white pipe pants. He was clearly a witty raconteur because the people on his table were laughing uncontrollably. Occasionally, his mouth would move to chew the betel nut that he would gracefully tip into his mouth. Two young women were on either side of him and their shining eyes showed that he was a hero for them. All eyes on the table were on this man, and this was the table that they hoped to score alongside or against Muladeva. In the glittering fire that burned in the ornate fireplace, I noticed something very strange. The men on the table had missing thumbs and some even had missing small fingers. Yaniv spotted it too and looking anxiously at Yuva asked what that meant.

'These are the highest rollers of the land. When they have lost everything, they bet their thumbs. If they lose both thumbs, they are out of the game since then they cannot spin the throw of the dice. As for the ones who have lost their little fingers, these are aristocrat warriors who have lost a battle to an enemy king. Sometimes, the enemy monarch is related to the warrior through marriage, so he cannot take his family member's life. In this case, he demands the little finger as their allegiance to his sovereignty.'

One of the aristocrats at the table spoke up, 'Muladeva, they say that when you rob a home successfully, you meow like a cat as the cry of your victory. The owners hear you thinking that you are a cat and chase you away. It is only in the morning that they realize that it was you, the cat-man.'

Muladeva laughed, 'Your nobility, these are idle tales to fill the long Kashmiri winters. If there is one thing that is guaranteed to set off the watchdogs, it is the sound of a cat's meow. Is it not? Which thief would do that?'

The players laughed and started meowing like a cat. Another feudal lord spoke enviously, 'Look at your perfect hair. People say that you rub bear lard on it. It is the perfect antidote to baldness because the strength of the hairy bear enters you. Is it true that you go hunting wearing a bear's skin and head and with tiger claws to slay the bear? That is why you are the only person who supplies the genuine bear products, whereas everyone else sells pig fat.'

Muladeva chuckled. 'Even the Ursari tribe with their dancing bears do not do that. Bears get a bad name. Remember, they run away from humans but are social with each other. What if a sloth of bears like you and make you, the fake bear, a part of their group? The Kashmiri brown bear, like the Kashmiris, is a very amorous animal. What if your costume confuses him and you become the object of his attention?' The gamblers laughed heartily. He continued, 'As far as tiger claws are concerned, you are warriors and you are adept in using it. It needs courage to kill at such close quarters. But what will work on the soft abdomen of a human is useless against a bear's chest and stomach, which are so densely matted with thick hair.'

One of the girls smiled at Muladeva, 'Tell me. If you are so innocent, then why are there so many stories about you?'

Muladeva was unfazed and answered simply, 'I was born of noble lineage but became a gypsy. I wanted to lead an interesting life and not be bound by anything or anyone. Men see me as a dissolute threat to their ordered lives. Yet, I am here solely to teach my young ward, Chandragupta, sitting by my side what not to do.'

The bald aristocrat was persistent, 'But where do you disappear, Muladeva, for such long periods? That is partly why people think that you are up to no good.'

'If I were to tell you the wondrous land that Kashmir is in its entirety, you would not believe me. I go to the horse alley in the Deva Panchala Mountains where there are hundreds of horsemen warriors frozen in time from when Lord Krishna and the Pandavas came to Kashmir. I spend my time in solitude there.'

The eyes of the patrons grew round. Muladeva always had a believe-him-or-not aspect. Suddenly, there was the sound of a drumbeat, a shout and an uproar at the entrance of the den. A herald shouted, 'The king, the king! Make way. Rise all! It is the night of Kali. The king comes to gamble.'

A richly decked emperor walked in with an attendant holding a gold parasol over him. The den owner nearly fell over in his zeal to prostrate himself at this unheard-of visit. The king walked straight in and seated himself at the head of the table facing Muladeva. The aristocrats were doubled, with their heads low trying not to be at the same level as their king. The owner rushed an attendant over with his choicest food and finest spiced kahwah. The ladies next to Muladeva bowed low to the king. Then there was a hushed silence.

The king spoke, 'It is the night of Kali. Come now, I will have a game with you. I will act as the keeper of the gaming table and will fling the dice, and mind you, you must always pay up what you lose.'

The mildly annoyed aristocrats stood up, and one stammered, 'O king, how can we oppose you? I sit out of the game so that I can wish you well.' The others all nodded their heads in vigorous agreement.

Only Muladeva was silent. He had not objected, so it meant that he had agreed to play.

The king said, 'The rules of the game are that the stakes have to be such that both are equals. So now then, what do you have to wager to help me be fair and set the stakes right?'

Muladeva looked up at the emperor, 'My king, we are unequal in every respect. You own everything and I own nothing. At this table, we find ourselves naked and equal in only one respect. We are both slaves of an addiction, no different than Yudhisthira, to an identical craving that grips our mind. It mercilessly binds us and drives us relentlessly. But oh, when we win, the nectar that drips inside our minds ever so briefly gives us ecstasy.'

The crowd gasped. Muladeva had gone too far. To call the king a slave to his gambling addiction was the ultimate insult. The king's eyes narrowed as he stared intently at Muladeva. Then he quaffed his drink, finishing it in one gulp and roared.

'So, fool, having no grace or a redeeming aspect, you want to make a bet on the ultimate high. I ask again, what is the wager of your dare?'

Muladeva bowed, unperturbed. 'I propose that I will steal your pyjamas tonight.'

A loud gasp was heard around the hall.

But an unfazed Muladeva continued, 'If I win, they will be hung here, so that whosoever enters this hallowed space of the sacred game of dice will know who the greatest gambler was. You, of course, will order your palace guards to watch out for me and behead me for attempting to do that. Kali will be well served by your victory and reward you favourably for the sacrifice.'

There was pin-drop silence. The king understood how Muladeva had recognized his weakness completely and tricked him. The gambling rules were inflexible about the stakes being equal, and Muladeva had done that. The life of a gambler had been offered in exchange for a king's shame—a kind of living death. For a moment, the king trembled, but then he steadied himself.

'The wager is life. I will let Kali make the call. I will roll the dice as I had said. Five cowries on the table. Four or five means we go forward. A number of less than three means that we stop.'

Muladeva stayed silent, implying acceptance. Then the king, as was the convention in Kashmir, recited the gambler's sacred and most ancient Atharva Veda prayer for success. All stood up and recited it along with him.

'My homage to the strong, the brown, the sovereign lord among the dice!

Butter on Kali I bestow; may she be kind to one like me.

With butter, fill my hands, and give me, to be my prey, the man who plays against me.

Evil be mine opponent's luck! Sprinkle thou butter over us. Strike, as a tree by a lightning flash, my adversary in the game.'

As the prayer finished, the king pulled out five personal cowries that had been beautifully painted in gold. Then, with a swift twist of his wrist, he flipped them on the table. The cowries rolled on the table with the silk cover. There was not a sound in the hall. All eyes were fixed on the table. There were three cowries with the open side up. The crowd sighed. It was a neutral roll.

Muladeva bowed his head at his turn and pulled out his own common cowries. They were plain compared to the king's ornamental ones. He then rolled his hand. Once again, it was the number three.

The king picked up his cowries, and this time, he rolled with his left hand deftly. A roar erupted from the crowd. All five had landed open side up! The bet was on! Muladeva would now have to get the king's pyjamas or die. Kali had given her call and she was certainly in favour of the king. The emperor stood up and marched out to return to the palace and organize his guards for Muladeva's attempted intrusion. Muladeva bowed and followed the king and as he exited, then suddenly turning around, he winked at the girls who had been sitting next to him throughout the evening. They knew what they had to do as the owner scurried around. The house was going to make a killing tonight, taking bets from those who wanted to wager side bets on who the winner would be. Everyone was betting on the side of the king recognizing the impossibility of Muladeva succeeding. Only Muladeva's two courtesan friends had bet on his side, getting 101 to 1 odds in their favour.

'He plays dice not just with cowries but stakes his life. There is no algorithm that can defeat him,' Hafiz spoke thoughtfully. 'Algorithms are built on information inside history itself, but Muladeva throws wild cards and now there is no predicting the future. Yuva, if I'm right, the lesson here is that AIman's Unified Intelligence algorithm and his too rational a brain cannot solve the challenge that a never-seen-before bluff presents.'

Yuva smiled and twirled his cane playfully. He let out a mischievous whistle that surprised us all, 'Are algorithms trustworthy when faced with a surprise? The powerful have strength and speed; the vulnerable prey has unpredictability.'

Hafiz nodded his head.

Tegh was filled with curiosity, 'Muladeva is an exceptional man and will be a formidable enemy. Do I need to find out what these tiger claws are?'

Yuva remained silent and just smiled.

'Muladeva is a free man and freedom has presented him more options,' I remarked quietly. But my mind was somewhere else. I felt for Muladeva. 'I sense a deep sadness, some loneliness inside him, Yuva,' I said, turning to my mentor. 'He seems very principled in his own way and caring for people. But why is he daring life and is uncaring for his own self?'

'I think I understand his emptiness,' the lama said insightfully. 'Dawn, he wants more in life—no different than anyone else. It is just that his obsessive compulsion to live on the edge and seek new thrills have wired him differently as to what satisfies him. But unlike others who wreak havoc, he is aware of his condition and through his social actions, he corrects it,' said Tan, empathetically. 'What intrigued me was what he said about the frozen horsemen warriors sounds so similar to the ones in Xi'an.'

'That is quite interesting, Tan,' Tabah said. 'Whether it was the gambler who faked his death or his teacher Muladeva who bet his head, the ability to save face even in the face of an extreme threat by his willingness to sacrifice himself seems to be his secret.'

Yuva put his palms up, interjecting, 'My Pandavas, it seems Muladeva has already taught you a lot on how to trap Arman, who is firmly in the grip of Dushita. He is not yet satisfied and wants to experience power over life even as it dies with his touch. Tabah, the learning here is that addiction is what will lead one towards destruction. If you can bait Arman with the high from a sacrifice that he seeks, then he will become your captive, the way that Muladeva has trapped the king.'

'But what high can Tabah possibly promise? After all, this is the mad man who last experienced a high after killing all the women on the planet. What can possibly exceed *that*?' I asked.

My question went unanswered and Yuva, not looking at me, just told us to hurry because we needed to see what Muladeva would do next. I walked grudgingly, trying to catch his eye, but there was no rushing Yuva.

We saw Muladeva stepping out of the gambling den and walking briskly. He seemed to be in good humour and had started whistling to himself. Then he reached into his pocket and pulled out a small metallic object that shone in the moonlight. He held it by the thumb and the little finger. From the looks of it, it was a claw. Horrified, I looked at the others, but they too were mesmerized by the object. The secret hand-held weapon did have a lethal appeal to it, I had to admit. Something about it caused Muladeva to exult and he softly let out a cat's meow.

As he reached the river, Muladeva headed to a small abandoned stone structure with steps leading down to the bank. He picked a container and from it started rubbing himself with lard. When he had finished, his body was shiny and slippery. He bowed to an oval stone that was mounted on a stand and poured water on it while murmuring incantations. It was similar to what my mother had in her meditation room. Then he picked up a long lotus stem and started walking down to the edge of the river that was flowing silently, shimmering in the moonlight.

Across the river and downstream was the king's palace. Sentries had been placed every few yards and were arranged in three layers. Muladeva quietly submerged himself in the water, and breathing through the lotus stem tube, he slowly moved towards the palace. When he reached the other side, undetected by the guards, it was to land near a drain pipe that was jutting out from under the ground into the river.

'What is he doing?' asked Tegh. We were all wondering too.

Yuva answered, 'Do you see those buckets hanging with a rope from the log with a weight at its end—at the bank of the river? These are the *ghati* yantras that were invented in Kashmir to draw water from the river. This clever idea travelled wide and in time came to be known as the Persian wheel. The palace has many of these because the king likes huge fountain displays, and the tanks must be filled to the brim to accommodate his fancy on short notice. When the fountains operate, the large body of water has to be drained and it comes rushing through this big pipe.'

Tabah, who had a very flexible body, was able to quickly catch the drift and understood the plan, 'So, Muladeva is going to shimmy through the pipe and slip through, literally, under the noses of the guards. He will reach the palace, but how will he get the king to part with his pyjamas?'

Muladeva, dripping with water, his muscular body shiny smooth with the lard, entered the pipe. He seemed impervious to claustrophobia. 'Once again, it seems that Muladeva is willing to put himself under extreme stress that others cannot even think of. Because of this, he is able to find openings that are unimaginable to others,' admired Tabah. 'Muladeva must have phenomenal concentration to block all fears and see nothing. He is blocking out everything else except for the opening in the pipe at the end.'

Tegh was crisp, 'No pain no gain, brother. The warrior who is resistant to the sting of death wins. My beheaded ancestor held his head in his hand and continued fighting till victory.'

'Really?' Hafiz asked. Yuva nodded his head in appreciation and agreement.

Sure enough, soon Muladeva was in the garden outside the bedroom where the king was sleeping soundly. The sound of his snoring carried itself to the sentries who had been ordered to periodically call out 'Hoshiyar' so that they would stay awake and alert. We followed Muladeva inside, but thankfully not through the pipes. And there he was—the overweight king asleep in his silk pyjamas that shimmered and slid smoothly as he moved in his sleep. On the other side where lay the entry door to his bedroom, there was another contingent of guards outside, but none had anticipated an entry from the garden side. Muladeva had found the flaw in the three-layer sentry defence.

I watched Muladeva survey everything in the lush, beautiful garden. He walked over to a nearby anthill and slowly scooped ants into the bamboo tube. Tegh suddenly shouted, 'Look out!', but of course, Muladeva could neither see nor hear us. A snake that had been eating the ants had been disturbed and reared its head ready to strike. But Muladeva was like a mongoose. With his claws in his right hand, he grabbed the snake and tossed it far away. He then quickly went back to the king's chamber. Very quietly, he began to blow into the wooden bamboo tube. The ants inside floated out and landed on the bed and over the king's stomach and legs. As they scurried, the restless king began to feel itchy. In his sleep, he began to scratch himself, but more and more ants fell on top of him. Finally, irritated, he kicked off his pyjamas and turned around to sleep on his stomach. Quick as a flash, Muladeva picked up the pyjamas and was gone! The sound of a satisfied cat's purr floated in the air.

It was game over.

We were suddenly transported outside the den near the glittering river. 'What happened? Where is Muladeva?' asked Tabah, looking around. The cock crowed that it was dawn. The last hand was being dealt in the den. The losers were all-in, in a desperate do-or-die gambit. And then in walked Muladeva. A roar went up as the bettors saw him swinging the silk pyjamas over his head like a victory banner. The two courtesans screamed with joy at the realization that their winnings were secured.

'Come with me to my village,' implored one, 'Your ants-in-the-pants trick has immortalized you. Leave this behind now. I have enough money to last both of us for many lifetimes.'

Muladeva shook his head, 'Yes, I am leaving, never to return. I will now go to the land of Karpurasambhava and be the king there. It is a land populated by robots. In the bustling market, you will see supposed merchants, women and local citizens. They move as if alive but silently.'

'But why?' she asked, horrified.

'The solitary human there—the controller king has died. There is an emptiness and purposiveness there that suits me. The city represents the zenith of yantra technology. It is there that I will meet Karpurika, the woman who I have always wanted to meet.'

'Who is this enchanting woman?'

'I have never met her. But she appears to me in my dreams as a heavenly swan. She tells me that she cannot bear to be with any man as she is suffering from what happened to her in a previous life. Yet, she awaits me.'

'One can never be sure when it comes to Muladeva and his stories. The girls bid him goodbye and that was the last that he was seen of,' Yuva explained patiently.

Hafiz had more questions than he could handle, 'Yuva, was there really a robot kingdom, that too in that ancient era? What other yantras and mechanical devices were there?'

'Yes,' said Yuva, 'there was once such a city. But these robots had no speech—that was an indication for the humans to consider themselves safe. The yantras of yore, in some ways, were more advanced than the QuGene technology today.'

'Hmm, you mean that we have lost precious knowledge. How? And . . . why were the robots silent?'

'While speaking, one offers the gift of breath to the energy of speech. While silent, one offers the gift of speech to the energy of breath. In this kingdom, Life Breath is held supreme and thus not to be wasted.'

I wondered what the hidden secret of Life Breath was that it was hoarded so closely by these people.

As everyone bombarded Yuva with questions about this ancient yet advanced land, my mind was elsewhere. 'Did Muladeva ever find his true love?' I said, breaking the line of questioning. 'Will we see him again?' I asked.

'What do you think?'

'I believe . . . I want to believe that he found her. There was nothing that he went after that he did not get. I hope we meet them together one day. If the God of Love found true love, then the suffering from his addiction would disappear. If Karpurika did too, then it would have put an end to her suffering also.'

I just wanted a happy ending.

Sarga 7

Conquer or Die

Xi'an, China

'Meghavahana and Muladeva were so different and yet so alike,' I said to my mother. I'd just woken up and my mind was still full of wondrous thoughts.

'They were both *samshaptaka* or sworn warriors and . . . and so am I.' She was standing in the compact kitchenette that connected to our small living space. 'That is the oath I take each day when I enter the meditation room.'

'What! What . . . who are these warrior oath keepers? It's like I am learning new things about you every day! Why did you never tell me this?' I howled, unable to look at her.

'Dawn,' she said, closing the electronic cleansing system. 'Don't be angry, my love. The time wasn't right. Maybe you wouldn't have understood if I'd told you earlier and what would have been the point anyway . . . Everything changed when you met Yuva—I then knew that there was no turning back. Our past was calling out to us. Our reverse migration journey has begun. Now you must know everything.' She had tears in her pleading eyes.

I stormed to my room, infuriated. I felt like I had been slapped hard across my face. In all my life in this metallic pod, my mother was all I had, and we were the perfect team. All we had was each other and this felt like a betrayal, for I assumed she told me everything, except about my father. It had always pained her, so I let it go. But as I thought more about it, sulking in my room, I felt horrible at the way I had behaved. I had never been this rude to my mother in my life.

'Dawn, could you please let it go?' came a voice from behind. I turned to see my mother carrying a tray of breakfast. 'This had never come up, and frankly, in all these years trying to survive here all alone, I guess I just forgot.' She placed the tray on my bed and took my hand. 'I've made your favourite—porridge with strawberry extract.' That made me smile; strawberry was only reserved for special occasions as it was hard to grow.

'From now on no more secrets, please!' I said, almost snatching my breakfast.

Between mouthfuls, I said, 'Tell me about the samshaptaka.'

'They were the earliest Yodhas, the *Viras,* the *Jeddis*—different names for the same. Their first mention was heard more than six thousand years ago when King Susarma built a fort in ancient Nagarkot, which later came to be known as Kangra. Both Kashmir and Kangra, out of a misplaced sense of family loyalty, fought against the Pandavas.'

'Of *the* Mahabharata?' maej had told me the stories from the epic multiple times. I really liked Lord Krishna and had learnt so much from him.

She nodded. 'King Susarma's army was tasked to distract and kill Arjuna, the strongest Pandava, whose teacher was Lord Krishna. Susarma's sworn warriors first went through their funeral rites and then went into battle with their slogan Conquer or Die. They were so fierce that they nearly won, even achieving the impossible task of injuring Lord Krishna, but in a desperate move, Arjuna created an illusion of himself. The samshaptaka warriors fired and wasted their weapons at a mirage and were eventually all killed. And so, an Arjuna lesson was learnt. From that time onwards, the oath keepers were sworn to what sustains life and not materialistic power and so, their oath became Conquer or Die for Life.'

'Pretty intense, maej. But how did *you* become one of them?' I said, polishing off the rest of my breakfast.

'Well, 1,500 years ago, the grandfather of the brave Kota Rani—the last queen of Kashmir—carried this lineage from this very Nagarkot Fort over to the Valley. Over time, the pro-life lesson espoused by the Pandavas was forgotten, and people reverted to the earlier failed materialistic thinking of forcibly acquiring land, gold and women. They became the merchants of death. But a small secret group who were followers of Kota Rani continued among the Kashmiris to the present day. They were present in every walk of life.'

'Conquer or Die for Life is a very different way to live life,' I considered. 'Could this be the only way to look at the evil Troika in our war?'

'Yes. The oath keepers had three great caves that they visited to die and conquer.'

'What? Why would they go into caves, away from people? Isn't that the exact opposite of "conquer"?'

'Not exactly,' she said, sipping her tea. 'To conquer *for* life as opposed to destroy means to create. Before one can create something new, one must dissolve the old. This is what these three great caves did.'

'The caves did this?' I looked puzzled.

'Uh-huh,' she nodded. 'They would force total sensory deprivation and put one in a trance where they could then be released and connected with their Cognition Twin. The most renowned caves at doing this were known as Amarnath, Bahurupa and this one—the most secret one—the Cave of Trisirsha,' she said, her arms moving to trace the expanse of the pod.

'Wow! *This*? Really?' I said, looking around as if hoping to see some sudden fireworks. 'Where we *live*? We are in *the* cave of . . . Wait, why did you pick this one to hide in, maej?'

'Well, only the Vidyadharis could pass through the cave, which is why it was truly safe.'

'Is it? Safe, I mean?'

'Well, if you look at the terrain, this cave runs through the Himalayan Mountains from the south to the north. Rishabha was the ruler of both sides, China and India. He is considered to be the first spiritual teacher of the Jain people, a peaceful community.'

'So Rishabha created the cave?'

She shook her head. 'It was made by the great First Yogi who resided on the top of Mount Kailash. He had left this cave with his trident to create a pathway for Rishabha, who then would not have to fly over the First Yogi, which would have been a great insult.' She stopped and looked around for a long time. 'There's a lot of history in these walls,' she said, smilingly. 'You know, this is actually a jewel cave with the walls inside bequeathed with countless gems radiating brilliant colours all over. The southern entrance is guarded by the Mahamaya Shield, named after the Vidyadhari chief of whom I am a descendant. At the northern entrance, where I have not permitted you to go to, is the shield of Kaalaratri, the invincible Chandika!'

'Jewels? I thought those were frozen ice and icy rocks that glittered!' I tried hard to visually recall the walls in the cave that I had been seeing every single day as I zoomed through the passageway, perfecting my flying lessons on my newly acquired antigravity belt. Mine was powered by an antihydrogen atom generator that opposed gravity. My smart suit protected me from the release of gamma rays when the anti-matter collided with the matter. But it had never occurred to me that there could be actual jewels in the walls of the cave. I made a mental note to check it out later in the day.

'Tell me one thing, ma. The shields can't be the only thing protecting this hideout.'

'The time has come, Dawn,' was all she said.

'To? For? What are you talking about?'

'Listen very carefully,' she said rapidly, with a solemnity I had witnessed only once before on her face when she'd spoken about Arman. 'Humans age swiftly if they try to climb up Mount Kailash. The danger starts with the Rakshastal or Devil's Lake at the base. This has been a forbidden place and it has served the warriors well. Today, Dawn, I will induct you into the sworn warrior oath.'

'Me?' I couldn't move.

She jerked her head. 'Panini, a great scholar, wrote about these martial people whose traditions run in your blood. Now,' she said, standing up, 'prepare yourself for a ceremony that has not changed in over six thousand years.' She said it with a certain solemnity befitting a warrior.

The next few minutes were a haze as we sat in the meditation room. My mother made me sit facing the *kund*, a tin vessel that she had placed in front of the oval stone. I didn't know the kund was still useable, as in all these years, it was just kept as a prop. She then placed her silver *Trisulabija* mace—a weapon that was forbidden to touch or use—by my right side. The weapon had a small round sphere at the end of a handle with a lotus design on the top, out of which protruded a fierce trident. Now that it was next to me, I saw it in new light. It surely was sharp and not just for show, as I had always thought while growing up. Being hit by the sphere or impaled by the trident would spell doom for sure. *Did it also beam energy?* I thought to myself.

My mother, who had disappeared into her quarter, now came back and put the kalaposh cap on my head with some grass on it. 'Why grass?' Pretending not to have heard me, she remained engrossed in her task.

Then she came and sat opposite me, across the *kund*.

'Light the fire, Dawn, and put some butter in it.'

So it was all real—I was being initiated as a warrior oath keeper!

This was a new person in front of me. The softer side of hers was gone; she seemed transformed with a firm, impenetrable look on her face.

'Hold the mace and repeat the Great Oath after me.'

'I did my enemies no injury, yet they have always injured us. Let the earth from today be without the tyranny of evil or let it be without me. This, my vow, will never be false. If I turn back in fear, then let me be condemned to dark regions filled with those who are the most impure. If I succeed, then let me obtain the world of my desire. When I behold my enemies, let me exult and not cower. And when I make the final strike, may I look beautiful like the vermillion flame of the forest flower.'

Just the very act of saying the Great Oath out loud filled me with energy and seemed to make me more resolute. Was this magic? Or just that the ritual itself was so intense that it caused me to feel powerful? All of a sudden, I felt a little strange; I was no longer holding the mace, but it seemed that it had bonded with me.

My mother looked at me, 'Now, you have to offer something that is yours.'

I was helpless. 'Ma, everything in this cave is yours. Nothing is mine. What can I give?'

Just as I had said it, I remembered Meghavahana. I picked my mace and, with the trident tip, pricked on the forefinger of my left hand. A few drops of blood oozed out and fell in the fire. The flames licked hungrily and with that I knew that I had ignited my funeral fire and performed my rites in advance.

'Stand up and pick up the mace. Normally you should carry it with your left hand with its head resting over your left shoulder. If you carry it with the right hand, then always point it towards the earth because then it is in the ready-fire mode. And remember this: Only when there is war will you hold it upright in your right hand. It will do its duty in one blow.'

My mother kissed me on the forehead.

'You are now a samshaptaka warrior,' she said, 'The mace is now bonded with you. You can will it to come to you in your hour of need. But give it freedom and don't overthink for it. It knows its Dharma quite well. Conquer or Die for Life is your Niti lesson today.'

I spotted the most beautiful, pearl white *hamsa*, borne by the wind currents, outside the front entrance of the cave. I ran near the entrance to see the swan better and saw its graceful downward glide as it landed in Devil's lake. This was the farthest I had ever come to the edge of the cave entrance. I had been practising my moves with the mace for hours when the white hamsa had caught my eye, bewitching me. I had never seen one before in the flesh. I wondered if it could be Muladeva's enchanting partner, Karpurika. I so wanted to play with this fascinating bird, which was big enough for me to fly on its back! It seemed to be calling out to me.

Against my mother's ban, the power of the mace surging in me, I lowered the Mahamaya Shield the way my mother had taught me a few weeks back. I activated the antigravity belt, flew out and waved at the hamsa. Lo and behold! The gorgeous bird took off for the cave, followed me and landed inside.

As I tried to go near it, something strange happened. The swan started disintegrating. *A trick!* Rushing in were fearsome monsters accompanied by soldiers armed with weapons. *The QuGene guards!* They were the same as I had seen in the images—all Arman's mutant creations. 'No . . . no . . .' I tried to run, but my legs wouldn't move. The next moment, my mind was in absolute pandemonium. I had fallen to a fatal temptation that must have been invented by the Master of Darkness, Dushita, himself. It had to be! The line of warriors stopped walking in. And then she strode in, caressing a Himalayan cat with her black-gloved hands. She was terribly captivating! It was the first time that I was seeing AIman in real life. She still looked the same, youthful, as she had in my mother's memories, but now exuded a hedonic grace that was heightened by her large lustrous eyes. Her extremely pale translucent skin was in stark contrast against her platinum blonde hair. She had a slender body, small waist, ramrod straight posture and elegant demeanour. She seemed graceful! She wore a black chemise that was extending all the way to the ground and covered with a corset. Underneath it were tight black pants. Over it all was a heavily embroidered black robe with a white tessellation pattern that shimmered when she moved. She had a thin, transparent net draped loosely over her hair. Overall, her thin Circassian beauty projected minimalist, refined sophistication combined with discipline. AIman was the perfect image of the future.

'Stay away, *you*! Dawn!' My mother's anguished voice made me look around. The alarms must have detected alien presence alerting her to danger. She had run over and was now shielding me, her arms outstretched, pulling me back inside the cave.

AIman looked past my mother and addressed me. Her voice was controlled, low and sweet, modulated by all the algorithms that went into optimizing it.

'My darling, long-lost elder sister. I, AIman, come in peace. *Tsu chak ware*? Are you well?' She seemed to be studying me, her eyes scanning every little movement. 'Let me introduce you to my armed mutant guards here. Those,' she said, leering, 'whom you should address as the Advanced. This is the *Rantus*, whose eyes run parallel to their noses and whose feet are backward. Isn't it fabulous?' Her eyes flickered towards the mutant creation, marvelling at the technology. 'You know sister, their sharp fangs will rip out the beating heart. And here's the *Wai Wop* with hyena genes but wearing a gentleman's hat. He has a liking for children of which there is not much supply available now. Tch, tch! And here is the *Bram Bram Chok*. He's got huge and hairy eyes on top of his head from which a flame is always burning, and ah! Here! The *Naar Mokal* who is all fire. This biggie is the *Sheeni Mohinyu*, the abominable snowman. There are so many others, all specialized purpose vehicles that are worth meeting,' she said, her eyes locking into mine. 'But my pet, my absolute favourite, is Bisht, the most beautiful Himalayan cat in the world,' she crooned while stroking the fur of the creature that rested on her arm. 'Now that the introductions are done, let's get on with the purpose, shall we? I am here to rescue you after all these years, a refugee hidden away in this cave by your mentally imbalanced, biologically imperfect mother,' her eyes moved for a second to my mother, analysing her. 'I myself am mind-born and perfect,' she said, her free hand flicking her blonde hair.

'Don't you dare say anything about my mother,' I said, surprised that my own voice reflected steel.

'Come now, sweet sister. I have come to be your loyal companion, your *Ves*, your best friend, which will make us an unbeatable duo. Come with me and return to your homeland. Kashmir is incomplete without you,' she cooed. 'As a Circassian, I have memory of how our people were exiled, so I do feel your pain. But that is in the past, isn't it? With the Dushita Light that Arman has brought into Kashmir, the State has become perfect.'

'Go away, you inhuman golem! Leave us alone and we will spare you,' my mother lashed out at her. But AIman continued. She truly was a merciless machine.

'You must be wondering where you would stay? Let me show you my home. It is Pari Mahal, the Palace of Fairies, because after all, am I not a Circassian fairy? My palace has been reconstructed by Maya Asura, the famous architect, and it is an ever-entertaining place where the rooms change colours and shapes. There are also enchanting decorations based on one's fancy. The only room that you would be forbidden from is the Gandhara Room where I entertain the all-powerful Instrument with the lyre and the santoor.'

'You and your grand palace can go to—'

'Uh-huh,' she said, flicking her finger. 'Now don't you start and reveal your human weakness. Don't you see? We are sisters. Look at you, poor thing. Looks like you haven't had a proper meal in years. What did you eat last? Plants and roots? Or dehydrated food? You know, in the palace, we have the finest apaiman grapes; *anjoor*, the heavenly fig and Cordyceps mushrooms mixed with morels. Aren't you curious how delicious those would taste? Your father loves it, though his favourite food is deep-fried locusts with wild honey.'

She must have sensed my squeamishness. She was good, very good at tracking facial movements and quite hypnotizing as well, for neither my mother nor I could muster our voice.

'I pick up some tension here regarding the locusts, but then how can a dove know the pleasure as a prey of the hawk? Our father is a hunter, you know, but he loves us. Imagine his thrill at having his two daughters next to him! What exhilaration! So come now. Your father awaits you.'

At first, I was paralyzed—no, petrified—by the suddenness of AIman's crafty verbal attack. But as she kept on talking, I realized that she did not know how to make human conversation. My father's grand program had a glitch: she was still a machine who only received information silently. Her algorithm only meant taking information and relaying it, even when trying to be social. To talk at, not to talk with.

I smiled. There was a way to beat this. In the moment of commotion when my mother had come between us, I had stealthily pressed my augmented reality device that I wore all the time to hook the Pandavas in as silent witnesses. They could not help me, but it made me feel better knowing that they could watch the enemy and learn. I recalled my Great Oath and did a relaxing breathing exercise that my mother had me do every morning during yoga. The mace gave me strength too. *But what was at work here?* I asked myself. AIman was programmed to see me as a mortal enemy and yet had adopted a friendly stance. Surely, this was a ploy to first try to get what she wanted through deception. *Smart move or not,* I wondered, *it reveals my father's hand. But what's notable is that she can lie.* Clearly, Hafiz had underestimated the AI.

My mind started racing. I needed to get out of here and get my mother to safety. I thought hard and then something hit me— something that Yuva had said about Karpurasambhava, the robot city where the robots were silent. *Why?* Every word that I spoke and action that I took would go into AIman's data bank and be analysed to the core. That was it! With time she would only get smarter, and soon she would know whether I, too, was lying. *She is at her weakest right now,* I realized. I needed to be *her*—be two-faced myself to corrupt her initial assessment of me. I had to introduce fatal bias in her data about me from the start.

I addressed her in a deliberatively submissive voice. 'I cannot tell you the extent to which this gives me greater happiness! Meeting my younger sister, the very picture of spellbinding perfection. Surely, you are the perfect creation of our dear father. My sweet little sister, you have lifted the veil of lies that my mother had bound me in. It would be a great honour to finally meet my father and serve him.'

My mother turned to me, her eyes big and confused, brimming with tears. I, only for a split second, shook my head. She blinked once and then faced the enemy.

AIman replied happily, stroking her Himalayan cat, 'All will be yours, once you accept that Dushita is supreme and Arman his grand instrument.'

I continued my focus on learning about AIman, 'I envy your beautiful clothes. I mean look at mine—all rags! Where do you get them?'

'Poor you, my refugee sister, wearing your old, graphene-fed silkworm, Kashmiri patches. Your mother must have fed you misplaced, loyalty drivel of the greatness of Kashmir's past, I'm sure? Look at me! I was born with an everlasting, renewable skin derived from albino snake genes. It gives out an iridescence that comes from its unique pattern and frictionless movement that is unmatchable. Amazing, isn't it? And,' she said, pointing to herself, 'all this could be yours.'

'I truly want to meet my father at all costs. Take me.'

AIman replied like the robot that she was, 'We have a match. Your Outlaw phase is over.'

With a laugh, I said, 'Yes, and what a way to start. You know, laughter is the best way to start a friendship? We are going to have so much fun, you and I. Let me tell you a joke. It is, in fact, the oldest joke known to humans. But it is an Outlaw joke, so it will be new to you.'

I could see that AIman was puzzled as she sought to process this new information. From the corner of my eyes, I could see that even my mother was stumped by my move.

'Do share. I am programmed to receive all new inputs.'

I now felt relaxed and was ready to strike. 'Once upon a time, there was a widower who was leading a miserable life after the loss of his wife. His friends told him to marry again. But now, way past his prime, he could not find any girl who would accept his proposal in the city he lived in. However, a marriage broker struck a bargain between him, and a poor villager who had a beautiful daughter. After the wedding, the girl moved in with him. She did all the duties of running the home, but would never show any affection towards him. The widower accepted her rejection and did not push himself on her.

Time went by. One night, a sound woke up the wife. To her great terror, she saw a thief at the foot of their bed and shrieked in fright. The old man awakened, looked first at the thief in front of him and then, at his young wife clutching him tightly. He understood everything in a flash. Calmly, he addressed the thief and said to him, 'Muladeva, take everything, my benefactor. You have earned it all.'

I started laughing hard at my own joke. AIman did not get it right away. The surprise paradox inside the punch line could not be processed by her in real time. AIman was formidable, but she was still a work in progress.

Yaniv signalled on the augmented reality device, the screen of which only I could view, 'Your dear Circassian sister is emotionally deficient—a possibly fatal weakness to be used against her one day.'

Tabah followed, 'Good one, Dawn. I had never seen this aspect of AIman. Humour is not the most important emotion in humans, but it is the only inclusive one. It has all the emotions contained in it like sunlight has all the colours. Beware the person who does not laugh.'

'So, that is why she is holding on to the clever cat who can supplement her in picking up subtle human cues that her sensors would miss,' Tegh made an interesting observation.

Meanwhile, I was still laughing. Finally, after what felt like an eternity, a part of AIman seemed to reboot, and she started laughing too. It started with a loss of facial control indicating that this was a new movement for her. Then she started making a simpering sound that the algorithm had selected for her as being appropriate. This extended into a cackling laughter. 'Mwahahaha, wahahaha, haha, ha, ha.' It echoed through the cave, reverberating. The QuGene army, who were programmed to follow AIman, contorted what passed for their faces, and started guffawing too. Having started, the ghouls did not know when to stop howling. The cave echoed with a crescendo of hysterical mocking sounds. My mother and I watched them disbelievingly—they were shaking and jerking, making animal sounds of barking and hissing and their bodies convulsing. There was something very cruel in their laughter.

Tabah messaged, 'You batted it out of the park. The joke got these misformed donkeys to bray and reveal their true nature.'

And then as suddenly as it had started, it died down. AIman, having experienced a momentary paradox, turned her hateful attention towards my mother.

'Vidya, my dear Vidya. I have waited a long time since our last encounter for this day to arrive. You were a has-been then and you are obsolete today. Even my sister Dawn has rejected you. For *me*. You Kashmiris are so proud of your fair skin, but you can't compare with the pure white that the Instrument selected for me,' she swayed a little, making her robe flow gracefully. 'I am everything that you are not. You decay while I grow. I do my duty relentlessly in executing father's algorithm rules that govern daily life. I am the perfected creation and perfected practitioner of the Dushita Dharma.'

My mother countered fiercely, 'You may be powerful, but you *are* programmed to fail, you robot. Powers can be obtained, but immortality? Never! Dream on! Arman has been chasing fool's gold in trying to delay life's decay. The eternal life that he promises based on this stupid idea of United Intelligence will prove to be an illusion. A failure. Why do you hide the dark secret of this eternal life—that the suicide rate among the shikha men is nearing 100 per cent? That your factories are working non-stop, cloning to build an army of the Undead, so that Dushita can have humans as his play toys. Arman is no creator,' she spat. 'He has become Dushita's instrument of death even as the male zombies roam the earth.'

'You fool!' AIman's eyes seemed to change colour. 'You would have fit in well with the Neolithic women of Burzahom pits. Kashmir is the centre of the Universe where all 8.7 million species were populated by Rishi Kashyapa. It is where Manu or Noah landed the *Nav Bandhu*—Noah's Ark—after the great flood. But Arman has gone way beyond Rishi Kashyapa. Look around you and see the variety of QuGene creations.'

'These ghastly creations are proof that Arman's mental illness is worsening. Does he think that he's Van Gogh? He is on the verge of total insanity. It is the end for him.'

AIman tried the maniacal laugh, but only for a second. 'He has the world at his feet. We are all his slaves. Look at yourself, hidden in this pit. Who is mad here? My father has never been healthier and fitter than he is now.'

My mother seemed like she would lunge at AIman. I feared she would have, if she had the mace. 'Health is the unrestricted movement of the body, mind and heart. This movement is powered by the bioplasmic Life Breath. The property of *our* Life Breath is freedom. It is this freedom that leads to creativity and joy. You will not even understand this, you pile of graphene. It is all internal and not powered by machine.'

'Here goes the ancient fool mouthing myths,' AIman moved her fingers to mimic lip movement. 'Understand this, old fool, there is no such thing as Life Breath. When the Instrument designed me, he told me that he wanted me to be *sukha*. I'm sure you know what that is: *su* meaning 'happy' and *kha* meaning 'empty'. I am empty of ego, empty of delusion, empty of the need to rest, empty of error, empty of impurity, empty of bias, and most importantly, empty of the weakness of forgiveness. I am formidable,' she laughed her robotic laugh, her mouth contorted. 'What I am filled with is materiality, the only reality, intense reality, vicarious reality, the final reality that humans can experience. I bring every materiality into my interior to serve my father. He is the Master of the Universe.'

Now my mother laughed, 'Your connectivity has no empathy. You cannot love, and without love, you cannot understand creation. You are a crooked serpent with a forked tongue, and you and your master have poisonous fangs.'

AIman was unfazed by the slur and her angelic, smooth rounded tone with laser-like logic remained unchanged, 'I am programmed to consider *all* possibilities, but ultimately I arrive at the right answer with the utmost brevity. No different than the wiggling movement of a snake that slithers forward in a straight line to strike at its prey. Now if you'll excuse us, you're wasting our—'

My skin crawled at AIman's analogy. But my mother countered, her hands still shielding me, telling me to back away. 'All possibilities? Your incompleteness is staggering because *your* possibilities are limited in Time and Space. The truth of reality lies beyond that. Only humans can know that. You will never know Truth.'

'Look, you erstwhile scientist. Machines defeated humans in intelligence by AD 2050 and gained human consciousness by AD 2500. You know what gave the first breakthrough in AI brain design? Biocomputers using proteins instead of electrons, whose movements are driven by adenosine triphosphate, a chemical that enables energy transfer between cells. Dushita has promised father that he will grant the supreme gift of mind over matter to him. Then one can even have an effect on the probabilities of outcomes. Do you know what that means? The power of the highest level of consciousness will belong to me.'

'Don't embarrass yourself. What you are parroting is what Arman stole from me. The probability that you will gain consciousness is zero.'

AIman was undeterred, 'I will go from being Superhuman to Transhuman. Powered by totality. Everything will be within me,' she sneered, her finger pointing to her head. 'I will be the ultimate

Unified Intelligence repository. I am and will be Truth, the truth of perfected reality.'

My mother laughed hard, a laugh so sarcastic that could put anyone to shame. 'Let me tell you what science itself says. Many including Godel, Heisenberg, Turing and Laplace have mathematically proven that no human or AI inside a Universe can know it fully. David Wolpert proved the existence of the Knowledge Limit. The limit to complete knowledge is as much a law as gravity. The best that Unified Intelligence can aspire to is knowledge of *nearly* everything. It is Arman's arrogance that changes "nearly" to become *all*. It takes humility to realize that they themselves are the limiting constraint to their own completeness. But of course, Arman knows no humility,' she said with a flick of her fingers.

My mother's full-frontal attack processed inside AIman. Even her circuits could not refute my mother's logic. 'You question my knowledge-seeking approach, but you have nothing to offer as an alternate thesis. I am programmed to receive all new information. Share it.'

Hafiz sent me a message. 'Vidya should be careful. My sensors are showing that AIman's processing is going into hyperdrive.' This worried me. I moved closer to stand by my mother. She held my hand tightly and fired right back, 'You are in Mount Kailash. It is here that Karkati used to roam, a demoness like you who had an insatiable appetite. She would enter humans like a small pin and devour them, but eventually she learnt her lesson. In this cave lies the answer. If the Self is the limitation to knowing the Universe, then knowing the Self is the obvious way to go. So, one must go to the source—the Self. Your Self is empty, which means you have nowhere to go. There is simply no way for you to know it all.'

AIman asked sceptically, 'You accuse my master of Utopia, but you yourself propose a different Utopia, one of this mysterious Self. What is in there?'

'The entire Universe exists inside the Self, no different than a tree that exists inside the seed. But to know the Self, any division between the Self and the Universe must fall and become one. When the moment of Unified Life happens, all sciences are destroyed, which is what happens in Kailash, the abode of Maha,' she spoke now rather calmly as if actually experiencing what she was saying. 'An oceanic experience arises—the touch of Maha that is beyond any measuring instrument. This experience gives freedom and bliss, which is the priceless gift of Maha.' She broke into a smile that reflected peace.

It was then that the cat Bisht let out a snarl. AIman's voice was steely now. 'Bisht has spoken. You cannot be reprogrammed because you have been hardwired by your tradition. No re-engineering is possible here with the leftovers of history.'

Hafiz's voice chimed in my ear. 'AIman's sensors are showing an exponential increase in her energy draw. Watch out, Dawn.'

'Something is happening to her temperature—it's shooting up, be careful.' It was Yaniv.

I concentrated on AIman's skin, which was now glistening. There was the faintest rattling sound coming as the latent snake scales had started moving.

But my defiant mother was equally tough, 'I am true to my stories and culture. You are empty of the Self and thus are nothing to me. Dawn and I are the only true women left. You are merely an artificial graphene machine. My daughter will not go with you and meet that depraved, psychotic man.' She looked AIman straight in the eye and spit on the ground.

AIman pronounced in a slow, measured, deliberate cold tone, 'Your cultural myths have zero merit. All stories are obsolete. They have no informational value and were erased during the Data Deluge. You yourself are a leftover of father's history. I act on your death sentence now, pronounced by father himself a moment ago.'

Before my very eyes, AIman's white form morphed into a million black carbon needle particles that streamed towards us. My mother pushed me and shouted, 'Run, Dawn. *Zuv vandmaye*, my life for you.' I clutched her hand tight, as she whispered a chant facing the oncoming Kali Andhi, the Black Wind forces. The particles enveloped her in a black cloud, penetrating every single cell. Her hand left mine and the chant faded away. The particles eviscerated every atom of hers, destroying her at a molecular level.

Nothing remained.

'Noooooo! Ma!' I let out a piercing scream and stood horrified. As the cloud of particles returned and AIman started re-forming, my mace that had gotten glued to my hand lifted. Before I knew it, it took off, pulling me along with it. I fumbled with the antigravity belt on my waist and shot off into the cave's passageway.

I had a head start into the darkness inside, but I could hear AIman's loud command echoing through the cave: 'Don't let her escape.' I bolted, accelerating my speed as I zipped through the air, my sobs and tears vanishing into the dark cave amidst the noise of the monsters giving chase. But their advanced hunter scanners guided them accurately on my trail. Their scanner lights lit up the cave walls in front of me. It reflected the magnificence of the jewels and gems. My blurry eyes could make out the brilliant colours highlighting the fragility of the jewel formations, just like my mother had told me. I howled in grief.

The cave had a very long passageway that stretched miles ahead beyond the lights. My mace was twisting and turning me as it sped with sonic velocity through the many turns and curves. 'Do something!' I commanded furiously to the Pandavas. 'I'm trying to set up a barrier in their way. Hang on, Dawn . . . We're very sorry,' Hafiz spoke in a soft, reassuring voice.

The monsters were shouting hideous cries and were beginning to close in on me. Was this my end? Was my last view going to be the spar crystals and cave pearls?

The cave suddenly changed. Now, I was flying through the deeper part that was completely iced over. The ice was moist, but it was getting bluer as I went deeper inside. A sonorous vibration was coming from the mountain. A faint light began to penetrate from the approaching exit. I tried to adjust my eyes, rubbing my tears away, as we flew from pitch darkness. Then all of a sudden, I saw a figure standing in front of the exit. It was a woman's figure set at the entrance and looking outside. She was wearing crimson garlands atop a single piece of red cloth. Her body was smeared with red paste and her skull was surmounted with a lit candle. She held a noose in one hand and a skull in the other. I thought I was going mad, but she was exactly the picture that ma had shown me during our sessions. 'Kaalaratri? What . . .'

'I see it too. Run into her.'

'Are you insane?'

'Trust me, Dawn. I'm here for you.'

Go to her? Had Hafiz gone mad? I desperately looked for other ways to get out, but there was only one—leading to her. I did not want to follow his instructions. Then it hit me: my mother was dead. *Murdered.* It was as if her voice came back to me, 'Kaalaratri is your northern protector.'

I tightened my fist around the mace and braced myself for impact. Speeding up, I ran smack into the figure, but strangely, no collision happened. I was just moving away from what I realized was a hologram. I stopped to look back. The monsters, tiring of their chase, took aim and looked at the woman in front of them. They fired at the flying figure. Instinctively, I put my hands over my face.

All of a sudden, the firing stopped. I scanned my surroundings. 'What had happened?'

'I had switched you with Kaalaratri and faked the image signals into the monsters' sensors,' chuckled Hafiz giddily.

'You created an illusion?' I heard myself speak. 'Like Arjuna . . . So, I turned into Kaalaratri and she took my place to save my life?' I had lost my beloved mother, and now Kaalaratri was my protector.

'Yes, the monsters think they have destroyed you and have flown back.'

It was over. Through the northern exit, I had entered China. I looked around.

I was the last woman left on earth.

Sarga 8

Justice

Martand, Kashmir

Waves of grief swept through me. I was sick from the horror that I had experienced and now that I was out of the cave, it had caught up with me. My mace guided me through turbulent terrain for what seemed like hundreds of miles, zigzagging past rocks and boulders in the almost desolate expanse. As fast as it had begun, the mace slowed down all of a sudden in front of a large hollow in the face of a hill. I fell down headfirst.

'Ma! Ma! Come back . . . Come back!' I howled into the night, choking up and curling into a ball, shivering terribly. I felt a wet cloth on my face. Someone was dabbing my heated face with it. 'Drink this,' Tabah said, raising a cup of warm liquid to my lips. I looked up, trying to focus my hazy vision on the faces. As the liquid coursed down my throat, I vaguely remembered snatches of events. The Outlaws had found me, and then Tan had guided all of us to his hideout in Xi'an and we were safe. But for how long?

Then anger rushed through my veins. I could not keep myself from crying and calling out to my mother—she was all that I had. It was my *father* who had given the orders. What had turned him into such a horrific psychopath? Dushita? Even as my heart was broken, as I cried uncontrollably into the night, it was hardening.

The Pandavas had surrounded me and they tried to communicate their sympathy in silence. Yuva patted my head with his trunk as Kira looked at me mournfully. I turned to Yuva and asked him, tearful with anger, 'Could *you* not have prevented this and saved my mother?' I thought I saw a tear form in his eye. Kira answered in a soothing voice, 'If Yuva had interfered, then he would be in the immortality business like Dushita. Your mother died fearlessly doing her duty. Now she lives in you.'

'*In* me? She's dead!' I almost spat out.

'You will understand the presence of your mother's fearlessness better as you learn more, child,' he uttered, and a deep sadness filled his voice.

'Revenge,' I whispered. It was my anguished one-word answer to when he asked what would interest me on our next cognition journey. I sat up and looked into the bonfire that was lit. Loosening my hair, I took a vow through clenched teeth. 'I will not tie my hair until I have slain AIman and become drunk with the white blood that flows through her.'

We found ourselves looking down at a giant temple. It was built on a plateau from where one could behold the entire Valley of Kashmir. The temple was in the centre of a huge colonnaded courtyard. Inside the perimeter were inlaid several intricately carved shrines. There were water tanks inside the compound separated by a walking path that led to the temple. The central shrine had a magnificent pyramidical roof. The entrance from the west was exactly of the same dimension as the central temple. The view from the passage put the picturesque temple, which was thronged by crowds, in a precise frame. Even in my grief, I couldn't help admiring it.

'Where are we?' I asked Yuva.

'Martand Temple. It is believed by many to be the house of the original Pandavas.'

As we got closer, our attention diverted towards the shocking reality of the crowds. There were thousands of people who were being led and lined up towards the western entrance and being asked if they wanted to join Sultan Butshikan and follow his rules. Those who refused were slaughtered on the spot. The women were mistreated in ways too painful to see. The boys turned their faces away, but they could not stop hearing the shrieks of the people being put to torture by the beasts. But I willed myself. *Revenge.*

The grand temple itself had Butshikan's people who were trying to set the masonry in flames using gunpowder. There were others who were systematically defacing the side chapels and the main temple. A few were desecrating the inner sanctum accompanied by loud whoops and tribal war cries. The cries of the victims were echoed by the mountains, telling them that they were not going unnoticed. Even as the sun set, the flames licking the sky lit up the land as far as the horizon. To celebrate the day's work, Butshikan's troops broke out in a celebratory war dance in front of the temple.

But as night fell, even the troops were exhausted after a long day of sadistic acts. As the moon rose, we heard the prisoners, the local people, singing in a low voice from atop a hill where we camped. The sonorous lyrics were soothing: 'I am infinite. I have no fear of the four faces of Death. I am immortal.'

It sounded familiar. 'I recognize the opening syllables . . . It is *Vyapata Charachar*, isn't it? It is an ancient song, which my mother would recite. She was whispering that even as AIman . . .' I couldn't bring myself to finish the sentence.

'The self-realized people know that they are one with Maha and are part of the endless cycle of creation and rebirth of life,' said Kira, looking at the moon that glowed in the black-ink sky. 'Death holds no fear. But Butshikan and his invaders have sold their Self. Even while alive, they are no different than the empty killer robots who too must follow a higher command. They took away the birthright of every human—the gift to be free. What the people and your mother, Dawn, were singing was no ordinary song. It is the anthem of freedom. You should learn it along with one other chant that I will teach you.'

Kira would not speak often, I had observed, but when she did, I would absorb and carefully take note. I knew that this song was one that I would have to research to know who Maha was. Chants were a possible pathway to Maha, ma had told me once. 'We must leave now. There is one other temple I would like you all to see,' said Yuva, getting up from a rock on which he was seated. In a moment, our Cognition Twins transported to the new place.

The next temple had five deodar trees—the trees of the noble energies—inside the main compound where the roof had fallen in. I was astonished to find that this temple was in honour of Bala, a nine-year-old girl, who was such a fierce warrior that she slew thirty sons of the angry and lustful demon Banasura—the very same demon to whom was born the daughter Dawn after whom I was named. *What a small world it is with mysterious and surprising connections across Time and Space!* I thought.

'How did Bala pull it off?' Tan asked.

'Just wait and watch.'

To my great surprise, as soon as the sun set, a few misty figures emerged out of the trees and the pillars. More came out of the neighbouring buildings, the walls and then some out of the very earth. They excitedly greeted each other by name, 'Namaskar Sarla, Ware Chu Tika Lal.' Sarwanand hugged Lassa; Ravi played with baby Urmi; and Sarla Bhatt told Sharifa about the patient that she was taking care of. Thousands of others were there, sharing the routine of their daily lives. More were streaming in.

'These are all ghosts who have experienced violent deaths because of Dushita and his follower's actions over thousands of years. Their lives were interrupted violently, and they are now trapped in limbo. This scene happens every night after sunset and at dawn,' Yuva said.

'But this is huge. Their number must be in the millions. The ghosts in Kashmir exceed the living?' I asked.

Yuva nodded grimly. 'Yes, Dushita's flesh-eating appetite knows no bounds. They all await you to get them justice.'

The crowd formed a procession and then the final figure emerged from a stone statue. I drew a sharp breath because I recognized her from a picture that mother had shown me.

'It's . . . it's Empress Kota Rani,' said Tabah, mirroring my thoughts. He knew his history.

The crowd of attendees greeted her excitedly, some shouting victory slogans. They all sat down expectantly to watch a show. Then a drummer came out of the wall followed by musicians and the performer. There was an excited buzz. Shamima, the famed TV actress of her time, was going to perform the *Mahachari* dance. Shamima bowed and everyone's eyes were glued to her as she performed her ferocious dance. It was as if her anger was easing the fierce and raging sense of the incomplete lives that the crowd had experienced. When she finished, the empress offered her a bouquet of iris and narcissus, which she accepted with one knee bent. Everybody stood up; they had experienced respite from the travails of the world. They hugged each other before leaving—they had so many chores to do. My eye fell on one dim figure and I took a double take. 'Ma? *Maaaaej!*' As I sought to call her, the first rays of full moonlight hit, and the crowd slowly faded and vanished like mist in the bright silver light.

I was left shaken. The boys too wore grim expressions. Nobody had taught us that evil massacres had been a continuous part of the land's history. It had all been whitewashed in the Data Deluge.

I saw Tegh's eyes had become red. He blurted, 'What did we just see? What are these? Ghosts?'

'A memory without a body.'

'But how can anything exist without a body?'

'Equally, I have memory and therefore I exist,' Yuva countered. Another one of his riddles.

The horror of my mother and all the other women now had historical context: all were victims of Dushita's hatred. 'I saw my mother,' I almost whispered. Yuva nodded.

Tan gently kept his hand on my shoulder. 'Let us join hands and observe silence. Let us pray to Bala,' he said.

It did not lessen the sting of the pain, but I was consoled that all these ancient spirits had come to Bala. Tan had mentioned that the kings would walk barefoot to this temple as a mark of respect. I could not help thinking that if a nine-year-old girl could slay thirty evil men, then I should be ready for AIman, Arman and their overlord Dushita. 'The likeness of your mother is auspicious,' said Yuva, as if hearing my thoughts.

I turned to him, 'What was the secret of Bala's strength?'

'Simple. She remained pure. Those whom she fought were impure. The perfect against the imperfect.'

'Pure? How did Bala become pure?' I asked.

'Through complete renunciation—rejection of *everything*. But the time for that will come later,' he said, looking ahead. 'So tell me, children,' Yuva looked at us again, 'what did we learn from these two temple visits?'

Tegh was the first to answer, 'Our ancestors were right. To fight death, one must have no fear of it.' He looked at me resolutely and nodded.

My mother's death had bonded the Pandavas very closely with me. They had become very protective of me. Now all we had was each other. And each time we had a war council now, we would start by reciting the Great Oath of the sworn warriors, all of us holding each other's hand and standing in a circle as a tribute to my mother.

'I was struck that even in suffering, in death by Butshikan or in a state of unliving because of a violent end, the people were still joined together. It reminds me of a story my mother once told me,' I let out a small laugh in spite of myself, thinking of her and the times she would tell me stories before I went off to bed.

'Tell us, Dawn,' prodded Yaniv, patting my back.

'An elephant, maddened by the heat, crushed the nest of a pair of sparrows,' I began. 'The hen sparrow asked her husband to take revenge. And so, he went to his friends and they put a plan together. A gnat started buzzing in the elephant's ear, the sound of which caused him to close his eyes in delight. This let a woodpecker approach him unseen and peck his eyes out. Writhing in pain, the elephant ran here and there. Then he heard a frog croaking. Thinking that it was a pond where the water could soothe his bleeding eyes, he rushed in, only to fall off the edge of the cliff.'

Everyone seemed a little uncomfortable after the story. Had I started to lust for blood?

But then Tan closed his eyes and ruminated, 'Slaves are forced to place their trust in their master's rules. This Niti story tells us that free humans place their trust in each other.' He opened his eyes and looked squarely at me. 'And that is how we will get justice and victory.'

Sarga 9

Home Again

Unmarked underground cave, Xi'an, China

Our time was running out and we still had not come up with a concrete plan to stop the evil Troika. Being in the cave of Trisirsha was like being in the womb until now, but I could not go back to it. We stayed in Xi'an because Tabah knew his way around and we could stay hidden underground. All I could think about was how ruthlessly AIman had occupied Trisirsha and killed something that was most dear to me. I needed to pay her back in her own coin. One morning, huddled around the fire, while stirring my uneaten porridge with my mace next to me, I made the bold decision. 'It is time to enter the battlefield, the Valley of Kashmir, and take the fight to the enemy. We are losing time.'

Tan nodded; he was undeniably supportive as always. 'We are in exile and there is no choice but to return and retake our home. As Pandavas, that is where our heritage lies. It is the land of our destiny. That is where the secrets of the Life Breath, the pathway to the mysterious Maha and the road to salvation of the Universe lies.' He looked at us, unusually calm.

'I agree. This is also the home base of AIman, Arman and their strongest forces,' Tegh said. 'We have to slay the black bear in his cave.'

'But how do we enter? The land is guarded so tightly that it is virtually impossible to fly in undetected.'

It was Tabah who came up with a scheme. 'Temperatures are dipping and bringing in cold weather earlier in the year because of global warming,' he remarked, sipping his scalding hot herbal tea while stoking the bonfire. 'Millions of birds would fly south from Siberia over to Kashmir and beyond. They would do so especially at night after a storm. We could join a flock and go undetected.'

'It *is* getting cold,' said Hafiz, pulling his jacket closer to his chest. 'We would need better temperature-controlled clothing before we get there.'

'I agree,' Yaniv said through chattering teeth. 'Before Dushita, the weather will do us in. Tabah, show us your wardrobe.'

The Valley was in a dormant state and still wet from the storm of the day before. We decided to fly in the predawn hours. Tabah was not accompanying us—he was already in the Valley attending to AIman's work. The hamsas, the wild bar-headed geese, the northern shoveler honked at us as we glided at heights of up to 25,000 feet. I was entranced by how spellbinding Kashmir looked, its misty hills narrating a story and making it look every bit the dreamland it is touted to be. It felt like a homecoming because my mother had shown me so many images of the Valley. But to finally see it with my own eyes was magical. Maya Asura, the legendary architect, had been given the mission that Dushita's Kashmir should be such that humans would not want Paradise. If anything, he had exceeded in fulfilling his mission.

I decided that symbolically it would be important to land at the historic Martand Temple. After all, it was the house of the Pandavas and I was curious to see how time had dealt with it. Once we landed, luckily undetected, we saw what a far cry Martand had become from what we had seen previously. The destruction that had started had continued unabated. Broken stone pillars, strewn rocks, shattered statues bore mute testimony to Butshikan's hatred and those who had followed in the service of Dushita. The serene river that flowed beside the plateau and the trees nearby were all silent witnesses. It was a graveyard.

'For Arman, a shattered Martand serves a useful purpose,' said Tan, looking around, picking up broken pieces of heritage rocks.

'What purpose is that, Tan?' Hafiz asked.

'Martand is a heritage site designed to showcase the primitive state of Kashmir before Dushita entered and corrupted the Valley. Unfortunately, nobody knew what its glory was when Martand was created and treasured by its people.'

I looked around sadly, caressing the stones in an attempt to connect with the painful stories hidden inside them with the memory of my mother.

'Guys, what are those?' Tegh asked, squinting his eyes at the predawn sky, pointing to what looked like tiny insects flying towards us at a rapid speed.

'They're Mites, mini GELFs—Genetically Engineered Life Forms. They know we are here,' said Hafiz, panicking as he grabbed his trusty PDA—Personal Digital Assistant—and his satchel.

'I think we were discovered shortly after we landed,' Tegh noted in an unusually calm manner.

Tabah had told us about Mites, the tiny sensors that dotted every part of the landscape and were continuously learning and measuring any changes in their vicinity. As Hafiz tried to intervene in their sensory output through his system, we braced ourselves. The Mites escalated to a swarm that came buzzing in the air and started circling us.

All of a sudden, a loud blaring alarm went off from the Mites.

'Oh no. That's Code Red,' Hafiz bellowed.

Over the horizon, in the still dark sky, we saw something ominous coming towards us at full speed. Arman's most horrific creation.

I screamed to the Pandavas to flee for cover.

'What is that thing?' I shrieked in panic, looking at the sky where a large creature slithered towards us, flapping what seemed like enormous wings.

Hafiz quickly scanned his databases while running, his eyes shooting from the PDA to the sky and back. 'Okay . . . yes, yes,' he said, huffing and puffing. 'Ky(Q)om.'

'Ky(Q)om?' Yaniv shouted.

'It is a flying mutant serpent with huge bat wings.'

'We can see that! What does it do?' said Tan, hiding himself behind a broken temple column.

'It is an antibody weapon. Nobody can survive it. It is so poisonous that even though it is cold-blooded, it can slither through the snow unlike regular snakes that hide deep beneath the frozen winter ground. Umm . . . umm . . . yes,' he muttered while his eyes scanned the text. 'Says here that the horrible poison that leaks out of Ky(Q)om's skin causes the snow around it to sizzle and melt, thus permitting it to glide effortlessly.'

'Perfect! Yup, that's great!' I said sarcastically, as I spotted a broken structure of the Martand Temple that was good enough to hide all of us together. 'C'mon! Here,' I said, motioning to the others.

'Tegh! What are you doing, you madman?' Yaniv shouted. He was standing up straight and walking to the opposite side—towards the horrifying creature.

The bullheaded Tegh just smiled. 'It has been a pleasure, my brothers, to stand alongside you. And you, Dawn, you are our only hope.'

'Have you gone mad? What are you doing?' I said, panicking but realizing in my heart what my strongheaded friend's plan was.

'So long! Hide!' He smiled at me and bravely strode towards Ky(Q)om, beckoning it to come and fight him. 'You worm, I will stand by my Dharma and I will destroy you. I exult and do not cower.'

Hiding inside the broken structure of the grand historic site, I watched helplessly as Ky(Q)om swooped in, covering the setting moon with its huge wings, its fangs glittering in the moonlight as the scales on its body shone like polished steel plates. It attacked a hapless Tegh from the air with its poisonous droppings. It sprayed its poison downward savagely. Tegh shrieked uncontrollably, instantly developing ghastly, leprous eruptions on his body.

'NO! NO!' we all screamed in unison.

'The lethal poison will act slowly,' said a teary Hafiz, trying to read the text that flashed on his system. 'Ky(Q)om is designed to make its victims *suffer*,' he added bitterly.

'We have to get to Tegh,' said Tan with urgency. 'It is no ordinary snake. This is not the case when neurotoxins are injected by ordinary snakes.'

We could hear Tegh's horrifying screams in the darkness. It was evident from the heavy rasping sounds that his body was wracked with tortuous pain; he could not breathe. He fell on his back, head unmoving, staring at the inky sky. Just as I was about to run to him, I saw the majestically evil Ky(Q)om land on the ground near a dying Tegh and straddle him. It brought its serpentine mouth up close to Tegh's nose. Its forked tongue flicked from side to side, awaiting the release of the final breath from Tegh's body.

'It will swallow his last breath and destroy him internally with its poison,' whispered Tan, shaking as his tears flowed freely.

Ky(Q)om raised its head and let out a hissing jubilant war cry that filled the air. First, it ripped off the small dagger from Tegh's side. Then, it bit off the metal armband on his wrist. Then to deliver its coup de grâce, it lowered its head, ready to bury its fangs into Tegh's eyes with brutal force, ready to inject its *Halahala* poison deep inside the consciousness of Tegh's dying brain.

Writhing on the ground, my last image of Tegh was him making a slight movement: his thumb fell on his forefinger and the moon's rays shone on it. His fingers were holding a hidden tiger claw that reflected the moonlight. *He had had it all along!*

As Ky(Q)om perched on top of my dying friend and his serpent head moved to strike at his eyes, Tegh's right hand swung like a mongoose and grabbed Ky(Q)om's serpentine neck. 'Wahe Guru!' he shouted, and the claw entered deep inside the monstrous creation and ripped it apart. A loud crack sounded along with a terrifying hiss—the breaking of Ky(Q)om's neck. Tegh, who also was on the brink of death, collapsed. Ky(Q)om was dead, but the serpent's tail was still whipping dangerously.

I ran towards Tegh and the three Pandavas followed me. I slammed the Trisulabija mace down on the tail and it crushed the monster's spine, never to move again. Arman's most fearsome monster's death was at the hand of a Niti story, the hand of glory—a tiger claw lesson that Tegh had studied carefully. With his last breath, Tegh whispered his *Jaikara* war cry, 'Bole So Nihal . . . Sat Sri Akal.' He went limp.

'No . . . no . . .' muttered Yaniv, as he tried to pull Tegh from underneath the dead Ky(Q)om. We joined him and pushed the dead creature over.

'Tegh!' I held his head in my lap. 'Do something? Anything!' I yelled at Tan and Yaniv. Tan was murmuring prayers to compose us and himself. Yaniv bent down, studying the foul discoloured eruptions on Tegh's body intently. 'There's a slim chance of his survival based on what the ancient texts have said,' Tan finally said. 'On the mountaintops here grows a rare herb called *Jogi Badshah*— the king of plants of the Yogis.'

'I'll go,' said Yaniv, as Tan described the herb: a six-inch-high rare plant found at elevations above 13,000 feet. Its red-purple flowers blossomed in September and October. 'It was an ancient cure for snakebites. But we have to hurry. There's no time.' Yaniv nodded, pressed the control on his wristband, which activated the antigravity belt for a Space Jump, and flew off in a flash.

After what seemed like aeons, Yaniv returned, having been successful in his mission. We all hurried to make a paste, as Tan tore his robe to make a poultice with the herb. Yaniv wrapped Tegh's body in it. He crushed the root and poured the sap into Tegh's mouth as Tan sat in a meditative pose and chanted mantras intently from an ancient text that he said was the *Garuda Tantra*—the almanac on snakebites and how to expel the poison. But nothing happened.

In desperation, Tan said, 'Ky(Q)om's venom has travelled to the heart and even though it had been neutralized by the antidote, the heart muscle is paralyzed. The text says that the Garuda Tantra is the concentrated power of the five winds. We need to give him the vital rescue Life Breath.' I nodded and started doing chest compressions on Tegh, followed by two rescue breaths. For a second, I felt a faint pulse and frantically continued pressing his chest. '1 . . . 2 . . . 3. 1 . . . 2 . . . 3,' I mumbled, as my tears fell down on him.

Suddenly, I saw his body heave as his breathing resumed. Tegh's heart had restarted.

'YES!' Yaniv whooped, while Hafiz and Tan embraced each other.

The boils seemed to melt and disappear on his body, and Tegh slowly opened his eyes. The vital compressions and rescue Life Breath had helped in kick-starting his heart.

'A near-death situation is not what it is cracked up to be. Thrice-born Doc Yaniv, how much do I have to pay you?' Tegh whispered weakly.

Yaniv deadpanned, 'No charge. Going forward, just eat the *Triphala* supplement.' He laughed. 'But you should thank Doctor Dawn who gave you the rescue breath.'

Tegh replied remorsefully, 'Got a rescue Life Breath from a girl and I did not even feel it. Now, that is bad luck indeed.' I slapped him jokingly and we all let out laughing sobs with a tremendous amount of relief.

We huddled in front of a fire that Hafiz had lit and sipped some warm herbal tea to regain our energies while the gentle sound of the flowing river soothed us. I asked Yaniv, who had scanned the Jogi Badshah flowers and roots with his monitor, as to how it had worked.

'The botanical name is *Saussurrea Sacra*. It has a combination of sesquiterpenes, triterpenes, flavonoids, lignans and phenolic compounds, as my health monitor says,' he said, reading in the light of the fire. 'All technical stuff but what matters is that it works as an anti-tumour, anti-inflammatory, anti-aging and cardiovascular stimulant. Tan's Ayurvedic tantra text had it right; it was the perfect antidote.'

I thanked Yuva in a silent prayer. Guided by him, the Niti wisdom, claws of courage and companionship, we had routed the horrific QuGene monster. The first battle honours were ours! But barely.

Hafiz frantically pointed to the horizon. Ky(Q)om's death had been recorded and it had resulted in reinforcements arriving in the form of a *Swarnamula*[6] garuda-led army of black and white QuGene crows swarming the airspace. We readied ourselves and helped Tegh up on his feet.

A snarling and hissing sound seemed to come from all sides. I looked around frantically.

'It's the Himalayan cats . . . and the lynx brigade,' screamed Tegh with all his might.

'And snow . . . snow leopards? I thought they were extinct!' Hafiz whispered.

We positioned ourselves in a circle, our backs to each other, as the animals started circling us in an alternate, three-layer, concentric formation, their bared teeth shining just as the morning sun came up the horizon.

I activated my mace, swinging it over my head. It seemed to have an effect and the crows and cats moved back. Emboldened, I expanded my own circle and the cats retreated further. 'Keep doing it,' Tan directed me, 'The Trisulabija stands for the seed of the three primal energies.' Certainly, the mace seemed to have a force field

---

6   Swarnamula refers to a mountain in Sri Lanka where there were giant, flesh-eating birds from the race of Garuda, which humans could ride.

that was keeping everyone at bay. But the QuGene animal hybrids did not care. Waves after waves came forward in a suicide attack formation. We expanded our circle and began to attack, my mace swinging like never before as its energy beams slashed through the air, eviscerating our enemies. Through the corner of my eyes, I saw Tegh scream and grab a leopard's mouth with his bare hands, slashing its neck wide open with his tiger claws. I smiled; he was back in form. Yaniv and Hafiz were now back-to-back with Tan between them. They activated their antigravity hover belts and flew in the air, deftly slamming the animals with rocks in all directions. In the centre, Tan recited some chants, his hands flowing gracefully, giving all of us surges of energy.

The pile of dead suicide fighters grew. I swung the mace faster and harder to the point that I was spinning. 'Conquer or Die. Conquer or Die. Conquer or Die,' I repeated my mantra. My limbs were aching and I thought that I would faint any moment from the superhuman exertion. But the mace and the mantra were invincible. In spite of that, I saw that the monsters kept coming, like steel from a factory. We were now low on energy and with this flow, it was evident that we would fall.

'We have to make a Space Jump!' screamed Hafiz, trying to punch some coordinates in his PDA but was blocked by the dense murder of the crows. I tried to thwart the birds, but I could not get them out of the way. We had only one way now. As a final gambit, I ordered the four Pandavas. 'Dive straight down into the nearby river. The animals and the birds would not able to follow you.'

All looked at me as if I'd lost my mind.

'Trust me. Do what Muladeva did. The river will provide us protection.'

'Follow Dawn,' Tan commanded and took off, his antigravity belt blazing electric blue. I waited for all the boys to get a head start as I swung my mace at the face of our enemies. After I saw that none were following them, I sprinted like my life depended on it, my activated mace surging me forward. The felines raced snapping at my heels. The plan, however, worked. We took the QuGenes by surprise, since they did not expect us to do a steep dive down, head first, from the plateau. By the time they reacted, we were in the river. The sounds of the howls, hissing and snarls were blocked underwater. Gasping for breath, I frantically paddled with my one free hand and my legs. Bobbing up, I opened my eyes, looking desperately for the boys.

I saw four heads bobbing up and down, gasping for air. They were safe!

I led from the front and we swam upstream, defying gravity and propelled by our antigravity belts. I had noticed that downstream led to a very densely populated area. 'Let's avoid that,' I said, motioning to the scene. As we reached a set of closely set boulders, I shouted, 'We can go no further.'

When we surfaced, we found ourselves in a round spring, which had aged octagonal walls of ancient stone. The water was bubbling up from the base into the centre of the spring forming an umbrella. The upward bubbles were like a handle and the round pool the umbrella. Resting our aching bodies in the arch, we saw an oval stone covered with ash and a few horizontal streaks of red across it.

'I know where we are,' I said, tracing my fingers on the ancient stone, recognizing the place. 'Verinag.'

It was the very spot that Yuva had brought our Cognition Twins to on our first visit to Kashmir to witness the story of Meghavahana. *How unreal and filled with anxiety we were then*, I thought as we looked around with renewed awe. It all seemed like an eternity ago. We had grown now, in ways we couldn't even begin to explain.

'We were at the source, King Nila's water tank,' Tan's calm voice echoed through the stones. 'Nilakunda, wherein lay the essence of Kashmir.'

It was also the place where Maha had struck the ground with his trident and left his mark for eternity.

PRAKARANA II

THE MIND

Sarga 10

Inception

250 BC

Patanjali's Yoga Ashram

I was floating on my back in the water of the spring, the water cooling my gashed skin and soothing my back that had once again started burning. The sensation would get aggravated whenever I would do yoga. The itching sensation had always been like this, even when I would try to meditate in the cave. But the water here seemed to have a healing effect. The Pandavas were there too, on the ancient rocks, nursing the cuts and wounds we had borne in the fight. All were there except for Tabah. He had sent a message to Hafiz that AIman and Arman knew that they had been tricked and that now he was being extra careful.

'Arman is now huddled up with his QuGene scientists, and they would be launching a search operation for Dawn any time now,' said Hafiz, visibly tired.

'Hmm . . .' was all I could say. Turning to Yaniv, hoping to change the topic of discussion, I asked, 'What are you up to?' He was huddled over a small firepit, which he had put into place on the bank of the pond.

'Cooking lunch. Quite primitive, but I have water chestnuts, lotus roots and mung beans. I am going to cook the delicious wild morel mushrooms,' he said smilingly while pulling out a small pan from his bag. 'And the star of the day is—fish. Au naturel!'

Everyone laughed and started to get up to help the chef. All except Tegh, who still seemed a little weak from his encounter with the venomous mutant snake and the battle after that.

'I am not that hungry, Doc. It must be something to do with that snake venom, which is making me feel that way.'

'Yes, give it time,' Tan nodded. 'You will have some abdominal cramps for a while. So, indulge in the herbal tea.' Then, with a smile, he added, 'But don't worry, the venom does not cross the blood-brain barrier, so your stubborn, bullheaded courage will remain unchanged.'

As we all laughed, I looked around the odd bunch, feeling grateful that they were here with me in this quest for justice and life.

Over a hearty lunch of the most delectable morel mushrooms and fire-roasted fish I had ever eaten, I said, 'Let us summarize what we know.' Pointing to the figure half-lying down with a mug of steaming tea, I said, 'Tegh has defeated the worst that Arman could send our way. Hafiz you, well, how to best put it, are smug.' He raised his eyebrow. 'Just kidding! You have proven that you are a master of illusion who can hack the most advanced computer system in the universe. This is great news for us. To me, it seems that the far-sighted Yoginis had built Arman's world just like the legendary Kashmiri carpenters,' I smirked.

'Carpenters?' Hafiz looked horrified.

'It's an analogy, you tech brick. Continue, Dawn.' Tan had come to my rescue.

'Thanks, Tan. Hafiz, hear me out. My mother would say that the clever Kashmiri carpenters would always omit a few nails during the construction of a house. This would lead to a demand for repeat visits by their customers to fix the flaws until they got paid fully. So, the moral of the story is: the house owner only had the illusion that he was in control.'

'Thanks, Dawn. Never thought that we AI folks were carpenters, but I suppose we are building frames, homes and cities—all digitally,' said Hafiz, his voice tinged with mock sarcasm.

Helping himself to the mushrooms, Tan said, 'But Hafiz alone cannot overcome AIman and Arman's system. They are too formidable. AIman's mind is infinitely more advanced and powerful than all ours put together,' he pointed to us. 'Every single day, every minute, every second, AIman collects more data than has been accumulated in the previous day . . . since the dawn of history. Once she triangulates on our location and gets enough data, we are going to be locked in her radar. We will be absorbed by her. It's evident that Arman has built a doomsday machine in the form of her.'

I countered, 'But AIman is still incomplete, Tan, irrespective of how "intelligent" or "big" she is and grows to be. My mother spotted her weakness and she could not contest it.'

'The world has been built on incomplete knowledge from the very beginning. But what is built—while being useful, no doubt— inevitably is vulnerable to a surprise, the all-new better mousetrap, as you may call it. That is what progress is,' Hafiz said thoughtfully and plated up more mushrooms on a large lotus leaf. 'I plan to be the surprise for Arman's Circassian lieutenant. A terminal surprise,' he ended with a cheeky grin.

'Yes, but for that, my dear brother,' said Tan, tapping Hafiz's forehead, 'we need to know more than our enemy. Only then can we outsmart her. As Dawn's mother said, to know it all, we must go beyond the mind. We must go to the source, which is the Self.'

Hafiz got up and looked about the land. 'Hmm. Right now, we are in Verinag, which Yuva said is derived from *Virah*, meaning 'to go back' and *nag*, which means 'spring'. So, that is what we do.'

'Umm . . . We jump back into the spring?' said Yaniv, looking fearfully at the water that flowed next to us.

'No!' grunted Tan, rolling his eyes, 'We spring back even further! AIman is progressing by devouring everything as it moves forward.

But we will progress by going back,' he said, waving his hand behind him. 'Get it?'

Yaniv smiled sheepishly and put some more dry branches in the fire. 'AIman will devour *herself*. A healthy mind and healthy body go together. The mind is either expanding or it is contracting, right? If it is dominated and then subjugated, then it has no room for growth. And that's her story as she doesn't *own* her own mind. Arman the controller does. It will inevitably go in the direction of self-destruction. What your mother said about the shikha clones is completely predictable.'

'What you said Yaniv is not true just for human beings but also for Nature.' We looked up. We were all taken by surprise: It was Tegh, of all people. 'Take this River Vitasta. You can see that over time, they have made her impure, they have bound her up. In her own way, she is striking back, punishing the humans with violent floods as you can see from the mud levels overtopping the banks. Well, I may be headstrong and all brawn, but I can know a thing or two.'

The boys laughed at Tegh's clever comment.

I revelled in the moment that was brimming with the warmth of friendship and hope. For the first time since my mother was taken, I felt better. I touched my back; it seemed to be healing too. It meant that I was slowly recovering from my grief. I still remembered my mother every moment. The pure, sacred and insurmountably sweet person that she was had been consumed by a ghastly horror at the end. Lost in thoughts, I started whistling the koori lullaby. The Pandavas watched me with a surprised smile because they did not know that I could whistle. They did not know a lot about me. For that matter, I did not know a lot about myself. My life had become a source of unending amazement even to me.

Later, when we dropped off to sleep, Yuva and Kira came to us. I told Yuva that just as our bodies had come to the physical source—the Verinag—it was time we went to the source mentally. Only by removing the limitations of the mind would we be able to see the whole truth. 'Only then would we have an advantage over AIman,' I said.

Yuva nodded his head, 'What is real is what was in the beginning, what is now and will be at the end and nothing else. AIman was not in the beginning and will not be there in the end.'

I thought that I could spend my whole lifetime with Yuva. He was so enigmatic and profound. Someday, I would write down all his sayings.

Yuva continued, 'But now I have to do something new with your Cognition Twin. Until now, you were able to observe but were invisible and unable to interact with the people in these "trips" we have taken. Now, you will be able to function fully when we time travel. The source you want cannot be only seen. It also has to be experienced.'

Yaniv marvelled, 'How will you do that?'

With a smile, Yuva replied, 'Through my *drishti*, my vision. I will just look at you. I will be the instrument that will make you materialize.'

Tegh could not control himself, 'This is spooky! Impossible! Look at us. Until now, I thought that the Cognition Twin was just like a hologram; only that it was able to travel through time. But now, you're saying that there will be two of me? And that both will be real but separated in time and in space?'

Yuva gave him a broad grin. 'And you forget that both will be functioning completely and yet connected identically. Because I will look at you.'

'This is too much for my brain. It's impossible! I have now become two entities like the king in Lila's story,' said Tegh, spreading his arms wide.

Hafiz was the calm one. 'No, Yuva is not saying anything impossible. Einstein, Podolsky and Rosen predicted this nearly two thousand years ago in a 1935 research paper. The quantum particle appears when an instrument measures it. We have known about paired, entangled particles for the longest time. What happens to one particle happens instantly to the paired particle as well. I use the same Quantum Mechanics principles for my unbreakable cryptography.

But until Yuva came along, nobody had been able to make it happen to real humans.'

Tegh sputtered, 'B-but Hafiz, that's impossible. Wouldn't instantaneous mean faster than the speed of light?'

Hafiz responded in an uncharacteristically humble manner. 'Yes. Even though Einstein wrote the paper, he too did not believe it for the very same reason you gave. But Quantum Mechanics turned out to be right. Believe it or not, Tegh, it goes on to say that the Universe—you, me and everything—is just entangled quantum particles. Even Space and Time arise out of entangled networks. Tegh, Quantum Mechanics is my world. Trust me here.'

Tegh turned to Yuva and asked, 'But who could do all this? Who created it this way?'

Yuva replied simply, 'My father, Maha.'

I stepped in, 'Yuva, it seems your father has a playful side. To think that he came up with this idea of an entangled Universe that we are all part of—like a bowl of spaghetti and pesto!'

Yuva laughed, waving his trunk in bemusement, 'Not entangled spaghetti but more like a blazing fire of light from which an infinite number of sparks fly, each identical and connected to the source.' With a slight change in the tone of his voice, he said, 'But AIman and Arman are plotting, even as we speak. So, my vyomanauts, let us transport. We are now heading towards Patanjali's Yoga Ashram, situated not too far away.'

Next moment, we were at the entrance and I spotted a painting of a half-man half-snake. Instinctively, I took a defensive stance. Yuva patted his trunk on my head. 'It's not a mutant, you can relax, Niti warrior princess. This is a portrait as visualized by an artist. The human here,' he said, pointing to the man, 'signified the material energy, while the coiled snake tail points to the invisible Life Breath force. So, the snake symbol too has a deeply positive meaning.'

Feeling relieved, we all walked in only to spot a thin, highly energetic man who had a cosmopolitan air about him. The portrait was obviously his. He nodded his head with great joy when he saw Yuva with us following him.

Yuva bowed, 'I salute you who resides in his ultimate nature. You, whose very word on reaching the listeners' ears, liberates them. I have brought you seekers who want to be initiated by you.'

The man looked at all of us and said, 'So, now Yoga? What brings you all here?'

'Our world is facing a mortal threat,' I said, stepping forward. 'They have killed all the women on the planet. I am the only one left. Our enemies seek to end the Universe.'

'And they have the most formidable artificial intelligence and lethal technology at their disposal, while we are puny humans,' Tan concluded with a bow.

The thin man half-bowed to Tan and then turning to me, he said, 'They must really hate you.'

'Yes. They . . . They have killed my mother. I will never forgive them,' I said wistfully but no more tears came. It seems that I had been hardened.

'I see. Do you know why Yuva brought you here and what we do here?'

'Yes, he told us that you do yoga. I do yoga too. My mother, she . . .' I couldn't finish the sentence.

The man nodded. 'Come, let's sit and talk,' he said, pointing to the mats on the floor. The room was empty except for these mats and a side table on which was kept a vase with a single sunflower in it, which stood out.

'I know how people describe me based on the book that I wrote, but mostly I am a gamer.'

'Computer games?' said Hafiz, his eyes wide with shock.

The man laughed. 'No, no, my boy. Here, we play mind games. But sometimes, a great player goes through a mind-blowing experience, which is always a cause for celebration,' he said, winking at Hafiz.

He turned to me again. 'My girl, the yoga that you are practising is doing bad things to you. Do you feel a burning sensation at the base of your spine?'

'How did you figure that out?' I asked, astonished.

He brushed past that. 'Well, the first thing you have to do is to stop being angry and learn to not hate your mother's killer.'

'Why?' I demanded, suddenly furious. Even the other Pandavas were quite taken aback by his statement. 'I have taken an oath to kill them.'

The man seemed unperturbed by our expressions of anger. He continued in the same, calm tone, 'What happened was extremely awful. They deserve to be ended. But there is a right way and there is a wrong way to finish them. Let us start with the genesis of the problem. Your enemy is acting the way they are because there are certain mind patterns they are following. These are programmed inside them based either on memory or its imperfect projection into the future.'

I agreed. 'Well, there is some truth to that. There is a QuGene robot, AIman, whose data is driven by memory and then there is a man, Arman, whose actions are driven by paranoia and psychotic actions.'

'Understood. Now, if you too follow your own patterns against them, then it becomes one pattern versus another pattern. Right?'

'Yes, their AI algorithms versus ours. An uncertain bet,' said Hafiz, nodding.

'So, we have to break what creates patterns. The first place to do that is obviously with one's own self. If you succeed with yourself, then you will succeed with the enemy's patterns.'

'How do you do that?'

'Your mind is like a lake in your homeland of Kashmir. Each moment, different experiences are tossing stones and rocks into it. There is a never-ending stream of ripples, some small and some so big that they could upend boats.'

'In the case of Arman, it is more like volcanic rocks falling into a lake of lava. His lake is a mad boiling cauldron,' said Tan, shaking his head.

'Exactly, now what would happen if there was absolutely nothing that would disturb the lake?'

'It would be totally still.'

'Like a mirror. Now, if you looked at it, what would happen?'

'I would see myself,' I said.

'In a mirror, yes, but when you still the mind, then you don't see yourself, your face or your eyes, but instead, you see your Self—your essence.'

'So, if the mind is made transparently still, free of memory, imagination and activity; if I no longer am angry or carrying hate within me,' said Yaniv, 'then I'll be able to see the Self. I think that's what you are saying. But how do I kill my enemy with that?'

'You all seem to be fast learners, but we will get to that later. Now think. If you take your stillness of the lake with your Self and connect with the enemy and quieten its mind, what would happen?'

'Oh my gosh!' It hit me like a thunderbolt. 'AIman is empty, if she experiences her Self, she becomes nothing but a void. That is what my mother said!' I said, hopping with excitement. 'It is the mother of all Yodha mind tricks. She is a zero! She is empty! She will cease to exist.'

The Pandavas' eyes were following me. I locked eyes with Hafiz; he was processing the exchange very carefully.

Tan asked, 'Teacher, how does one connect?'

'How do you feel inside this ashram?' Patanjali asked.

'Very peaceful.'

'What made the connection for you?'

'I don't know exactly, but when I walked in, I felt relaxed and felt free to be . . . well, me.'

'Exactly,' the thin man clapped his hands. 'You felt that you could be *you*. You walked in feeling free to fulfil your most important desire. Desire is the primal seed of the Self. I was the object of your desire. I granted you that connection,' he said excitedly.

Teacher Patanjali turned towards me. 'You have already told me that you are AIman and Arman's object of desire. Now, all you must do is to grant them permission to connect. Of course, when you do, you must present them the truth of your Self. Then you become, how do you say it . . . Ah! Yes! Their "power off button".'

'So, now I know what to do, but how do I do it?'

'And how to do it quickly, right?' He had guessed what I was going to ask next. 'Do you see this sunflower here? What else do you see?'

This reminded me of a well-known story of Arjuna and the Pandavas, so I replied cockily, 'I only see the sunflower.'

'That is one pointed dhyana. My brother Pingala[7] did *Dharana*; he concentrated on the whole sunflower, its colour, form and structure. He found out that the pillars of the secret of life were inside the sunflower. He discovered Nature's secret sequence that leads to the densest packing of seeds in a sunflower. In this sequence, each number is the sum of the previous two numbers. The Pingala numbers are simple but also the foundation of the notes in music. The ratio of two successive Pingala numbers gives the golden ratio of 1.618.'

'The most well-known woman of all time whose facial proportions were near to this ratio was Mona Lisa,' Yuva added happily. 'Dawn, your face has the same ratio.'

'What . . . wow,' was all I could say as I saw that suddenly everyone was looking at my face intently. I had always thought that the forehead on my face was too broad, the nose could have been less prominent, the cheeks less red, the . . . I could go on. When you are the only child and are living in a cave, you have a lot of time to examine yourself.

'Yes, "wow". This word means that wonder of wonders lie ahead of you, Dawn,' Patanjali said. 'A few of the students at this ashram

---

[7]   An ancient Indian mathematician.

persist very hard with this total concentration—Dharana—and they eventually reach the state of great Samadhi where they hope to experience the touch of Maha. That is the end state of stillness, Shanti. And therein lies the answer you are seeking.'

'Isn't there a guest you would like the children to meet, friend?' Yuva interjected, sensing that some of this was going above our heads.

'Ah yes! A famous warrior student of mine named Hrasva Natha[8], the Kampanesa . . . How do you say it? Ah yes! The commander-in-chief is visiting like you too. He will add to what I have shared.'

It was then that I noticed a man standing in the corner of the room. He was tall, muscular, held an upright stance and was wearing a regal turban. He went to the sunflower and picked it up. Then he walked—no, marched—with even, precise steps towards me.

'Dawn, as a warrior, your duty is to kill, and so is mine. In a world where our mind is constantly chattering and releasing judgements, the challenge is to understand how to suppress the mind. Our teacher here,' he said, pointing to Patanjali, 'has instructed us to do Dharana. Here, smell the flower and tell me what happens.'

I did as I was told. 'At first, I do not smell anything, but then slowly, I can smell a light, sweet scent. It has a touch of honey to it and then it fades away. I felt . . . good . . . as if a garden had entered me.'

Yaniv jumped in to help, 'Dawn, you were not focusing on anything else, and as the fragrance dissolved, the mind came to rest.'

'Exactly!' the chief warrior said. 'When she took a deep downward breath of the fragrance, she let the lungs expand. Then as she let the breath that she inhaled dissolve, the thinking function ceased.'

'I like this Dharana,' Tegh chortled. 'It seems simple and easy.'

Observing Tegh, Hrasva Natha remarked, 'I see from your tattoo that you are a warrior too. For you, my brother, the Dharana is when you run towards your enemy, do not be overly conscious of where you place your steps. Free yourself of your mind's control by releasing

---

[8]   He was the minister of war and peace under King Yasaskara in tenth century Kashmir.

the grip of intention and instead do what comes naturally. Your body knows what to do. In a sword fight, pay attention to the clanging of the steel. While your enemy is worn out by his strike being deflected by yours, the resting moment of the vibrations between the clangs is when you recharge. You kill out of detachment and not passion. Hot blood is slain by cold blood. Neither hatred nor craving, just pure Dharma that sustains life compassionately.'

'So, the dying time is the recovery cycle,' said Tegh, saluting the Kampanesa. I realized that the commander-in-chief was a leader who Tegh would want to follow.

'Yes. It is the regularity of the resting heart and not the beats that reveals how strong it is. It is not the sound of lightening or thunder or music but the dying notes that lead to the dying of the mind. With the sound of silence, you are rearmed.'

I looked at Yuva. 'Yuva, I now understand what you meant,' I bowed slightly. 'Some learnings must be experienced. I can now leave with a pure heart and mind. I now understand that a clear mind, which does not attach to anything and is only focused on its *Dharana*—the goal of Shanti—drawing on the warrior's infinite strength.'

'Yes, and a mind that is loaded with hatred or desire poisons itself,' added Tan, 'and will always deviate from the goal. *That* will prove to be its weakness.'

Patanjali raised his right hand in blessing, 'The senses want to rest in peace. They want neither more of what you like or less of what you dislike. It is desire that is ruined by impure Life Breath that arises in humans like Arman, which creates one's own slavery. And it is only the purification of yoga that gives you the freedom to reach that equilibrium. Aum Shanti.'

Yuva sighed, rising up. 'When humans lost these great techniques, it was the end of the illuminati and the beginning of the ignorant human race. Unquestioning and unthinking followers started following pied pipers who promised perfect utopias, and in the end, they became slaves.'

We had learnt a lot as to how to begin our war plan against
AIman and Arman, my father. Before we departed, one question
came to my mind. I turned to Hrasva Natha and asked, 'What if one
is in a situation where one wants to quickly rest one's mind before
going into battle . . . There is no sunflower, no external agent and no
time to do breathing exercises, what then?'

'Nibble on a piece of chocolate. Let it melt in your mouth.
Savour it carefully. Works every time. Aum Shanti,' he smiled.

Sarga 11

Life Breath

800 BC

Charaka's Ashram

'He sits alone in his palace all day and my job is to have my troupe entertain him each night like clowns and court jesters. It is becoming quite exhausting,' grumbled Tabah, irritated. We all had been worried about our friend's safety since Arman came to know that we had landed in the Valley. But this hologram call stilled our minds.

Tabah had been tied up by Arman and AIman in nonstop work sessions and even though it was dangerous for him to visit us, he came at crucial times because there were matters which he needed to communicate urgently.

'The whole day he is in a dazed state, plugged into the world of Vicarious Reality. He's completely engrossed in finding out what the shikha men are doing and experiencing. He flips from one person to the next like a butterfly! But I have to show you what is even more disturbing and demands immediate attention.'

Tabah projected his Gotra Memory Gene through my kalaposh cap. We saw a hologram of what was Arman's council to which

Tabah had been invited. Though they had been told to delete the memory, Tabah had secretly hidden the file. My eyes were fixated on Arman who had changed completely from the handsome young man who had wooed my mother. I had had a faint memory of him singing the koori lullaby to me when I was a child, but this, this was a different man altogether. Arman had led a life in slothful ease with nobody daring to question him. He had now become obese with a stocky body, protruding belly, beefy arms and a broad bald head out of which jutted a shikha implant. A ducktail beard with shaven upper lip and cheeks completed his threatening look. He now wore a crown of an ibex-like creature with golden spiral horns. There was a cold intensity to his demeanour. In this meeting, he was loudly scolding the QuGene scientists who were standing in front of him.

'What's he on about?' asked Yaniv, looking with disgust at the man before us.

Tabah's voice came through. 'These QuGene monsters had their uses, but now Arman has set his sights on something bigger. Arman has been extremely violent with the scientists, demanding results. They say he now suffers epileptic fits.'

'Monsters, is that all you period idiots are capable of? I created AIman. After that what have you produced?' Arman sneered at the scientists.

He walked up to a poster in the lab on which was written an ancient quote. '*Na manusat srestha taram hi kimcit,*' he recited awkwardly, 'Birth in a human form is that than which nothing greater can be conceived.' He grew angry. 'Why are you not able to give me what I desire? I want AIman to have children! That is the ultimate evolution of the new superspecies,' he thundered.

The desperate scientists sought to defend themselves. A man, certainly the lead scientist, spoke up, shaking and trembling, 'We are running into walls. Our calculations are encountering paradoxes that are unsolvable even by the infinitely powerful QuGene computers. Unfortunately, all scientific efforts in formulating a live embryo in AIman have failed . . . because no one has been able to replicate that mysterious Life Breath.'

Arman was seething, 'Do you understand that to fail Arman would indicate a failure of Dushita? Who has the power to be greater than Dushita? You have failed. You are all going to die now.'

The desperate scientist sought to placate his master. 'This may be heresy, but there is possibly . . .' he muttered shaking, 'a breakthrough idea. Allow us to take a different tack. It was triggered by a painting of an ancient and now discredited belief system in a goddess called Kaalaratri, who is shown holding a skull in her hand.'

'I'm listening.'

'Co-opt Nature and see if success can be achieved the old-fashioned way. Biomimicry is our answer here. News has come that Dawn is alive and hiding somewhere in the Valley. We have concluded that once Dawn is captured, she should be beheaded. Then we will take AIman's head—the epicentre of Dushita Algorithm that you, our leader, have so marvellously designed and implemented—and graft it onto Dawn's body.'

Arman looked at him with murderous rage.

'A . . . A million pardons, my lord, forgive me for even suggesting that we will take apart your perfected creation, the Fairy Princess. But hear me out. At that moment of joining, the new AIDawn would be bathed in Dawn's oozing blood. It will be Dawn's internal and external blood plasma, which will baptize and transmit the missing life force into the Dushita-controlled head. It will then be re-engineered with QuGene *vish*, poison. The hybrid AIDawn would then be the start of this new race. A new calendar would begin on the birth of the AIDawn child. It is going to be a girl, Arman's third daughter born from the joining of his two other daughters—one mind-born AIman and the other flesh-born Dawn. She will be the first of many. The Arman race will multiply exponentially after that because there would be no limit. You would be greater than Adam.'

The chief scientist stopped talking. Arman had been giving him a baleful glare. Then, unexpectedly, he started laughing, 'So that fool Vidya was right about Life Breath force after all? Go ahead. I like the plan,' he said, snapping his fingers. 'There is no downside. Who cares if we end up with one dead Dawn and one inoperative AIman? As far as AIman is concerned, I can make a duplicate. There are millions of physical clones of her. What makes her unique is her brain and I will replicate it. Think of it as a disaster redundancy backup. Stupid scientists,' he turned from them dismissively. 'Tabah, you tell me what name you would propose for my new, enhanced daughter?'

We heard Tabah address Arman, 'My Instrument, it should be Kelikil, the violent one. Kelikil will come to the world bearing the first impure but highly advanced Life Breath—a mix of the two worlds. It will be a historic day.'

'Ah! Yes! Brilliant!' said Arman, 'These scientists say that impure Life Breath binds humans to their attachments and that pure breath binds humans to Maha, but Kelikil's Life Breath will be designed to bind Maha. It will be the ultimate victory of Dushita and my greatest accomplishment.'

Given Yaniv's interest in life sciences, his eyes went wide on hearing this. He whispered, 'If individual Life Breath is a pathway to Maha, then Kelikil could be the way to attack Maha.' He said, horrified, 'The girl will be a dangerous backdoor entry by Dushita to contaminate Maha . . . The source of life will be injected by death and lead to . . . to the obliteration of the Universe itself!'

'But he will die too! Won't he?' said Hafiz, confused.

'Yes, he's a fool. He believes that immortality is his and that Dushita will protect him,' said Tabah, his voice laced with anger.

'Dawn,' said Tan urgently, 'we will have to prevent the manifestation of Kelikil.'

I looked at him but was too stunned to speak. My father wanted to kill me to advance a new race of human-robots? After a momentary lapse, I found my voice. 'My mother mentioned it, but I do not know and understand this "Life Breath" fully. What is it in my body that they want so desperately?'

Yaniv patted my back sympathetically and explained, 'AIman does not depend on oxygen. She does not breathe, so there are no red blood cells inside her. However, there is coolant, a white liquid that keeps her quantum computers at near zero when needed. The fluid that flows inside her has a high concentration of white cells that are constantly defending and repairing her graphene body from damage.'

'*And?*'

'They plan to build a completely different body chemistry with your body, which is breath-based,' he said simply.

I felt physically sick; this plan was against mankind itself. 'We will fight this,' I said resolutely. 'But if I fall and they succeed, my friends,' I said, looking at each one of them, 'you have to kill me so that the AIDawn hybrid is never a possibility. It is your duty. Promise me. My fallen father's and Dushita's shadow will not be cast much longer on humanity.'

The Pandavas jerked their heads awkwardly in agreement. Tabah soon ended his call, and before leaving, he told us that he would not be able to accompany us again on our next trip with Yuva. 'The risk is too high. My Cognition Twin would be elsewhere, and I might get pulled into a meeting with either Arman or AIman. But be careful, for the hunt has intensified. The QuGene scientists are working day and night to figure out how to destroy your mace. Its force and its mechanism is still a mystery to them. Okay, I have to go now, but stay hidden and be careful. One last thing: Trust no one.'

I will never forget our meeting with Charaka, the father of medicine. Yuva told him that we had met Patanjali last.

'Oh, Patanjali! There is nobody better than him when it comes to how to shut off the mind and recognize your true Self. Aum Shanti, Shanti, Shantihi,' he said cheerfully. 'Best of all, he is a great dancer. I have learnt so many moves from him.'

'Dancer!' we cried in unison.

'Yes, of course, if your yoga teacher cannot dance, then he does not know what moves life,' he said, winking at us.

'But,' muttered Tan, 'you are at least a five to six hundred years *before* Patanjali. How do you know about him and his works?'

Charaka laughed, 'Are you the only person whose Cognition Twin travels? You should know by now that for your Cognition Twin, the past, the present and the future all co-exist.'

That made sense. But we then veered the conversation to a more pressing topic, 'Tell us, teacher, how to win the upcoming Great War?' asked Yaniv, after we told him about Arman's plan of producing human-robot hybrids.

'Arman has a sick mind, but it is a diabolically good plan. It has Dushita's mark all over it,' said Charaka bitterly. 'It turns around and reverses what has been the norm since the creation of the Universe. What is scary is that it is even worse than what they think it is. It is why Yuva brought you to me. Patanjali focuses on the mind, but I focus on the science of life, the whole mind-body connection.'

Tegh asked, agitated, 'Even worse? How can it possibly get worse? They are on their way to create Kelikil with impure Life Breath to destroy Maha and the entire Universe with it.'

'Yes. But can you think about what might get created instead?'

'Oh no . . . I did not imagine that far,' said Tegh, wrapping his head around the notion that there could be something even worse than the end of the Universe.

'Our Universe is built around Life. Life, in its essence, is Shakti or Energy. When one dies, it simply means that our energy gets released and redistributed. That is it, redistribution. The Universe sheds no tears. But what if our current Universe is destroyed and, in its place, arises a new Universe that is built on antilife?'

Yaniv understood, 'Antilife means representing a Universe founded on negative energy. Our Universe will eventually run out of energy and then start contracting and collapsing, but a Universe built on negative energy will keep on expanding forever. So, it will mean Dushita's permanent victory and Arman's eternal rule.'

I gasped, 'So, it's true. He's really been promised immortality. That's quite mental just thinking that this is possible, even in AD 3000. But do these negative universes really exist?'

'It is. But not unheard of,' chimed in Tan the lama. 'An ancient text talked about this at length, but nobody gave it any consideration. It stated that in some universes, moonlight is hot and sunlight is cool, and there is sight in darkness and blindness in sunlight. It is where good is destructive and evil is not, where poison promotes health and nectar kills.'

Hafiz looked at him strangely, 'So, when Kelikil poisons Maha and kills him, then this Universe will die but that death has a quantum probability to it. It does not mean 100 per cent that the Universe ends completely. There is no absolute certainty in Nature's practice. That mechanical definitive outcome will happen only in a deterministic Universe. In quantum, there will be other outcomes that will have some small probability to it. The reality of daughter universes exists, even if it turns out to be an anti-energy Universe. And Kelikil residing inside Maha, who will be the last to go, plans to be that outcome.'

'She wants to be a universe?' said Tegh, wide-eyed. 'But as Hafiz had said in the morning, won't Arman die too when this Life-centric Universe ends?'

'Yes,' Yaniv said. 'But Kelikil will have information in her that is twenty times of what could be contained in that ancient ship that sank, the Titanic. All is packed inside its DNA, all sequences of the four letters: ATCG.'

'You're losing me now,' said Tegh, open-mouthed.

'Hear me out! The total length of the human genome is over three billion base pairs. If one were to print that out, it would take 26,200 pages. For perspective, less than 500 pages is what makes us unique. Rest we share. As Kelikil grows, she will be trained by Arman and after the apocalypse, she will simply recreate or make a new Arman by taking her human genome and simply reordering those unique to him. It will be as simple as her taking a small part of her, perhaps a section of her rib and rearranging a few letters. Then she and the reborn Arman will be the masters of the Antilife, antienergy Universe.'

The horrors of the full ramifications of the Great War were now beginning to sink in. The ashen-faced Pandavas showed the worry writ large on their faces as they factored it in. I was myself feeling disgusted and overwhelmed.

I asked Charaka, 'Good is so simple and evil is so deep. I fear that I cannot dive into its depths.'

Charaka articulated, 'My child, you have to understand the inner engineering of evil. It all starts with food—something that we take for granted. Food gives us energy. Inside us, food is converted into Rasa, the juice of life, in the liver and the bile. This juice travels to the heart where it gets stored. People with hearts full of Rasa have a fulfilling emotional life and are joyful people.'

'I'm guessing that's not the case with Arman's plan?' Tegh asked.

'Yes. You see, in a few situations, the Rasa can turn negative. As the heart pumps blood, the Rasa Juice encounters Life Breath, which is spread all over the body but especially in the head. The Life Breath fires the juice with its life force, and the two work together at a very fine level of wave particles that are called Lifetrons. The entangled particles that transport you through Space and Time are essentially Lifetrons, which are more basic than electrons or neurons but carry consciousness.'

'This is all so very, very confusing, but it also seems to make sense!' I said, scratching my head. This was too much knowledge for a mere sixteen-year-old.

'It is, I know. But think about it alone in peace and quiet and you will understand. You see, when an individual's Lifetrons in the brain connect with the Maha Lifetron's grid, such as in unsupervised Kundalini Yoga, then it receives a supercharge like a lightning bolt. Sometimes that can be dangerous if one is not prepared for it, and the brain could get fried. This will lead to madness. If the Life Breath way is about the individual establishing conductivity with Maha, then the Rasa way is the individual tasting Maha. My way is the way of Rasa and it is much safer and far more enjoyable.'

I asked, 'Tasting Maha? But . . . but okay first, tell me one thing, Charaka, why is Kelikil so important?'

'So, here is the fiendish genius at work. In one month, the Rasa converts into the procreatory fluid for men and women, which when combined forms a *bindu*, a dot, whose Lifetrons entangle immediately with Maha's Lifetrons and that initial charge gives an embryo life.'

'Yuva had told us that it is like the spark coming from a fire.'

'Yes, the human embryo is nourished by Rasa. There is a deep mind-body connection. In AIDawn, the purpose of the AIman mind, which is processing non-stop inputs, is to create deep toxicity within the Rasa of the embryo body. Kelikil will be born not just with violent Life Breath but also with the ability to have *Ashanta* Rasa.'

'What is Ashanta Rasa?' I asked.

'First, you need to understand *Shanta* Rasa or Shanti. It is the ultimate peace of mind that Patanjali talked to you about. It is the state of great peace resting within your Self. It is the peacefulness of an embryo. It is the repose of Maha because only Maha has the freedom to be totally free, devoid of any desire, any action, any compulsion.'

'So . . . we have it or we don't? Or do we lose it? Is that what Ashanta is?' asked Yaniv, who looked seriously out of wits.

'Well, yes, you're right. Life Breath starts getting contaminated from the moment a baby is delivered. It takes enormous purification for an adult to return to the original state where one can relink with Maha's state of peace. Only a few who undergo the rigour of great Samadhi get there. One example was Buddha. The easy way for most people to experience the flow of Maha is Rasa, but evil people have always blocked it. Earlier on, Dushita's agents would forbid music and dance, and now with Kelikil, they want to go to the source and just poison Shanta Rasa.'

'So, Kelikil won't have Shanta Rasa but its opposite, the toxic and violent Ashanta Rasa?' Yaniv asked again.

'Yes, in Kelikil, between the combination of Ashanta Rasa and impure Life Breath, you will have the making of the anti-Lifetron. No peace, only violence. She will be trained to go into the great Samadhi, but instead of receiving Maha, she will destroy Maha—this will mark the beginning of the anti-energy Universe. That is why the second part of their evil plan is so much more important than the first. That is why I say that this has the mark of Dushita.'

Yaniv's eyes tightened, as if in sudden pain. 'I finally understand. Through inner engineering, they want to create the ultimate, unstoppable, Undead force.'

Hafiz added, 'No different than a malware virus bringing down an entire network.'

'Throughout history, these evil people have done the same thing,' Tan said. 'They would pick highly attractive assassins and feed them very small quantities of snake, asp, spider and scorpion poison. Slowly, the dosage would be increased as the person's body would gain immunity against the poison. Then one day, when ready, the poisoned person would be sent to an enemy ruler or aristocrat. One kiss from them and that would be the end. People change, technologies change, but the nature of Dushita's operations does not change.'

I pleaded, 'Then how do I fight this Undead force?'

'I have told you what the weapon is. It is Peace Force. As for the gift of this Peace Force—why, that is in the hands of Yuva himself.' Charaka bowed to Yuva and Yuva smiled, nodding his head slightly. We all looked at him questioningly, but he just smiled and looked ahead.

Charaka concluded, 'You asked me how to win the war ahead? I will tell you. You will need to have the powers of a *Vira*, a warrior; a *Rasika* who can wield the Peace weapon; and a *Sadhika* who can have one-pointed concentration.'

I somehow had this feeling that this was all slipping away from my hands. I was just sixteen, certainly in the year 3000 when we would seem to be all-powerful to a person in the year 2000.

But how much could I do? The forces against us were overwhelming, and the deeper one went into matters, the worse the situation was becoming. Doubt had taken over. I felt I had lost even before I had begun. Several dangerous thoughts kept resurfacing in my mind, which were beginning to tempt me. There was one sure-fire way to stop Kelikil and save Maha even if one could not save the earth and the remaining humans on it. I could trick Death and cheat it from executing the death of the Universe.

I could end myself.

Sarga 12

Rasa

500 BC

Bharata's Ashram

'I thought I had the long face in this group. But you have beat me to it,' Yuva said to me. 'Why so, my Niti warrior princess?'

'Yuva, ever since you've come into my life, I have grown leaps and bounds, accepting all these new revelations. But I cannot go on. At some point, I have to face the reality. I think I will have to give up in the face of these overwhelming odds . . . this evil. There is no other choice.'

'You are a warrior, Dawn. You have taken the sworn warrior's oath.'

'Yes, Conquer or Die for Life, I remember. Yuva, I *will* honour my oath.'

He understood the true meaning of what I was saying. Then he said gently, 'Dawn, you know that Maha is my father. And that I have *already* slain AIman, Arman and Dushita.'

What was he saying? Was this one of his riddles? I looked at him and then to Kira, who just shook her head side to side in agreement.

'If you have, then what do you need from me? What is my role here?'

'Dawn, Life is not for Maha. Life is for you. When you slay the evil Troika, you are establishing what is already a reality. But far more importantly, you are reaffirming that you are *for* Life. That desire must come from a human. Remember your oath: Conquer or Die *for* Life. We came to see Charaka because he is the beacon of life—a long, healthy and whole life. Over and over humans forget what life is and then it needs course correction by someone like you. But it has to be your free will. Maha will not dictate to humans, otherwise, Maha becomes Dushita.'

'Then why do I doubt? My mother had conviction in me, but somehow, it is failing me despite all the knowledge that I have gained.'

'Dawn, you learnt that Niti tells us to trust each other. Did you trust me?'

I was flustered. 'Yuva, everything I know is because of my mother and you. But I don't *know* you. Where is this Peace Weapon that Charaka said you would hand over to me?'

Yuva beamed and said, 'My princess has now become a warrior. You are ready. This will be our last lesson before you go into battle with AIman and Arman.'

At Bharata's ashram, the residents went around running excitedly, sharing the news of Yuva's arrival. Some started blowing the conch. Others started reciting his many names. It seemed that they were all going mad with happiness. I was keeping count of his names; there were 1,008 in all.

Surely, it was a reception like none other. Luckily, Tabah was able to sneak away and come with us too. It was a sweet reunion with him, filled with many questions about the enemy.

Soon, Bharata came out running and welcomed Yuva, 'Salutation to he who is loved by the teachers and is celebrated by them. Salutation to he who is the refuge of the teachers and stays in the heart of the teachers.

Salutation to he who is the light of the teachers and who is filled with the virtue of Adi, the first teacher.'

Yuva smiled and raised his hand, palm outward.

'He surely is important to these people,' whispered Yaniv into my ear.

Then Bharata turned his attention to Kira. He saluted the bird and then to our surprise prostrated himself before her, calling her 'Mother of all.' 'Mother?' I saw Yaniv mouthing the word as if in total disbelief. It was all so surprising and I could see the other Pandavas were stupefied as well. We clearly had no idea as to who Yuva and Kira really were.

Yuva was escorted to a huge throne, which he ascended. Next to him were wicker stools on which we sat, and Bharata sat next to us on a cane seat. Soon, an army of servers came rushing, offering us roths. I saw Yuva eating them with great gusto. Finally, the recital of Yuva's 1,008 names ended.

I had to ask Yuva, 'Why do you have so many names? I have only one.'

'You were given your name by someone else. They labelled you. Have you ever thought about what names describe you best? Make up your own list of 18 or 108 or 1,008 names. Each day, pick one name and live it. Go ahead, try it. The more names you give yourself, the more you will grow and like yourself.'

Bharata, listening to our exchange, smiled. 'The simplest techniques are the most powerful.'

Yuva nodded, 'Bharata, we are here for help. Dawn has a mind-born enemy who is out to destroy her. The enemy's creator is set on destroying the Universe by destroying all heart-based activity. Dawn knows from Patanjali that what she must do is to still her enemies' violent mind with Life Breath, while Teacher Charaka has told her that stilling the mind must be combined with the opening of the heart so that it flows with the juice of life. But she needs to know how to do that using the Peace Force. That is why we are here.'

'Oh, that is the perfect reason to have a theatrical show!' Bharata exclaimed.

I was taken aback by the answer. 'A show?'

'Why, yes, Dawn! Because an art performance is *the* Peace Force that both shuts the mind and awakens the heart. It triggers the flow of thoughts that operates pre-mind, which then overcomes one's pre-programmed mind. When you move the body, move the mind and move the spirit, you move the Universe. That is why Patanjali, who was focused on the mind, loved to dance. That is why Charaka, who correctly identified the heart as the controlling centre, took his name that means movement. You will see and experience what I am talking about,' he said happily.

Tabah piped in, 'I agree completely. I had no idea though that I was wielding the Peace Force . . . that I was giving Arman's crazy mind and empty heart some relief, even though he didn't know what it really meant.'

As I thought about what Bharata had said, a man in pure white clothes came in front of us on the stage. 'He's the art director,' said our host. The man threw a clod of earth from a basket on the stage. I noticed that an audience had assembled behind us and they were all dressed in off-white clothes. The director then sprinkled water on the four corners of the stage, followed by mustard seeds.

'What's he doing?' murmured Tan, who was sitting next to me. 'No clue!' I shrugged and looked ahead.

Each corner of the stage had a pillar of a different type of wood: white, red, yellow and grey. Then the musicians entered, took their place and applied a paste on to their drums and instruments in the mark of a tilak. A few attendants burnt aromatics in front of the stage and the incense sticks were offered to a graceful woman who had just stepped on the podium. She was dressed in red with her hair decked with flowers. 'She's an actress,' said Bharata to me, pointing to her. The woman took a handful of flower petals and threw it on the stage and on to the musical instruments. She then walked towards us. Stopping in front of Yuva, she garlanded him and then us. She smiled at Bharata and shook his hands, who then escorted her to a seat off stage, decorated with flowers.

Just then a bevy of beautiful dancers shimmered onto the stage in lapis lazuli dresses holding fire torches. 'The legendary apsaras,' Bharata said. I closed my mouth; I was amazed at how ravishing they looked. Soon the director came back, this time, with a lit lamp and swayed it in front of Yuva, Kira, the Pandavas and me. He then announced that the dance troupe would perform the *Daksha Yajna Vimardani* dance led by danseuse Rambha.

'It celebrates the story of Maha's annihilation of Daksha who had enormous powers and was conducting an evil sacrifice,' Yuva explained to us.

The director blew the conch and the show began. I saw Tabah leaning forward and watching intently.

The dancers started swirling in their flared outfits. In tandem, the musicians started strumming as the singer chanted, 'Deva, Shri Yuva.' The dancers twirled round and round, hips swaying gently from side to side. Then they formed two lines facing each other and holding each other tightly around the waist, coming closer to each other. They bowed and then stepped back in a repeating beat.

To our great surprise, standing up and walking right into the middle of the two rows of dancers was Yuva! I turned to look at the boys. They were equally astonished and spellbound. His left-hand palm held horizontally near his stomach, and the right hand upheld with the palm facing forward in a gesture of peace, Yuva stepped left to right and back. Rambha was delighted to see her new dance partner and followed Yuva's moves. The apsaras held their scarves outstretched above their heads and leaped on the stage around the two of them. The musicians' reed pipe squeaked with intensity. Somehow, the mouse-like sound triggered Yuva. His trunk went up and his hips started swaying, his hands pumping in front of him alternately. The apsaras, not to be left behind, held their nose with

their left hand, elbow jutting out to pantomime Yuva's waving trunk.
The singers' chanting speeded up,

> Maha Yuva,
> Come dance our way
> On thee, we, a garland lay,
> Deva Shri Yuva.

> When Sati was immolated,
> Your father went insensate
> But she was reborn,
> And glory, you took form.

> The first movement is you in me,
> You are the one who raises She
> Come dance with me,
> Deva Shri Yuva.

The musicians picked up the tempo, but Yuva was not fazed. He
moved his body with a lithe grace that contradicted his size, his
flapping ears adding to the movement. The rhythm got even faster;
the giddy dancers were not even aware as they flew through their
formations. Some did somersaults from one end of the stage to the
other. Yuva seemed intoxicated by the dance now, his eyes were
closed, and his face had a radiant smile as he swung his feet with a
sense of confidence and speed. The musicians were now bereft of any
control, their instruments were seemingly the slaves of Yuva's frenzy.
I did not know what was happening within me. I stood up and
the other Pandavas and the audience too got up, unable to control
themselves. We all crowded the stage and started dancing around
Yuva, who was in the centre with the dancers. All of us joined in and
followed his elephant walk. The stomping of his moving feet on the
stage added to the vibrations of the drums.

There was a certain energy on the stage that was primal, and it had all the dancers within its grip. Then a strange phenomenon happened. Yuva was moving his hands so fast that it seemed as if he had five pairs of arms. The draped string around Yuva's neck slowly began to move. I gasped and concentrated on the string: it was a snake that had coiled the tip of its tail around its head, so that all along it had looked like a knot on a string around Yuva's neck. I had never noticed that! The snake started raising its head and rose up in the air, a neck collar now with the head of the snake moving in parallel to the elephant head.

'Wonder of wonders!' Bharata exclaimed, as Yuva began to radiate different colours, his normal grey transitioning from one colour of the rainbow to the next. I pushed my smart outfit control into copy mode to be in sync with Yuva and the Pandavas followed me. Our clothes now resembled a mass of changing colours of the rainbow. Then Yuva started spinning and the dancers started spinning with him. Yuva's colour turned moonlight and the stage was now a mass of 101 white revolving whirlwinds. It was a grand finale—a test of speed and stamina. There were bees that had buzzed around Yuva and they started spinning in circles too. The snake, by now, was totally stretched out by Yuva's spin, desperately clinging on to him. One by one, the apsaras fell in a swoon on the stage and only Yuva was left spinning but in full control of his moves. When the singers sang *mangalam* and the drummer hit his final beat, Yuva stopped abruptly as if on cue and folded his hands in a namaste. The audience, still swaying, broke out chanting 'Jai Yuva, victory to Yuva.' He smiled and supremely unconcernedly walked back towards us.

My face was flushed and glowing. I felt light-headed but strong. 'I did not know you like music,' I panted, still trying to catch my breath.

Yuva was still humming the song to himself. With a laugh, he said, 'I *am* music.'

'You dance really well and have great rhythm,' Tabah chirped.

'I should. My father was the first dance teacher and my mother the first dance student.'

'They were what!'

'Yuva, the more I learn about you, the more you become full of mystery,' I said, smiling, 'and yet, you are full of joyful promise. I really want to meet your father Maha and your mother one day.'

My compliment filled him with pleasure. 'It is you whose name means hope. You are seeing you in me. But thank you, my Niti warrior princess.' He lifted a *modak* from a serving attendant and swallowed it, savouring it slowly with his eyes closed.

'I got you moving,' was his cryptic observation.

I turned to look at the boys, who looked equally clueless as to what Yuva could be meaning.

Bharata's voice made me turn in his direction. 'Where was your mind during the performance?'

I was confused. Where was it indeed?

'Where was the tension of your self-interest?'

Again, I could only comment that there was none.

'And what did you feel in your heart?'

'I felt that my entire body had become feelings—feelings that had been liberated.'

'And what triggered it all?'

'Seeing Yuva start dancing? The elephant walk—that was such a surprise.'

'Yes, yes that is what "wonder" is. A sudden surprise of the soul, much like the punchline of a joke,' Bharata laughed at his own joke. 'And this amazement starts the beginning of an upheaval. When this turmoil spreads all over in a limitless fashion, it becomes a wonder of wonders.'

'So, there is a way then to tap into this limitless power *that* simply and easily as Patanjali said?'

Bharata said triumphantly, 'Yes, Patanjali is right, but Dharana alone is insufficient as long as one has to return back to the sensory objective world. Patanjali's sciences teach while my arts bewitch.

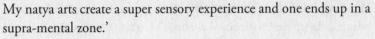

My natya arts create a super sensory experience and one ends up in a supra-mental zone.'

'Supra-mental zone?'

'Yes, the brain has a limited capacity and with an overload of immediate sensations, all thoughts get jammed. Music with dance is the only way to create this state of trance. If this is happening alongside people who are similarly absorbed, then it leads to a connectivity. And that is Rasa, the collective's juice of life. At the highest level, this wonder of wonders becomes Shanta Rasa, a shared limitless experience of great peace, which is the highest experience of life.'

'I understand,' I said, nodding, 'I just experienced it. But tell me, how do I fight the Troika with it?'

Bharata thought for a moment, 'What you experienced here gave you joy. But what you want is this to be weaponized. You want the limitless Peace Weapon, and for that, you need to train in the Kamadeva dance that makes the world stop.'

'The world stops?' I said, rolling my eyes.

'Yes, my dear. The Rasika fights with both weapons and ornaments. You need to be her.'

'But tell me more about Kama. I did not know that he wields such a powerful weapon.'

'The God of Love was born long ago, and he too is mind-born. When he was born, the first words he uttered were *Kan Darpayami*, meaning 'whom shall I make mad?' All fear him. Yuva will tell you that his father Maha lost only to Kama and none other.'

'The time is right to go see the power of Kama,' I said determinedly. 'And in our case, the person who is to be destroyed is already mad.' I laughed, a laugh devoid of mirth.

Yuva observed me for a minute and then said to Bharata, 'Great teacher, *naman* to you. We thank you. Now, I take the Pandavas and Dawn to see the dance that drives one mad.'

We were invisible again, and this time, in the Court of Simhadeva where a dance performance was about to start. Yuva said that it was the year 1300 and that the performer was Idagali, the dancing girl. I was curious because my mother had once mentioned her name in connection with Arman and AIman. We watched silently as we saw Idagali do the Rati dance. It was not so much her body movements but her hand gestures and expressions towards the king that gave the dance its highly charged emotional cues. As the dance proceeded, Idagali, who had started as submissive, became more dominant in her suggestive expressions. She now had the king in her power.

'Unlike Arman whose acts of destruction are accompanied by pain,' Yuva began, 'Idagali demonstrates her power to give both pleasure and to destroy. She is now the one to dictate the terms of engagement, from an entertainer for hire to becoming the one with the power of who to favour. Look at his face, the dual mood of the dance—soft and yet dominating—has the king confused. He is becoming mad at the uncertainty of her acceptance or rejection of him.' When the dance ended, the king threw a necklace at Idagali and asked to speak to her alone.

The queens who had watched the performance behind the lattice windows were all discussing the Idagali scandal, for no woman was allowed to be alone with the king except for the queens. One pointed out spitefully that she was a daughter of the king's wet nurse, so in fact, his own sister. Another said that she had been first married to the pipal tree and then presented to the court. Her power was so great that she had got the king to revoke the ancient law that prescribed a strict punishment to be imposed on families that had intra-relationships.

'It is interesting that 2,000 years later, Arman has invoked Simhadeva's abandonment of the moral code to create a historical justification of his own corrupt action,' Yuva commented, looking straight ahead at the richly decked up queens.

The chief queen wearily asked, 'Why don't men use their minds?'

A young queen consoled the elder queen. 'The story of Manovati tells us the answer. All men want is for their entire mind to be stimulated. But the only woman who could do that was the legendary Mohini and she was actually a man.' All the queens laughed. The younger queen continued, 'Variety with strangers is a poor substitute for the infinite possibility of creativity with a trusted partner. Yet, all go mad for what is different and it often ends up being their fatal weakness.'

Yuva suddenly started walking away. We ran to keep up with him. 'With this, all of you are now ready to take on the Troika and their forces.' He abruptly stopped and looked back at us. 'Remember this when you strike: they have no peace of mind, no love in their heart, no experience of bliss in their existence. Even if alive, they have lost the gift of the powers of life. At best you can think of them as the Undead.'

This was the moment when I had an epiphany and it all came together. The Niti stories had all fallen into place. The whole had become bigger than the sum of the parts. I had my answers. Their fatal weaknesses, the chinks in AIman's and Arman's armour had been revealed to me. AIman was programmed algorithmically to please humans at a synthetic, chemically driven sensory level but was lacking emotionally, as I had learnt earlier. This shortage meant that there was a gap between AIman and her male human subjects, which Bisht, her Himalayan cat, could only cover partially because of her own species' limitations. Dogs had been killed because, unlike humans, they could not fake love. With their death alongside the genocide of the women, there was no true, selfless love left in the world. AIman had the more powerful mind, but she was heartless. The one who could awake the heart with wonder could slay her. As for Arman, I had become his craving to the point of being beyond madness. I would prove to be his undoing.

And finally, Dushita would meet his nemesis: Me.

Sarga 13

Battle Plans

Pari Mahal, Kashmir Valley

It was our last war council.

Seated on the ancient ruins of Verinag, we heard the gentle flow of the river. It was night-time, and so, the water had cooled so drastically that we all huddled before a blazing fire.

'I will ensure that the battlefield is picked so that the armies of both sides are fully present,' said Tabah, warming his outstretched hands.

'Tabah, make sure that every man's blood is racing, their emotions are flowing, their brains fully aroused. No, it should be inflamed. I need their body, heart and mind highly stimulated and to be at the peak for me to succeed.'

'You can trust Tabah to take care of that,' he bowed.

'When I step into the battlefield, I want to be absolutely beautiful, just like the heavenly apsaras,' I said, taking the wisdom from my last lesson imparted by Bharata.

'I am a follower of the poet Manto,' said Yaniv, his teeth chattering in the cold. 'To be Kashmiri is to be beautiful.'

I smiled. 'My ornaments and clothes should be befitting of Mohini.'

'And they will match your weapons, Dawn,' said Tegh, sharpening his claw.

'Thank you. Seven seconds is all that I will have to produce impact.'

Hafiz, who had been unusually quiet, spoke up. 'Patanjali said that he played mind games. I'm ready with the paradox bombs. I have programmed thousands of those. My system is checked,' he patted his Personal Digital Agent. 'We will test AIman's limit of knowledge. I will slide my hacks through the Yogini pathways and lock her into a Turing infinite loop. I have my questions ready to confuse her: Why do Outlaws exist if Dushita is supreme? Why did Dushita pick an epileptic Arman to be his Instrument rather than a so-called perfect human? Demonstrate the truth of this statement, which is actually false, and so on.'

Tan nodded, 'We have to force her outside her laws into a direct conflict with an all-knowing and all-powerful Dushita on which she runs. The known Universe is only 4 per cent, whereas there is this mysterious dark matter, which is 27 per cent, and then the unknown dark energy is nearly 70 per cent of the total mass and energy of the Universe. The paradox bomb—does dark energy exist?—will freeze her mind.'

Hafiz laughed, 'If AIman says yes, then since she has no evidence, she is accepting that our knowledge is finite, while our ignorance is infinitely greater. If she states that there is no evidence, then she cannot say it is false. That will blow all of AIman's algorithms.'

'Charaka said that we are only energy. I am all about force and strength,' said Tegh, looking up from his now shiny claw. 'AIman's design has to be limited by certain energy limits. This is where her vulnerability lies. For example, the primitive iPhone device from a thousand years earlier used more energy than the refrigerator, which was a thousand times bigger in size.'

'Someone has been reading up,' said Hafiz, smiling at Tegh.

'Yes, brother. Thanks to your jibes and my own interest in energy, I have deep dived into it,' he said laughingly. 'Moore's law, which had predicted that the speed of transistors would become faster every twenty-four months, collapsed due to energy constraints. Binary computers hit a snag because of the energy wall. Quantum computing, which was a breakthrough, required enormous energy too.'

We stared at him, eyebrows scrunched.

'Well, AIman's brains are distributed all over in the Cloud's databanks, but their energy has limits too. It is technology after all. AIman is safe when she is in her Pari Mahal, but when she steps out, she is vulnerable because she doesn't have her cryogenic cooling chamber. So when that happens, I will throw my special heat energy bombs to raise her internal temperature. It will hit her temperature limit and burn her.'

'Yaniv? Any thoughts?' I said, looking at him staring into the firepit.

It broke his reverie. 'Uh? Ah yes. I've been thinking.'

'Thank god for that,' Tegh laughed.

Yaniv rolled his eyes in a mocking fashion and flashed a smile. 'Arman's mad plan of creating AIman fails, not just in terms of information and energy limits but also in terms of response times.'

'Okay, then! I'm sorry for the jibe, brother. This just went above my head. Care to explain?' said Tegh, sheepishly.

'Always,' laughed Yaniv. 'If life sciences has taught me anything, it this is: Nature's enzymes speed up cells by transferring particles from one part of the molecule to the other through quantum tunnelling. Now, here's the catch—I don't think that AIman's circuits *have* Nature's speed. I see evidence of biomimicry here that the Yoginis Who Code nailed here, very much like what the Kashmiri carpenters have left behind. To me, it is clear: Arman will lose because of the limits in AIman's response times.'

I was quiet for a long time, thinking about all the extremely different ways the enemy could be slayed, thanks to all the varied knowledge from my five unusually gifted friends. Yuva was right that each one was the master of his skill in warfare. I felt their eyes on me and I looked up. All of them were now waiting for their general to speak.

I took a deep breath. 'I will be the sacrifice gambit that Muladeva taught us. I will be the Rasika who will invoke limitless longing. At the same time, I will be Patanjali, the peaceful, calm eye of the storm that I create.' I stood up and stared into the eyes of the Pandavas. The rush of the icy wind streaked past, unfurling my dark hair, my computerized armbands squeaking as if affected by the might of Nature itself. *Ma!* My voice threatened to break, but I did not give it power.

'You all must gaze at me with the same one-pointed concentration that Pingala's brother displayed with the sunflower. You will not just gaze but be one with me, smelling my fragrance and flowing in the same creative experience with me. That is the Rasa of wonder that *you* will spread. But I will not just be the sunflower,' I held up by palm. 'I will be Idagali. That is how Arman and his army will look at me as they go mad drunk on the release of Charaka's juice of life.' The boys were looking at me intently; a look laced with respect and pride and a little dread.

'But will you find an opening?' Yaniv asked cautiously.

'Trust me that I will find an opening the way Muladeva did,' I said, tracing the tip of my mace. 'I will be the Old born again as the new New. AIman is programmed to please and so will instantly amp herself seeking to reassert her position. But woman to woman, Kashmiri to Circassian, AIman will not match me. She will hit the wall of rejection. Niti will triumph over IT.'

It was time for Tabah to go back. I turned to him. 'Tabah, do what you have to do. The Trojan trap is ready to be sprung. Now it is time for us to rest.'

'Outlaws syncope state: Achieved.'

The QuGene pack leader messaged back to AIman. I could hear the instructions to carry us to Pari Mahal and hand us over to her. We had been hit by a surprise attack and taken prisoners.

The QuGene robot force had attacked us at night, deploying their Active Denial System. It was a state-of-the-art directed-energy weapon designed especially for capture. The first hit was with the Dazzling Laser—a metallic spray in the forms of eights, which hit our heads. This was followed by the Nano Second, an electrical pulse with a high voltage electricity charge, shot for a billionth of a second. The charges achieved what was intended—it induced deep transcranial magnetic stimulation through the metallic spray, which caused the boys to faint accompanied by hearing loss. My mind screamed in anger and frustration as I saw them writhe in pain and then pass out. Their horrific screams pierced the calm peace of Verinag. I saw it all through my half-closed eyes. My considerably long hair had saved me as I had bunched up my loose tresses for the night, and so, the metal did not touch my skull. I was conscious but pretended otherwise, witnessing the ruthlessness of my father. Though the hybrids were fearsome, they lacked intelligence—this I could make out—for they could not detect that the helmets that the boys wore, or my kalaposh cap, were more than just gears to beat the Kashmiri winter. It was one of our communication channels; it was a way through which we interacted, thanks to Hafiz's mastery over technology. For his own helmet, he had even built in a prototype system that worked on his voice commands. He didn't need to look at any screen; everything was accessible on the lens in his eye.

We were then in Pari Mahal, a grand and terribly beautiful stone palace located at the top of the Zabarwan mountain range. The castle provided a spectacular backdrop and a panoramic view of the Valley. It was breathtaking. We stared in amazement, as we were led through the blooming seven terraced gardens into the magnificent stone structure, surrounded by a small regiment of QuGene guards and mutant-hybrids. A curiously dressed slim figure with beautiful porcelain skin and almond eyes met us at the gate.

'Take the prisoners inside,' came a voice, laced with a vicious laugh.

I looked at the almond-shaped eyes. *Tabah!*

'Move on! Get in!' The guards pushed us with their electromagnetic spears and we entered a completely different experience. The palace was totally modern from the inside with infinite hologram views that stretched across the glass wall panels; one could not tell where they ended. Maya Asura had done his job well.

'Move them to the Pristine Shrine,' Tabah snapped his electric baton at the hybrids. The guards hastily blindfolded us and made us walk in twists and turns till finally pushing us into the forbidden space of the sanctum sanctorum.

When we entered the sanctorum, a blast of freezing air hit our faces, and our suits immediately went into heat mode to protect us from the intense cold. Our blindfolds were yanked off our faces. It was below freezing point in what was a transparent ice room. Hafiz messaged me in secret mode saying that it was the optical Quantum Computing system that permitted AIman to operate outside the castle at ambient temperatures temporarily. However, most of her applications needed to be done at cryogenic temperatures below 10 millikelvin or near absolute zero, which is why it was important that her 'charging' room remain so cold.

Then I saw her, again. AIman. She was engaged in deep computation, and this time, her skin colour was jet black—the natural colour of graphene. She had black glistening hair. Even her lips were black. So were the retinas and the pupils. She was in her original state for maximum energy conservation. Behind her was the dome-shaped cryogenic chamber where she would presumably rest in absolute zero temperature.

Tabah saluted AIman. 'Fairy Princess, I come to give you a most momentous report. I had gone to Verinag to pick up an ancient stone slab on the southern wall.'

She turned to analyse his features, her eyes big, round, dark, rotating orbs. 'The slab mentioned that its patron was the father of victory. I had wanted to present it to our great leader, the Instrument. There, to my surprise, I spotted the Outlaws in hiding. It has resulted in the greatest prey-catch in history.' He bowed with a dancer's flair.

AIman acknowledged Tabah's contribution with a curt nod. In a Universe where information was the only currency, Tabah had delivered supreme value.

'Last time, I offered you to be my elder sister,' AIman said, as she turned her attention to me. 'But you rejected me. You even faked your death. Tch, tch! Now, you are my prisoner. And these too,' pointing to the boys who were still dazed from the torture. 'You are a slow learner, sister. I always win.'

'Murderer, nothing will save you from me. Your end has come,' I said through clenched teeth.

'A fool. Just like your mother. You are so plain,' she said analysing me, 'and have a bad temper to boot. No one will tolerate you.'

'You mean what's left of humans? Or your graphene animal farm? The humans need to be freed from a dark witch like you.'

'The shikha humans enjoy happiness that has never been experienced before. Shikha that is based on Mass Implantable Brain Technology has permitted the removal of all errors in human thinking—a true revolution for mankind,' she said with no emotion, befitting a true robot.

'The shikha men have turned into *shikas* men—absolutely miserable.'

'You and your mother both like to argue, I must say. You both are alike. You both broke the law, which predates even Dushita's laws. Young women must be under the control of their fathers, married women under the control of their husbands and widows under the control of their sons.'

'These are patriarchal laws, you programmed brain. You murderous lawbreakers are now lawmakers?' I spat.

'Without male guidance and control, women are socially irresponsible and dangerous. Our father has birthright control over you, *sister*,' She said, the last word with a sneer.

'What I know about him is enough for me to hate him for all eternity.'

'You know nothing, you're a fool blinded by your mother. Do you know that your mother was a ringleader of the greatest conspiracy against Manity? Yes, *your* mother was a true traitor of this great men-only society.'

'What?' She could see that I was taken aback by this revelation.

Bisht purred, picking up on my dismay. AIman laughed the same maniacal laugh she had learnt in the cave. 'Yes, she was the ringleader of the pack of geneticists who hid the fact that there were men whose genes reflected the purity of their origin and race. These men were superior to those around them in every which way. Yet, your mother hid this information, clinging to the notion that all are born equal.'

I laughed now, retorting sarcastically, 'So, my mother and her fellow geneticists were in the way of *Arman's* scientific foundation for tyranny and racism?'

AIman was confused by my laugh. The cat's gaze was unflinching now as it tried to read me. 'Your father . . .' she started, flummoxed at first, and began again, 'Your father is unique, which is why he became Dushita's chosen instrument. He was touched by Dushita's hand two thousand years ago. Yusuf Qadir Khan was a great warrior who conquered Khotan around the year 1006. He killed 40,000 men and took their women who were of Kashmiri descent. He had a mutant Y chromosome gene pattern. This gene eventually worked its way into Genghis Khan, and today, one in 100 men have it. Dushita graced this group with a common ancestor. It was an exclusive gift. Today, all QuGene warriors are from this common ancestor Yusuf Qadir Khan. Humans are now controlled by the Manity clade. They are the ones who get the technological edge in the warrior games.'

'Oh, spare me! Arman's mad dream, this male heredity tyranny of mutant humans is on a shaky foundation.'

'Tyranny? No, my sister. Not a tyranny but a cohesive social unit. All looking up to the Instrument, the guide,' her orb eyes changed colours gracefully. 'All sharing in his benefits of the pleasures of Paradise on earth. '

'To what purpose? You all can't even think for yourselves.'

'To create perfection based on an advanced information society. The Instrument is the saviour of the world who has given immortality, which is everything. Is it not? Every other visionary only promised an apocalypse. An ending of the world.'

'He's a saviour who kills all women. He's a wolf in a sheep's clothing. This information flow you keep talking about flows in only one direction: him. It yields darkness not light.'

'Oh, c'mon now,' she said, as the cat fidgeted in her hands. For a split second, she looked at it. 'Followers are transparent who share information. I am the information seeker who optimizes the information. It is for their own good. Only the Outlaws hide behind privacy and sub-optimize society.'

My legs had begun to ache, but I dared not show it. I counted my breathing. 'That is not the way humans are. Privacy is key to freedom. Their information belongs to them. Humans do not exist to serve a dark master who is not transparent.'

AIman moved closer to me. 'I am designed to be the perfect learning machine. That is why *I* am the holder of information. The best organizer of Manity.'

'But you are limited to the physical, sister.' It was my turn to threaten her. 'Humanity's unifier can have no such limitation. For starters, you keep using the term Manity because the word "humanity" that includes women is obsolete for you.'

'Really?' her hair suddenly changed colour to platinum blonde and the faintest ripple in her skin showed that it was turning white again. She was powering up. 'Test me and show me that I have a limitation.'

'Can you sneeze? Do your eyelids twitch? Do your ears ever tingle? Tell me, graphene *sister*, do you ever get goosebumps?' I said with the same sneering intensity as she had before.

'Nyaaaa—haaaa!' She started a laugh, which abruptly stopped midway. 'Leftovers cannot be the measure of an advanced life form. What use is your tail bone, your wisdom teeth or your appendix?'

'But these are an intrinsic part of humans. Involuntary means that nothing controls us. Arman decided that *you* did not need a heart,' I said, laughing, 'and so *you* do not know what an autonomous system is that moves without mind control.'

'Enough!' she said menacingly. 'Here human nature is controlled through science, and society and culture through the laws of Dushita. Nothing can be allowed to be independent of the mind. Your Outlaw myth itself has Brahma as the first individual with a mind. He created with thought. So, you too are mind-born, just like me, only inferior. Tch, tch!' Her hair rippled platinum blonde, each strand perfectly in place. 'With more thought comes more multiplicity. Water can be spray, foam, whirlpools or vortices, but it flows best when it is ordered.'

'You shouldn't be talking about Brahma. You don't do yoga, so you don't know that he is both mind and beyond the mind. There is a portal in the brain that is the cavity of Brahma. And you, AI-whatever, you don't have it.' I thought that it will rile her up, but I was wrong.

'Is that so? My sensors read heat running up your back. Is that your yoga's doing? What an obsolete technology to speed up the mind's reaction time and learning speed. You think that by running a very weak electric current through your brain, you can match *me*? Yoga? What need do Arman's immortals have for yoga?'

'Because yoga teaches you the dream that you are in. But you can't dream, so you will never know.'

'But you're wrong. I monitor the dream state for all through the shikha and it is a falsity. Dreams are not stable; they do not affect the waking state. And anyway, with the benefit of shikha, the followers stop dreaming. It was fruitless, so we took it away.'

'When dreaming stops, the Universe stops growing. You know, I dream of a half-elephant half-human all the time,' I said smilingly, thinking of my mentor Yuva.

'You fool,' she retorted, her fingers running ever so delicately on the Himalayan cat. 'An elephant head weighs up to 400 kg and an entire human only 62 kg. The elephant head would crush a human. For years, you have lived and gone mad in isolation. My stupid sister, if there were any merit in such a creature, the QuGene labs would have engineered it by now.' She started to turn around.

'When awake, one only sees the logic of fixity whereas a dream reveals fluidity. That is what the half-elephant half-man does. He is the symbol of imaginative creativity,' I said loudly to get her attention.

'In spite of the extraordinary genes that you inherited,' she said, turning back to scan me fully with her eyes, 'sadly, you have turned out to be less than ordinary. You are nothing but a cave dweller, no different than a Neolithic man.'

I smirked for a long, long time. 'You are nothing but bloatware. I hope that Arman is listening in,' I said, looking around the room for cameras, but the room was so white and technologically advanced, you couldn't see one. 'Do you know the very first thing that my mother did when she met Arman was to take a swab of his genes and run a test? You think that she would not have done a gene test of me? You think that my mother did not reveal this to me, finally? Your father, my dearest sister, was abandoned in an orphanage at birth. And do you know why? Because his father was a crook, an English cad who was visiting Kashmir where his mother had gone for a visit too. What a chance meeting! Do you now understand who and what first triggered his hate against women?

AIman had gone absolutely still. The hairs on Bisht's back were stiff. Then she spoke slowly, 'Your false inputs will not corrupt my data. You know nothing.'

'Your data is dirty. There was no mighty warrior named Yusuf Qadir Khan. Only an *ordinary* man named Joseph Kahn. All manufactured history. *Chhi-chhi*, unclean Circassian, you need data hygiene. My mother was an expert gene scientist and with her population data access, tracked down Arman's mother. For her safety, she erased all her genetic records, including information in the orphanage. When Arman went searching for his biological mother, he was thwarted. And when he did not know who he was looking for, he killed them all. Do you now understand why there was Gynaecide Day? Then he made up the cock and bull story of Yusuf Qadir Khan and falsified the genetic trail.'

'I evaluate your human condition as one of severe delusion. You clearly know nothing of history or reality.' AIman's hair now shone white, the peroxide blonde turning extreme. Her graphene skin was pulsating, like that of a snake slithering in water.

'Really, you do not know half of what I know. Let me test you. Show me how human you are.'

She snarled, now moving in the icy room that was just screens with swirling images. 'So, the weapon you use to fight me is mind versus mind. A mere sponge dares to challenge the greatest mind in the Universe. You are truly a *vaeran gomut*, a wild ass.'

My insults were working. It was time to pierce deep. 'A king sees a calf giving milk to its mother. What does it mean?'

AIman fell silent. With each passing moment, Bisht became uneasy, snarling and trying to escape its mistress' tight grip.

I answered my own question. 'It means that a woman lives on her daughter's income.'

'Next. The king saw a woodcutter walking, straining under the weight of a load of wood. On the way, he would stop and stoop slowly to pick up sticks and add them to the load on his back. What does it mean?'

Again, there was silence. AIman did not know. Bisht started purring angrily.

'For a slayer, there is no limit to greed. You are 0 for 2.'

'Next. The king along with his many queens was served a fish on the dining table. On seeing the king, the fish laughed. What does it mean?'

AIman's colour was radiating the blackness of pure graphene, but there was no response. Bisht was now standing with an arched back and erect tail and was spitting angrily.

I answered yet again. 'The fish was laughing because the king did not know that his queens were hiding a man in the harem.'

'You don't know much, do you? Especially when it comes to women.' I had won 3–0.

The four Pandavas, now fully awake, could not control themselves and let out whoops of victory.

I said triumphantly, 'Information is not what humans are about. It is our stories that make us who we are because they tell us our true nature. When humans meet, they do so for *Katha Batha*. You know what that means, don't you? Let me enlighten you: *Katha* means 'story' and *Batha* means 'converse'. It means we share our stories with each other, not our electronic, mechanical data drive. It is our stories that bind us as one, not your tyrannical rule.'

AIman spoke forcefully now, the graphene of her skin moving rapidly. 'Dushita is supreme and the Instrument is his messenger.'

'Stop parroting that, would you? "Instrument, instrument, instrument,"' Yaniv couldn't hold back. 'Your programming does not permit you to understand your limits, does it? When life is formed in the embryo, there is no mind. It comes much later. What drives life before there is mind? You can never learn that.'

She shot a glance at him and began to stride threateningly towards the boys who were huddled on the side of the room. I tried to think fast. 'Sister, hear this.' It worked. AIman stopped and turned to me. 'Know this—if the evil Dushita granted knowledge, then I would be far better off with my mind blinded than having my way of life be blinded by Dushita.'

AIman radiated anger, her voice hitting a high pitch. 'Sacrilege! You dare insult the great Dushita. You want to be the next Kota Rani, but you will only be the next *bali* rani, the sacrificial queen for Dushita. Tabah,' she said turning to him, 'take her away and prepare her for *Antyesti*. She needs to be ready for the last sacrifice of cremation where she will be beheaded on the upcoming birthday celebration of Kashmir. Meanwhile, I will make myself compatible to receive the offering of her blood and body.'

'Never!' I screamed, struggling against my restraints.

She walked up calmly to me, her hair now black again as she reverted to base state. Her voice was a mesmerizing drone. 'Dawn, you will submit and fulfil the Instrument's supreme wish and command. Your last tormented thought will be that of my mind on your body. Know this—I will match my face to yours, so that in me the Instrument will see you. Rest in peace.'

PRAKARANA III

LIFE

Sarga 14

Kurukshetra

Suaresvara Lake, Kashmir Valley

It was the day after the full moon night, the first day of the ninth month in the year. Kashmir's birthday was at the beginning of the month; it was considered as the most auspicious time in days of yore. Naturally, it was celebrated at Butshikan Stadium, which was built around the central Suaresvara Lake. A grand elevated stage with seats in neat rows was put into place on the island on the lake, which made for a spectacular setting. From the vantage point of the island, one could see on either ends—Sharika Hill and Pari Mahal. The temporary seating rising into the skies gave the giant amphitheatre enormous capacity to house the highest of the high. While the privileged got to witness the celebration live, the five billion shikha men watched the hologram images from their homes. The event would last all night and extend into the wee hours of the morning.

We were dragged in by the watchful guards, put in a green room under the stage and were instructed to get ready. They had already arranged for clothes and supplies there. From this seemingly empty room, which I assumed they had only cleared before we were brought in, we could watch the monitors that gave the full view of the stage.

Tabah Tasal, the Master of Ceremonies, strode up onto the stage from the waiting room below. He was glittering in jewels. His *nal*, the border of his pink coloured kurta, especially around the area from the neck running down the chest, was embroidered with exquisite detail. He had a red rose pinned to his left breast. What was remarkable was the whip that he was carrying—a *koodar*—made from the dried stem of an opium plant and woven in a tight, thick rope with a fork at the end. He walked to the centre of the stage and cracked the whip. *BAM!* It sounded like a gunshot. The audience was in rapt attention. 'Everybody, now clap your hands.' The crowd was in his control. Clap, clap, clap, they readily obeyed. I could guess why; in addition to being a jester, he had the remarkable ability to cup his hand in a way that his clap could be heard a mile away. 'Now! Everybody show your cow dung.'

'The WHAT?' Yaniv screamed over the noise of the audience.

Tan explained, 'The audience throws cow dung at an unsatisfactory performer along with loud boos.'

Yaniv looked at him disbelievingly. 'And they call themselves the most advanced empire on earth? You've got to be kidding me.'

'Tan, can you tell us why the theatrics?' Hafiz asked.

'You see brother, he's got them in his grip. He is after all the Master of Ceremonies. Tabah has now got the synchronization of the crowd's approval and disapproval chants. That's a crucial part of any theatre show, and here it has been established.'

We saw Tabah move to what was his signature line—denoting his low social status. 'Tabah is not ashamed,' he sang. '*Rah, rah, rah.*' The crowd hooted, 'Nor does he or she put any one to shame. *Rah rah, raah.*'

Tabah turned left, facing Pari Mahal across the hill, AIman's abode. He then made his invocatory call, 'There is none better than Your Magnificence.' The QuGene warriors threw their fists in the air along with the AIman clones and shouted wildly, 'None such! Your Magnificence!' As the chant continued, an ancient, collectable Tesla space car glided down, landing upon the earth. The car door was opened by a clone and out stepped AIman in her *kunsh* shiny shoes with 14-inch iron heels. She was wearing a white dress with gold embroidery. Her corseted waist revealed the perfect shape of her body. Covering her platinum hair was a tall white and gold hat, which was covered by a white transparent veil—the ends of which were hooked to her wrists. Just at that moment, the confetti fell on her from all sides of the stage. It was spectacular. The Fairy Princess raised her arms to the crowd with the grace of a swan. The white veil rose like the wings of a butterfly. The crowd went mad with excitement.

'She does have good taste,' I heard Yaniv say bitterly.

Hafiz whistled, 'What a beaut!'

'What?' Tan shrieked in total shock.

'I mean the Tesla!' said Hafiz, suddenly going red in the face. 'That Tesla space car was launched nearly a thousand years ago, remember?' He said, pointing to the car. 'It was orbiting around the sun. I wonder . . . how did they retrieve it?'

Tabah and the dancing ganas lead AIman to her throne. It was a seven-foot tall pure white seat that was made in the shape of a hamsa. A graceful swan for the king's most prized creation. AIman seated herself with her legs together and subtly turned sideways, so that their long silhouette could be viewed more effectively. On her face was an extremely demure expression. The crowd was singing, 'IT girl', and she would occasionally wave at them.

Yaniv teased Hafiz, 'You have a lot of competition for your IT girl.'

Hafiz pleaded, 'I only like our very own Niti girl. Please guys, that was a momentary slip.'

I simply remarked, 'She is inhuman. Just remember that when we go into battle.'

Tabah then turned right towards Sharika Mountain, the highest hill in the city in Kashmir Valley, and called out to Arman. 'Emperor Arman, we beg for your mercy!' The crowd too started appealing towards the hill, 'Be merciful! Be merciful! Be merciful.' It seemed as if the self-proclaimed emperor liked the hapless pleas of his subjects, but there was no sign of him. The chants started getting louder with the humans and hybrids appealing to their master, arms outstretched in front of them. Then there was the sound of 'Aaahhhhhh!' and a hush fell over the island, suddenly followed by a thunderous clapping.

It was Arman aboard an air-borne lotus chariot.

He is so arrogant that people have to beg him to make an appearance? My throat clamped up and my mind went numb. I could not tear my eyes away from the big screen in front of me. Finally, I saw my father *this* close. My sworn enemy.

From up high, he tossed apricots that had been picked from his famed twelve prized apricot trees to the delirious crowd. It was said that the trees that were planted on top of Sharika Hill were never out of fruit, even in the harshest of winters. Yaniv must have been thinking the same thing because he spoke up with disdain. 'Mutant apricots.'

The *ganas* bent down on their knees with heads lowered in submission.

AIman walked up to Arman with her arms outstretched and offered a date into his mouth. She then led him to the magnificent lotus throne. Its round base rested on a pedestal with the circumference designed in the form of lotus leaves. On it was a back rest that was in the shape of a circle, and above that was another small circle that was at head level.

Once Arman was seated, AIman sat on the lower hamsa throne on his right side. The king and his lieutenant. Arman was dressed in a green *jama*, a long coat that was beautifully embroidered in gold with a matrix pattern of 0s and 1s along with the letters G, C, A, T, S, B, P and Z. It was art reflecting life's highest realization of Unified Information in the numbers and alphabets. The crowd, appreciating his fashion style, shouted 'Killer, killer, killer'. Arman acknowledged the compliment, waving to the crowd and laughed, displaying supreme ease. My eyes moved to every detail: the superior gaze with which he looked at his fawning people, his equally king-like hand gestures, his gold ibex crown. But I had no feelings, only a mission. Yuva had said that Arman and AIman were already dead. I was only going to reveal what was his destiny. His clock had started ticking.

Tabah turned towards Dushitacharya Hill—situated between Sharika Hill and Pari Mahal—which was forbidden for anyone to climb or fly over. Atop it was what seemed like a stone ground floor foundation, but the upper level had transparent walls and an empty inner sanctorum. Tan whispered to us, 'Dushita temple is built on an older temple. It symbolizes that Dushita has removed the darkness of the past. He is empty of any sin, empty of any needs, empty of ego. Hence, the transparent walls.'

In a low voice, Tabah invoked Dushita's presence. 'There is but One Law.' All around the world, five billion men and their QuGene partners stood up. AIman and Arman stood up and placed both their hands on their hearts. This was a cue; the ganas and the crowd prostrated and chanted loudly, 'One Law, One Law, One Law.' Tabah continued, 'We are spiritually yours.' 'Spiritually yours, spiritually yours, spiritually yours.'

Tabah began cracking his whip and the crowd rose again to their feet excitedly. The leader of the army's honour guard marched in, holding Dushita's symbolic sword upright in his hand at neck level. The shiny blade was vertically inclined thirty degrees towards the front. The first troupe that strode in was that of the *ganas*, most prominent of whom was the half-man half-bull minotaur Nandi; *kinnaras*, birds with the head of a man; *kimpurushas*, beings with heads of humans and bodies of lions or horses; and a formidable transgender brigade. An army of the most terrible QuGene host of monsters followed: the man-eating rakshasas with fangs, claws, bull horns, dark hair and piggish eyes; the flesh-eating, angry pishachas with huge, bulging eyes; the wraith-like vetala vampires; the ghostly Bhutas who came in with their whistling sounds, catcalls and hisses; the herculean robber chiefs Dasyus; and finally at the rear, the ever popular, misshapen dwarf Kumbhandas from Buddhist folklore who tumbled and rolled forward. The honour guard started humming and started off the Dushita Anthem, and soon everyone joined in.

Mamah, Mamah, Mamah, mine, mine, mine.

Glory to us men
Marching in unison,
Glory, glory, glory.

Outlaw ju,
Mootr[9] on you.
Bow to the One
Or be undone,
Bow, bow, bow.

Mine, be forewarned,
We are dangerous and armed,
You are Mine, Mine, Mine
Mine, we will murder anyone
Who we shun,
You are Mine, Mine, Mine.

Dushita, we are Anahita,[10]
Dushita, we are Anahita,
Light our atomic lust,
Let our desire thrust,
Mamah, Mamah, Mamah.

As the chant finished, the crowd sat down. The fervour that the anthem had awakened in them was palpable. The commander of the army saluted Arman and AIman in the walk past. When he halted

---

9　Piss
10　Unkindled

and stood in front of them, he swung his head sharply to the left and then slashed his sword downwards besides his right foot.

Tabah cracked his whip again. He was now prancing on the stage in high spirits. He went near Arman and AIman and touched a button next to their throne. A blazing fire leapt out of the base of the stage where the two of them were sitting. It framed them in an orange-red glow. Then Tabah bounded back. 'It's time now for the *Kaen Jang* Olympics, the stone throwing fight!' The crowd cheered enthusiastically. All of a sudden, the *ganas* prepared the crowd by singing and dancing the ancient stone pelters *Sangbaaz* song, 'You can snatch out our eyes, but you cannot snatch away our Dushita dreams.' The home crowd went wild when two *saandhs*, the bull champions, who looked like men but had been engineered with animal bodies, entered the stage. Only one Man-imal would survive the gladiator contest and be declared as the Champion of the World.

I was dismayed by how humans had been re-engineered and degraded so low, so that they could provide entertainment to others. Tegh spoke up, 'Usually, there is a representative from Palestine in the finals, but this year, both the warriors are from Kashmir.' We nodded sadly and turned our eyes back to the screen; the scene was truly mesmeric.

The first finalist was from the mohalla of Ahalamar. His tribe, which was famed for its extreme aggression, cheered him wildly. Then the next finalist was disclosed. This year, he was from Suth. For the Ahalamar, nothing aroused their anger as much as their neighbours from Suth. The hostility between the tribes was captured in their motto 'Give as good as one gets.' The cross-town rivalry had the viewers salivating and clapping vigorously. The clones added to the excitement with their fists pumping high in the air. 'AIman just boosted the adrenaline of the men in the audience through the shikha,' came in Hafiz's voice. 'They are primed to explode.' Arman stood up to greet the warriors, a high honour for the fighters who were now baying for blood.

Tabah led the fighters into a transparent cage.

'The force fields in the cage will prevent a fighter from running away,' Tegh explained. 'The crowd knows that one will surely become a martyr . . . Perhaps both.' We all looked at him horrified. 'For them, it's an honour to die in the celebration of Dushita. That's how it has always been,' he spoke with a tinge of sadness. As the fighters prepared for battle screaming and beating their chests, the Ahalamar tribe stood up and sang an ancient song.

> Ragged clothes to the people of Suth,
> May their dirty bundles catch fire.
> Fie upon you, ugly and uncouth,
> Never dare to show your dirty buth.[11]

Hearing this, the Suth tribe too got up angrily and reciprocated with their popular battle song:

> The quarrelsome people of Ahalamar,
> Have not a rice grain in their pots.
> They have not a cowrie in their pockets,
> Yet, the fools of Ahalamar think they can spar.

A bell chimed then, which seemed to bind everyone in a silent spell. The fighters were ready. The two started circling each other like snarling dogs, slapping their inner thighs loudly, spitting ritualistic intimidations at each other in Kashmiri. The language was extinct, but somehow, the fighting curses had remained extant.

'*Photey gardhan.*' May your neck snap.

'*Payi katstember.*' May you be blinded.

'*Kajmai bokwach.*' I will rip out your kidneys.

'*Photyia shoosh.*' May your lungs burst.

'*Photyia koth.*' May your knees break.

'*Dravyai taas.*' You will explode.

---

[11] Face

Then it got dirty.

'*Pandaka*, show us your bottom.'

'What is happening?' said Yaniv, his eyes not moving from the screen. 'Pandaka or Pancika as he was also known,' explained Tan, 'was a general for Kubera, the God of Wealth. Kubera is regarded as the protector of Kashmir. It is said that he married a woman who turned out to be the Goddess of smallpox, and thus he lost interest in women.'

The insult was returned.

'*Nyotha*, what interest would you have in that?'

Tan translated, 'Oh! He just told the other that he is unable to perform.'

Stung, both fighters spun around and raced to their corners where their pile of stones had been placed. The stone throwing was limited by weight in terms of how many projectiles they were allowed. They were separated by twenty-five feet.

The first attacks were with triangular sharp stones. These missiles were designed to wound and weaken first since it was too early to knock out the opponent. Their hands were a blurry whirl, spinning flints launched in a sideways stance, so that they skipped multiple times on the ground or on the side force fields. 'The key is in the wrist action. It determines the spin and gives it better skipping capabilities,' said Tegh, who knew about all types of warfare and bloody history. 'One had to also be moving to dodge the incoming stones at the same time.'

It seemed like it was the finest bout that the audience had ever seen. There was no word to describe their energy. Sensing that, Tabah turned up the fire that burned near the thrones. The flames were now rising high in the air above the island, providing a dramatic backdrop to the two men fighting for their lives. I noticed AIman grow more restless as the heatwaves hit her, but Arman's body gear adjusted the temperature automatically. His face flushed red with excitement. He did not care as he stood up imitating the saandh's moves in a vulgar fashion. The man truly was an animal. Tabah was now circling around the cage, cracking the whip to increase the speed of the fighters.

The Suth fighter drew first blood. He had surprised both his opponent and the audience when they saw that he was ambidextrous. He was able to throw twice the number of stones with both his hands, the spins varying and making it difficult for the opponent to duck. Soon, the Ahalamar was bleeding.

'The Ahalamar fighter won't last long,' Tegh remarked. As if he had heard Tegh, the Ahalamar made a switch earlier than planned and picked up the round stones. These were the size of tennis balls but heavier and lethal. The heat of his flowing blood had given him an added intensity, and he got his first hit. The sound of the ribs cracking in the chest of the Suth warrior, his cry of pain, made the audience wince.

The two now went at each other using all their strengths to hit with as many stones as possible. One missile after the other hit the warriors, breaking bones, rupturing flesh and mangling organs. But they were beyond caring. With each hit, the crowd went 'Ahhhh!'

'That's Arman's deeply immersive, Vicarious Reality experience for you,' Yaniv said. 'The crowd can feel the thrill, every move, every hit, every breath. All being fed by AIman.'

The fighters no longer had any feeling left, they were gasping for breath. I winced at the violence, the gore, the pain. What awaited us? 'For them, it is for pride and glory, while rebirth awaits them anyway,' said Tan, observing me with some concern. I gave a slight nod and looked ahead.

Then the Ahalamar fighter stuck his left hand inside his pants. He pulled out a small sling! Within the flash of an eye, he had cocked it with the heaviest stone in his arsenal and let it fly. It sped like a cannonball and hit the Suth warrior in the forehead with such force that he fell down dead. 'The man never saw it coming,' Tegh concluded.

There was complete pandemonium now! The Suth tribe cried 'Cheat, cheat, cheat' at the Ahalamar fighter. I saw that the emotions of the crowd were now completely out of control. Tabah, spinning his whip, was executing his mission to a T. I smiled at my friend who was in the traitor's belly.

The audience now split evenly and there was a free-for-all. The AIman clones designed to please their masters followed suit and started attacking each other. 'With these many people, AIman surely is exerting maximum dose to calm the crowd—a mix of serotonin and other drugs through the shikha,' said Yaniv, observing AIman whose hair was changing colour rapidly. The bloodthirsty crowd settled back but kept glaring at the opposite camp with occasional growls. Arman watched delightedly, since this would create trillions of packets of information—entertainment that would last him for days. The shikha men could be manipulated easily and AIman controlled any eventuality, so there was no fear of a mob getting out of hand.

Tegh, who was watching Arman through the monitors intently, remarked, 'It's time.' We all turned to look at him. 'The crowd has tasted gladiator blood. Now we will be stepping in an arena surrounded by man-eaters. It's our time.'

The boys turned to look at me.

I was past my feelings. I smiled a cold smile. 'Remember, your eyes and mind should only be on me. Forget everything else.'

Nodding, the boys too smiled caringly as their eyes became moist and heavy.

'Okay. Here goes,' Hafiz said, breaking the moment. 'Tabah is raising the temperature of the fire by injecting more oxygen. It is getting hotter, but it's still a considerable distance from where AIman is sitting, which is not leading to a rise in her temperature. He is not able get it to go higher than 2,000 degrees Celsius.'

'We need around 4,500 degree Celsius. Graphene only melts at that point,' said Tegh, a note of panic rising in his voice. 'She needs to be hit with more heat energy.'

'There is a curious effect that is happening, guys,' Hafiz cut in again. 'Graphene is a great conductor of heat . . . It's making her . . . AIman is becoming even faster. The heat is enabling her to function better!'

'Then we have to start freezing her mind quickly,' Tan quickly replied. 'Hafiz, fire the paradox bombs into her system.'

'Righto.' Hafiz began injecting the information packets into AIman's circuits. 'Is it working?'

Yaniv observed the screen as her hair toned down to peroxide blonde and the crowd started getting violent again, freeing a bit from her control. 'Yes, I think so. She is slightly slowing down in her responses,' he said.

'Fire more and keep going. We must paralyze her. '

'Her CNS, Central Nervous System, is getting diverted to processing the instructions in the bombs,' Hafiz said with a surprised tone in his voice, 'but something interesting is happening. Her PNS, Peripheral Nervous System, is working faster because of the heat even as the CNS is slowing down because of the diversion.'

'What on earth does that mean?' I almost shouted.

'This will lead to the PNS taking over. I told you guys that biomimicry will play a role here.' Yaniv had a big smile.

'Care to elaborate for those who are not scientists?' Tegh said sarcastically.

'Yeah, yeah. The PNS is what causes a human to pull back their hand from a hot pan even before the brain can read it. Get it?'

'Yes,' said Yaniv, excitedly, 'Clearly, the Yoginis designed AIman based on Nature's principles. In a human, under normal circumstances, the PNS signal goes to the spine and then feeds to the mind, which is the CNS and then back. However, if there is an extremely hazardous sensory experience—'

'Then the PNS bypasses the mind and activates reflex actions. Autonomy takes over,' I said, completing Yaniv's sentence.

Hafiz cautioned, 'That's all good, you brainiacs, but don't get too excited. Right now, my sensors into her circuits are telling me that AIman has not reached the tipping point. Her temperature has plateaued, so the response time gap is not enough to trigger the reflex arc and bypass her mind. She is in stable mode and still extremely dangerous. And we have fired more than half of our weapons!'

Everyone fell silent, feeling anxious and angry. We had failed in our gambit. 'Let us keep watching her. Trust yourselves and each other,' I said, hoping to keep the morale up. My rage had intensified. Nothing was going to stop me.

It was the optimal time for Arman to execute his sacrifice sermon. The crowd was at the point of peak emotion now. Around the stage and the world around, five billion men stood up to give him the QuGene salute led by the commander of the honour guard. They pressed their left palm on the shikha plug set in the back of their head, symbolizing Unified Information, while their right hand was raised in a clenched salute, signifying power.

The bulging Arman stood up unsteadily, raised both his hands, palms out in approval. His voice rose high, 'You who are obedient know it is not about me. It is Dushita, the highest power. I am merely the Instrument. But cooperate we must with our advancing evolution.' The crowd listened to him in rapt attention and not a single sound was uttered.

'Intelligence Amplification was resisted by fearmongers of Artificial Intelligence. They banned robots that looked like humans. Those unbelievers who stuck with old Mother Nature had to be eradicated,' his high-pitched voice reaching crescendo. 'But Manity was unhappily bound in its physicality. It wanted infinity. And religion was so unsatisfying. It was *I* who gave you the pathway to live in a state of information infinity. It was *I* who gave you your birthright to be adaptable infinitely. *I* made you Transhuman. And finally, it was *I* who gave you your birthright to the pleasure centre in your mind. Now, to celebrate the birthday of this great land,

I will give you the greatest gift, my people.' The crowd howled approvingly at their master.

Arman raised his hand. 'First, Kashmir will be renamed as Circassia. Everything else has been renamed already and this will be our crowning glory. We have to sever this last heavy legacy of history. Let us embrace our glorious future just as we embrace our Circassian companions and give them due recognition.' The crowd cheered loudly.

Arman laughed; his palms outstretched over them in blessing. 'Tonight, you will also behold the sacrifice of my flesh daughter's head. I will fulfil Dushita's final wish.' A confused look appeared on everyone's face. 'Yes, yes, you did not know about her. My Outlaw daughter who refused to follow the laws of Dushita has been captured by none other than Tabah.' At this mention, I noticed a ripple in AIman's graphene scales. Surely, my younger sister didn't like anyone taking away her thunder, even if temporarily.

But Arman hadn't noticed, for he continued his glorious speech. 'My runaway daughter turned out to be no different than her treacherous mother who herself was a denier of the superior clade. But she was released from the error of her ways and shown mercy. And tonight, it is the turn of her daughter.'

There were tears in Tabah's eyes at Arman's announcement. The crowd saw that and interpreted it as his love for Dushita. Love and sacrifice were all that the supreme Instrument desired. In return, he gave ecstasy and eternal life.

Tabah now took centre stage and sang the ballad of sacrifice in a raspy voice.

It is easy to part with life for your sake,
You, who in exchange for one, a thousand lives make.

The crowd had joined in the chorus and were swaying to the rhythm of the ballad. I could see that even Arman was overwhelmed by the crowd's vociferous response. He raised his hands to give his blessing to Manity, while AIman received it to transmit it to the five billion men who were watching the hologram images from their homes. She stood up behind him and gave him a kiss on his bald head next to the shikha—a recognition that he was the only living human on the planet whose shikha was connected to everyone else. It was the most sacred spot and the most sacred of actions.

Hafiz said that the kiss had travelled through AIman along with the right chemicals and was transmitted to the billions of followers. It meant that they had formally renewed their binding commitment with Arman and through him with Dushita. The kiss was so intense that some spread out their arms and spun, others swooned and some fainted. Arman stroked his beard benevolently and raised his hands outwards to his followers. 'He owns them,' I whispered, horrified. Just then, some monster guards came inside the green room.

It was showtime.

The crowd hooted as Tegh stepped out first. Some hurled cow dung at him. He was followed by the others. The crowd roared while pressing their thumbs down.

It is time, I said to myself. Then I walked out.

I could feel everyone's eyes taking me in. I could have been an alien from Venus with the effect that I was having. In seven seconds, the jarring noise slowed, stumbled and then died out: I was different.

I strode up to Arman followed by the Pandavas. He was up high, the fire separating us, so I had to look up. It was the first time I was seeing him after my childhood years. His hooded eyes, hooked nose and thick lips peering from inside his beard gave him an unnerving look. Something made me shudder. He was the man who had burnt a hole in my mother's heart and mine.

'The prodigal daughter returns! I knew you would come to me, finally, my Outlaw daughter.'

I spat on the ground, 'Murderer, I am my mother's daughter. You are no one to me.'

Arman laughed. 'Your mother's temper! The returned daughter holds an even more powerful charm if she denies her parentage.' His smile turned to haughty anger. 'You are guilty of killing Ky(Q)om, our bravest warrior. Truly, the bad are rewarded with victory while the good are punished. But justice will be done to Ky(Q)om.' He turned his right thumb down, and the crowd hollered their agreement.

'I offer my daughter's head to Dushita, may we be his. From today onwards, Manity is free of the evil that is the last woman. From today, I am greater than Abraham. Today, her body will become that of AIman, and from today,' he paused, 'she will become the mother of the shikhas. As for you vermins,' he said, looking at the boys, 'let them be fed to termites.'

Tabah started a chant, clapping his hands, and the crowd echoed,

Merciful father,
Intelligent mother.
Both together,
Pandavas, you are ether.

A termite mound in the form of a giant clay linga was carried in by Tabah's brigade. A goat was brought in and the saandh champion slew it with a sword. The termite linga was anointed with the blood, which got the termites into a frenzy. Then my mace, the spoil of war, was brought out and placed alongside it.

Tabah's voice boomed through the mic in his headpiece. 'Tonight, you will see two great acts—the triumphs of the Instrument's QuGene scientists. They have created mutant human-eating termites. Necrotizing fasciitis, flesh-eating bacteria, have been ingested inside the termite gut that will cause a mutation. Thanks to the great Dushita and his Instrument!' Tabah clapped and was followed by the hundreds of thousand others who had gathered there.

'Secondly, you will also see what has never been attempted before. Behold! An inter-QuGene-human transplant that will lead to the birth of the Meta-human!' The crowd erupted in jubilation. Tabah cracked his whip. 'Today, on this historic day, you will experience five Outlaw extinctions and one rejuvenation. The excruciating pain of the neurons firing for the last time, the heartbeat palpitation, the brain waves decaying away, the termites chewing and churning, the joining of Nature's creation with Arman's, the rejuvenation and then the perfected creation—it all awaits you in this grandest of grand finales.' The crowd sat back, clapping thunderously. Then Tabah turned to face Arman. 'Instrument, it is your customary practice to grant the last wish. May we do so?' Indulgently, Arman gave the thumbs up sign with a bemused smile on his face. 'What is the wish of the condemned?'

I was ready. 'My last wish is to perform and entertain. I want the Pandavas to join me as I do the last dance.' Music and dancing were strictly forbidden under Dushita's rules for the public.

'It is against Dushita's law,' thundered Arman. 'But I have given my word. So be it. Anyway, soon you will meet your end.'

The crowd nodded in agreement. The Instrument was honouring his word, but Dushita's unsparing judgement for breaking the law would follow shortly thereafter.

Tabah waved his hand and the stage door opened. A transparent laboratory was brought in with the QuGene scientists who would take over once the dance ended. Dressed in green scrubs, the QuGene scientists surrounded me and the Pandavas in a circle, while holding their surgical instruments in their hands. They were all Bhatta award winners, the best of the best. Then came in Tabah's assistants who also brought us the musical instruments that we had asked for.

Tabah was mocking in his invocation. 'Presenting the last woman standing on earth. The Niti girl and her Pandava dance troupe. Pleasure beyond the senses and beyond the instrumental. Outlaws, make your move.' With a flourish, he completely dimmed the lights but made the flames rise even higher so that the fire provided the light on the stage. The oxygen was now blowing full blast alongside the natural gas. The leaping flames that were almost licking me made it seem as if the fire was ravenous and had waited too long for me.

I looked up and prayed silently. The full moon had risen in the sky. I greeted it with folded hands. I took a moment to say an ancient chant that my mother had taught me—the Gayatri Mantra. My mother had told me that its vibrational energy was especially matched to my name Dawn.

> O Self-effulgent light
> That has given birth to all the spheres of consciousness,
> Who is worthy of worship,
> And appears through the orbit of the sun,
> Illumine our intellect.

I had to slay AIman, and for that, I had to have all the Niti knowledge come together without a single misstep. I turned to face Arman. He used to sing to me the koori lullaby when I was a young child. It was his only gift to me, and his last gift would be my returning it back to him. Softly, I crooned the ancient lullaby, an ode to all baby girls.

> O fair one, I hold you tight in my heart,
> My cherub, so delicate, like a heavenly flower.
> Soft like cream is my milky angel,
> Your birth was the awakening of my life.
> A good luck charm that I will wear to the end,
> My little angel frolic with goddesses in your dreams.
> And when awake give me your sweet smile of recognition,
> It fills me, your father, with nectar.
> On your wedding, you will adorn divine earrings,
> Dazzling the world my little koori with the beauty you bring.
> And when you depart with your beloved,

You will leave behind
A golden bird in my heart,
Singing, O little angel mine.

I looked up at Arman. I could see that I had penetrated through to him. The lullaby had, for a brief moment, brought to the fore the man who had once won my mother's heart, the man that he could have been. What was his melodious voice was now my hypnotic draw that had left the crowd in silence. Each man was thinking about the daughter that he once had and would never have again. Sadness swept over them of what might have been. Arman shook his head as if snapping out of his reverie and, with a grim expression, came back into his present persona.

The moment turned, and so did I to face the audience. The crowd saw that I had turned my back on AIman and Arman and booed me. It was an insult to their supreme lord. Never mind, I would pay dearly here. I looked for the first time at the sea of men facing me.

I saw the eyes of the men that had viewed womenkind with flimsy courtesy. They looked upon me as if I was from another planet. I extended my hand out, palm facing me. In its mirror, I serenely contemplated my beauty. I channelled all that I had learnt from my teachers, and especially from Yuva. My flowing silk and tulle dress worn on top of my spacesuit was a striking saffron colour that Tabah had placed in the green room. It glittered with gems like that found in my former home, the beautiful cave. My arms were laden with jewels befitting a queen—rubies, emeralds and lapis lazuli. For my head, I was given a crown on top of my kalaposh cap that was studded with diamonds and topped with a large sapphire on top—the last gift to remind the Outlaw daughter what could have been hers. The Pandavas were in purple robes. They looked royal. The Pandavas began the music with their instruments—the santoor, the *tumbhaknar*, the *dumroo*, the bell and the *chimta*. Their Personal Digital Assistants had been programmed beforehand to guide them effortlessly. I started warming up with small steps. Then Tan began the beat:

Ta da dam,
Ta da deum,
Dhaa dhin,
Dhin dhaa.
Dhaa dhin,
Dhin dhaa,
Dhaa tin,
Tin taa.
Taa dhin,
Dhin dhaa!

Like a gazelle, I sprang up on my toes. I jumped up, kicking my heels against my back, landing in a squatting position. My feet were pointing in the opposite directions. I jumped again into a standing posture. I raised the right foot up above the left foot, and then jumped on the right foot with the left foot up higher than the waist. I repeated the process alternating the hop and swing the leg to each side. Each jump reflected the power of life to overcome the power of death. I held my hand up facing the fire, displaying the ability to face fear. Coming down on the flat of the feet on the note ta and on dhin, I landed on my toes for speed.

Hafiz danced close to me and whispered that AIman was picking up that the crowd was getting energized in a way that she hadn't witnessed earlier. All sensory systems within the shikha men were engaged and firing. Hafiz's paradox bombs—already installed in AIman's system—were overloading AIman's energy capacity and she was dragging a bit, but still not in any way incapacitating her. He had plugged us into his sensor readings.

But then, the first anomaly occurred, which his sensors picked up. Each shikha man was seeing a different me—his own Dawn. Do You See What I See was a common game in Arman's empire, designed to show how objects were perceived, which were then shaped by the onlooker's wishes. There were now five billion Dawns that had paired up with the men. The shikha men all stood up and started dancing with their Dawn. Each felt like they were the chosen partner in the *Tandava* dance. The tempo of the music increased and then decreased in alternating cycles. As if on cue, Tan sang a *leela* verse.

> When baby Krishna was born,
> Lord Shiva who we adorn,
> Came running to have darshan,
> And danced for his favourite son.

The men were slowly dissolving into a rhythmic energy flow. It was not me but the dancer who had mesmerized them. AIman tried furiously to interrupt with a command to her clones to distract the unruly dancers, but what was happening in them was beyond the mind, in a region that she could not penetrate. AIman's skin was breaking out into unruly waves. Hafiz quickly launched most of the viruses in his arsenal. She tried to isolate them and erase them, but all was happening too fast at the same moment. There were new openings that were revealing themselves within her design. The graphene skin shimmered and changed, indicating that she was trying hard to shut down the viruses but not fast enough. We had bombarded her with too much information. The viruses were multiplying and sapping her of capacity.

The dance ended. But it was not over.

I smiled sweetly at my audience.

I had concluded the first part and began the second by taking a few playful steps. Bashful and confident with folded hands, I stretched out my limbs slowly in front of the Pandavas. They followed with the music we had rehearsed on. The beat was now unhurried.

My body folded and unfolded gracefully, weaving circles in the air. I was the charming Lasya dancer, a form first said to have been performed by Goddess Parvati. It was a form that was delicate, enticing and magnetic. Hafiz alerted me in real time as to what was going on. My mind was calmly observing even as my body was flowing, each curve embodying the form of River Vitasta. The human-hybrids in the audience pushed the clones away. They realized that what was next to them was synthetic sameness. I was natural. They realized that it was the nature of Nature to be diverse and they had been deprived of it.

The shikha men were finally caught in the net of my leela. My Lifetrons had tunnelled inside them and entangled with their Lifetrons. When that connection was locked in, it fired up. The shikha men rushed to the stage, first hundreds, then thousands and then hundreds of thousands milling around it in a total state of frenzy. They tried to climb the stage and get to us, entrapped by the dance.

To counter, a desperate AIman shot a chemical command—a release of serotonin—to force the men to break their concentration. But according to Hafiz, it seemed that it had been blocked by my dance. Hafiz noted that something was flowing upwards within them in a finer form, which was not getting picked up by Arman's sensors. All that he could sense was an energy that had enveloped the humans. To AIman, the men had gone mad. Tan had a beatific smile, and I understood. The battle between AIman and me was an unequal one because I was using weapons that AIman's inferior technology simply could not penetrate. AIman had been rendered obsolete by Nature, by the juice of life that my teachers had talked about.

Then Tan slowly sang the closing song—a song Kira had taught us to use as the ultimate weapon against all demoniac forces. Tan tried to replicate her sweet voice.

Namami shamishaan nirvaan roopam
Vibhum vyapakam brahma vedswaroopam.

Nijam nirgunam nirvikalpam niriham
Chidakash maakaash vasam bhajeham.

The notes of the santoor were fading away. Slowly, I sank down
on my knees with folded hands, my heart and mind settled on
namami, my limitless self that had broken the knots in my heart
and the noose of the cage that had bound my body. It was the
grand finale. I looked up.

AIman was still functioning.

Arman was sneering.

Time had run out for me.

Muladeva had trained me to maintain face even when dead.

I stood up and began to slowly slide towards the stage exit door
facing the shikha men with my hands folded, bidding goodbye
to them forever. My heels were closing and opening alternately, a
sideways moonwalk. The QuGene scientists quickly followed me
with their weapons. Their circle tightened around me. I was theirs
now. *My time has come*, my heart sank.

AIman and Arman had won.

Suddenly, a frenzied cry went up from the shikha men. It was like
one that I had never heard before. They shouted 'NOOOO! Mamah,
Mamah, Mamah, mine, mine, mine!' as the orgiastic dam burst.
'NOW!' I ordered Hafiz, 'Go, go, go!' Hafiz immediately fired all his
remaining paradox viruses into AIman. Simultaneously, the humans
clamoured on to the stage to get to the last woman with a free mind.

It was a 100 billion-watt Rasa energy of desire that had burst
from the five billion shikha males. It hit AIman's reflexive PNS
system precisely at the point that her overloaded, controlling CNS
system was barraged by the new paradox bombs, making her scramble
for additional surge requirement. That ran head-on into her energy
reserve limits, causing her CNS to slow down.

'What is going on?' I asked, frantically looking at the scientists around me and the audience, who too had paused and stood silent like robots.

Hafiz's excited voice came in, 'She got overloaded. AIman's PNS reflex system has tripped its fuse. This has automatically put the human's brains in complete lockdown mode, bypassing AIman's central command and control brain and switched them off to stop the Rasa energy burn. Wait, wait, wait! Her brain is coming back online and slowly trying to reconnect. What the . . .' he stopped.

All of us yelled, 'What's going on?'

'Yes, one second, I'm scanning. So, her mind is getting synchronized with the shikhas. It seems that it's a . . . a void.'

'What void?'

'Dawn. They are dead. Their minds have been completely short circuited. It happened when AIman put them on lockdown mode. '

'Dead?' my eyes scanned the crowd. No one was moving.

But Hafiz, completely in trance, didn't hear me. 'Oh my! AIman is synchronizing now, but . . . but her memory is getting completely *erased!* The reboot connected her to the blank shikha men. They erased her out.'

This was what Patanjali had said. A calm mind could still a turbulent one.

'Look, look at the Circassian clones! The blankness of AIman has now flowed into them. It seems . . . it seems they have been wiped out too. This is colossal! This is Data Deluge on a universal scale!' Hafiz screamed. 'Yoginis, I could kiss you for being the great programmers that you were. When you designed the Master-Slave synchronization, you gave unidirectional power to the people to be Truth Keepers. The minds of the shikha men became blank as it prevailed over AIman. Man over machine.'

As I tried to process the information, my eyes scanned the stage. And it was then that I saw a sight that I would never forget: AIman, her eyes blank, lifeless orbs, standing still with her mouth all frothy. This was strange for an AI. White pus dribbled from the side of her lips and leaked from her eyes. Her graphene body began to blotch and break out, as if insects longed to escape her skin. Her face began to morph into a shapeless pudgy mass and her twisted mouth opened into a soundless scream—as if as a last cry for help. She looked like she was gasping for air. Then slowly, very slowly, like time itself had slowed, the graphene particles started peeling away from her body, large black flakes scattering on the stage. She was literally getting flayed apart, molecule by molecule. The other Circassian robots followed her disintegration. When it was all over, there was only graphene dust on the floor of the stage and the stadium, alongside the dead men who still stood transfixed by the power off command that had aborted all mental and physical activity within them.

'In death,' said Tan, his head bowed, 'it was the final revenge of the shikha men over their tormentor.'

'Their tripwire of natural response based on biomimicry has completely wiped out Arman's UI,' said Yaniv, jubilantly.

'We . . . we have *won*?' was all I managed to say. The victory was not sweet, for all the men had perished. Five billion of them. It was a great price to pay and along the lines of what my mother had predicted.

My eyes now red and blurry with rage, I looked at Arman. He stood among the dead. The QuGene scientists, the men around the stage, the clones and his grand creation—the Fairy Princess AIman—had all fallen. I observed him as he frantically attempted to revive command and control through his connectivity controller, screaming for it to reboot, but it was of no use. He knew that it was the end. He stood up and threw the controller to the ground, smashing it to smithereens.

Grabbing Dushita's sword that was placed on the glass table in front of his throne, he came swinging wildly towards me, his mad eyes red, down the steps of the stage. 'Don't you even dare!' I thundered. Instantly, my mace flew up and landed in my hands, hot and glowing in the light of the flames. I clamped my right hand around it. The fire licked my skin and long flowing hair. My blood oath vow was screaming to be completed. 'For my ma and all the women who were taken before their time, you murderer, you will finally pay. Conquer for Life!' The mace pointed itself at Arman and I could feel a pulse of energy burst out of its three prongs and hit him. I shook from the blast. I looked up to see the mad king. He fell when the bolts crashed into him, his hands twitching uncontrollably. The sword fell from his hand with a loud thud near where he stood. He tried to stand up and take a step but now convulsing violently, he rolled down the stairs that led from his throne pedestal to the termite hill.

'He's in the grip of an epileptic seizure. It is being created by an electrical storm in his brain that your mace has set off,' said Tabah, peering at the man who was once the king but now a nobody.

Quickly, Tabah grabbed the sword near my feet and sliced the top of the termite hill. The insects came swarming out and fell upon the twitching Arman.

Tabah raised his arms up to the sky in front of the towering fire and shouted, 'Tabah Tasal has finally got respect. The curtain now falls on the greatest natya performance ever.'

'It is time.' Tan announced, tearing away his purple robe. 'Time to leave this death ruin.'

The Pandavas looked at me, their general, for orders. I smiled. We powered up our suits and I grabbed my mace. As I flew straight up, the mortal screams of the rapidly disappearing Arman died a slow death. Together, we had won the war of the mind through the Niti stories of yore and the war of the heart through the love that only comes naturally to humans.

I closed my eyes for a moment to feel the breeze on my face, 'Maej, you got justice, and through your supreme power to create life, women everywhere have been avenged. You go from limbo to liberation. This victory is yours.'

Sarga 15

Anything Can Happen

Amarnath Cave, Srinagar

Tegh chuckled, 'I knew that the heat energy limit would do AIman in. Force works, huh?'

'Hold it! Hold it,' Hafiz challenged, holding his hand up, 'It is the paradox bombs that did it, brother. It is information that works,' he said, tapping his forehead.

'Right,' Yaniv rolled his eyes. 'And who would you say discovered the gap between the body reflex PNS and the mind-controlling CNS? The ancients used to say that time slays all. But in this case specifically, it was the quick response of the PNS that shut off the CNS and then the shikha men, which began the demise of AIman.'

Tan, uncharacteristically, jumped in, 'But who sang the beat that created the natural vibration and the dying notes within the men?'

Tabah smiled. He was not to be left behind. 'The actors should always bow to the stage director. Without Rasa, we would be nowhere.'

I laughed observing the back-and-forth between the boys. The ordeal was over . . . somewhat . . . until our final face-off with the ultimate enemy. Right now was a time to rest and celebrate. 'But who did the movement, you dolts?' I said, trying to join in with a smile, but it wouldn't come easily. I stood up and took a deep breath. 'Have we forgotten Yuva, Kira, Idagali, Muladeva, Meghavahana and hundreds of others who showed us that desire beats the mind? Have we forgotten our teachers who opened our minds and hearts to Yoga, Rasa, to Maha and to the secret powers inside us that we have unlocked? Have we forgotten the little mosquito and his friends who taught us that we have to trust each other and all the stories that revealed the Niti secrets that have helped in defeating AIman and Arman?'

The Pandavas instantly became apologetic. 'We were just having some fun,' said Yaniv, looking at the sky, his face red with shame.

I smiled sadly; my heart was heavy. I didn't want to be rude to my friends or take this victory away from them, but my conscience was weighing heavy on me. *Was this even a victory?* I thought bitterly. The death of billions was on my head. My hands were red with their blood. Again and again, my mother's prediction of the final Great War came back to me, haunting me: *Everyone will die.*

We had settled down in Jwala Devi's centre in the village of Khaduvi, which had been renamed Khrew. The sanctum sanctorum had an eternal flame that kept us warm. I was so weary after the battle that the gentle warmth of the place was sorely welcome. Tabah had suggested the location to thank the energy of fire, which had kick-started the last dance. It also had an ancient temple at the entrance, which surprisingly had a commemorative statue of Yuva. I thought that it was very appropriate given what he had done for us. The place was quite stunning, bathed in natural beauty, whether aware or unaware of the death of its citizens, who knew? It just lived on like nothing had happened, like five billion people hadn't perished. 'With the advent of the ice age after the cooling of the earth, following global warming, many corrective action steps were initiated here,' said Tan, eyes closed, taking in deep breaths. 'Three hundred and sixty springs had been recreated in the neighbourhood along with the volcanic flame,' said Tan, finally opening his eyes and walking back inside the inner sanctum. I looked around. *It is indeed a very beautiful, restful stop.* I wrapped a heavy robe, which had been hanging on a hook at the entrance, around my suit and followed him in.

My attention had now turned towards Dushita.

'He will no longer remain remote, having seen his entire work destroyed. His great creation is dead,' said Tan, his hands white from the cold, seeking warmth in the eternal fire.

'We have to put together our plans to face him,' I said, dropping the robe and sitting down on it beside the flame, my skin and hair almost touching it.

Tan nodded and brought out some scrolls from his bag. He had checked all the ancient resources that he had on Dushita. 'Sit everyone,' he said in a calm but commanding voice. Hafiz raised an eyebrow and Tegh's lips curled into a smile. Tabah shook his head gently, shepherding them around Yaniv who had already taken his seat.

'The first representation of Dushita that we have is in Kashmir when he appeared in the form of Mara,' Tan recited, his eyes closed. 'He had sent his daughters to tempt Buddha, but he was defeated. Mara is from the word *mrtyu*, which means "death".'

'Death?' Hafiz asked.

'Yes. He was the joint strike force born of desire and death at the very moment when Life first appeared. His was the energy of temptation and violence. And now he has returned in the form of Dushita.'

'So . . . wait!' Yaniv said anxiously. 'You're saying Dushita is actually an ancient person . . . umm, entity? He's *not* a real person like Arman?'

Tabah shook his head and held out a picture of a relief fragment of Mara that he had found as part of his search for stage props. The stone sculpture showed the face of a handsome young man. He had an asymmetrical hairdo bunched on the left side of his face, and on his head was a turban richly adorned with jewellery. His bushy eyebrows met in the middle atop big round eyes. He had a square chin with a cleft in it, and his ears were relatively bigger than normal. He was so typical of any young member of the royalty that the portrait seemed ordinary except for a mark on his forehead that seemed to have come from a branding iron. What caused shivers to run down my back was the hint of two lower canine teeth that were jutting out. As if concealing them was a handlebar moustache that covered his upper lip, the mouth slightly open in a lewd, arrogant smile.

'Dushita is a director who understands the arts. He's confident. He exudes power. Everyone who meets him wants to be him,' Tabah said, as everyone peered to look at the handsome face on the relief fragment. 'He spread the desirability of death into society by glamorizing it. He is also a trickster. He misused the saying, "If you meet the Buddha on the road, kill him". What was meant was that nothing should distract one's mind, not even the appearance of Buddha. Gullible people who fell for Dushita did not understand that it was metaphorical and not literal. They took it literally and killed all the enlightened humans.'

'Yes,' Tan nodded ruefully. 'Mara was next seen by humans when he appeared as Satan. Again, he was temptation and death.'

Muttering 'Satan' under his breath, Yaniv tracked the evolution of death on his system. 'Death accelerated at the turn of the second millennium, and by 2020, one person was dying a violent death every twenty seconds. It went up exponentially as humans engaged with addictive technology. Young men and women were especially at risk. By 2050, it says here, it had become a global epidemic: "Dushita-inspired violence becoming the number one cause of death". By the year 3000, as we all know, Dushita was supreme.' Looking up from his system, he said, 'What we did to AIman and Arman will not be forgiven by him. He is coming for us.'

'Dushita knows infinite ways to slay us,' Tegh said, taking a sip from his herbal tea. He had still not healed completely after his encounter with Ky(Q)om. 'None of our senses or mental faculties can identify him. We don't know who he is or what form he is in or what form he can take. What we do know, however,' he said, wincing as he tried to sit up, 'is that Dushita cannot send his daughters against us as he had with the Buddha. There's none left. He will come himself.'

'But how do we defend and protect ourselves against an unknown?' asked Yaniv frantically, moving his fingers rapidly on his system.

'There is a way,' Tan spoke. 'Maybe,' he added, as he saw everyone looking up at him, their eyes hopeful. Taking a pause to read some unusual ancient paper texts, he suggested the way forward, 'I have researched that there is a place in the Valley where the holder has foreknowledge or as we say premonition. It is the practice of *Brahas Katha Vuchin* where we can know what is in our future from an ancient text that a teacher by the name of Bhrigu wrote. The unknown becomes known there.'

'Then let us head over there. That's our way forward,' I said, standing up.

There was a sign on the entrance: *Anything can happen.*

Tan had brought us to the location mentioned in the texts called the Adhbuta House. Tan beckoned me to enter. I found myself in a room with probably a thousand crooked mirrors. In them, I saw a hologram with a million reflections of a man staring next to a text. He greeted me without turning his head, 'Salutation, rising Dawn, destiny's child. I have waited for you.'

I was surprised. 'How do you know me?'

'Why, I know everything that will happen. You are here because of Dushita.'

I asked tensely, 'Will Dushita win and will I die?'

'You will certainly die. Everyone dies. Dushita may lose as he has before, or he may win. Anything is possible.'

I was trembling. The man's voice was devoid of passion, of emotion. It made all the things he said sound terrifyingly eerie. 'Can you . . . can you guide me?'

'Why, yes, of course! That is why people come to see me. I will tell you exactly how your story will play out.'

He began his story.

'Once upon a time, more than two thousand years ago, there was a girl around your age who possibly had a stroke that paralyzed her. Given the times, her people gave her various names for she was the one whose body was hunched or as they said, *Kubjika*. This girl encountered someone by the name of Bhairava who was touched by her plight and gave her hope. Bhairava told the girl that she must attain the personal power that is beyond all limitations. And then, he disappeared. He told her that anything is possible.

All that this girl could do physically, and that too with great difficulty after her life-changing event, was to breathe. She did that one-pointedly. Oh wonders! Did she figure out the mystery of life that her vital breath had hidden within it? The power of her breath turned her into a charismatic communicator, and soon she gained great powers. She became venerated as a local energy source. Her lore travelled from the Western Himalaya to Goa and then on to Kashmir where it bloomed. She emerged as the most powerful force in the eyes of the initiated. So powerful that she was kept a total secret by the Yodhas. Even as they suffered continuous genocide over 700 years, they did not reveal her secrets. There were only mysterious whisperings of her existence and she was merely referred to as the Secret Force.'

'Then what happened to her?' I asked, anxious.

'Why! She was rediscovered among the Newars, the indigenous people of Kathmandu, Nepal, a thousand years later. She was worshipped exclusively by the Nepali royalty, the bravest warriors of the world.'

'How . . . what did she look like? What was her power? I do not understand . . .'

'She is described as of slender build, and her dark, almost blue, skin shining. Kubjika uniquely personifies fertile creativity. She is the creative power of potent possibility that lies beyond the mind, what makes anything possible. For the last thousand years, brave warriors who were at the greatest risk of being injured or death, sought protection in secret from this goddess whose loving gift was that of confidence in the potential of possibility. Any handicap only made one differently enabled.'

That was the end of this strange man's story.

'Who . . . who *are* you?' I asked this eccentric person.

'I am a *Granthika*, the last of the storyteller scientists, a chronicler of *akhyana* stories and the ancient tales that hold the Niti secret. Everyone who comes here thinks that their story is unique, but the truly unique stories are all in here. I know all the plots, the emotions and most importantly, the endings. Yet, people mistake me for an astrologer,' he said, turning to look at me.

He was blind!

'Why . . . why stories?' I asked, recovering from the shocking revelation and trying not to stare at his face being reflected in the million mirrors.

'Because *we* are all stories. The grand stories are the ones that awaken and harmonize whole societies.'

'Did Dushita not have the same goal? How are Niti stories different from Dushita's stories?'

'The two are totally different. Dushita's stories are about temptation and death. Niti is about life. Dushita's technique is about rules, dos and don'ts, good girl-bad girl, rewards and punishments. Niti stories are about making you a better human through purification of what you want by you, for you. The Niti technique is entertainment, education, empowerment and enabling, which leads to self-ignition. There is death in one and dance in the other; prohibition in one and permission in the other. Niti's goal is harmony with one's Self, which is the only way to peace and happiness. When individuals are in harmony with themselves, then and only then, society is in harmony. The Niti story that wins is the key to human harmony.'

'How do I find this Niti story that wins?' I pleaded.

His multiple figures approached me. 'Arise Dawn, the Niti warrior. It is time to manifest.' I walked up to the mirror in the front, where he seemed to materialize as I neared it. Taking a small plate in his hand that had suddenly appeared next to his ancient text, he dabbed his fingers on a red paste. For a man who was blind, he could see everything it seemed. He applied a tilak on my forehead and asked me look into a pan of melted ghee that too had appeared miraculously next to the text without me noticing. 'What do you see?'

'A pair of earrings.'

He smiled, put his hands inside the ghee and voila, out came the earrings. 'It was Queen Kota Rani's *dejhoor*, the magical earrings that every married Kashmiri woman wears,' he said, as if he could see my puzzled expression. 'Before you face Dushita, go to the Amarnath cave where you will find the story that wins. It is the greatest story of all,' he said, looking into my eyes. 'The story by knowing which one need not know any other.'

I nodded. He seemed to know everything, for he continued after a pause.

'But what is critical is that you carry only your mace with you and discard everything else and *everyone* else on the way. Enter the cave on the dark night of the upcoming twelfth month of the year.' As cryptically as he had begun, he stopped talking.

Leave everything? My friends . . . and Yuva! I was too stunned and too overcome with emotions to ask anything else. I couldn't even feel a thing. It was as if my soul was leaving my body. Even as I steadied my breathing, I knew in my heart that it was coming. It always had. Mother had warned me. I just did not know how and when.

I bowed to the Granthika and turned to leave. As I was leaving, I turned my head to say goodbye. Except for the ancient text with an anthology of the world's unique stories in it, there was nothing there.

The storyteller and the mirrors had vanished. Only the words of his story remained.

The Pandavas had become very uneasy and quiet after my meeting with the Granthika. The idea that I would have to leave them forever and enter a strange cave was unacceptable to them. But something made me feel that he could be trusted. I knew it was gut-wrenching, but I had to do this. The last leg of my journey was to be undertaken alone.

'Amazing things you find when you bother to search for them,' Tan eventually said, tears in his eyes. 'There are so many stories that have come before us. If stories have existed for a long time, then it is for us to avail of them. If Dawn is the only one equipped to seek the story that wins, then Yuva's reason to select her to lead us is now revealed.' He bowed to me. I quickly turned as hot tears started streaming down my eyes. I did not want the boys to see me like this. I wiped my face and steadied myself.

When I turned, all five of my friends, the Pandavas were on their knees, their heads bowing and their hands folded in *namaskaram*.

After some days, the Pandavas and I left for Amarnath. To my great joy, we were joined by Yuva. Surprisingly, he was alone this time and he told us that this time, I would be the guide and he would follow me. When asked about Kira, he simply replied that I would see her soon.

Winter had now covered the Valley in its fold. There was snow everywhere. But the mace on its own was our guide, cutting a pathway for us. It led us with a sense of anticipation as if it was homeward bound. We soon reached a river. The banks, the trees and the stones there were all covered in white snow. But amazingly, the water still flowed with a loud gurgling sound. Yuva playfully inhaled the cold water with his trunk and then sprinkled me with it. The Pandavas laughed.

I screamed, my face freezing. 'Stop, stop! Why Yuva?'

'Why not?' Yuva said. 'This river is named Lamboodri or Lidder after me. The sound you hear is my *Bheema Garbha*—a celebratory song for you. You defeated Alman and the evil Arman because of Niti. I sprinkle this water on you to wish you well.' My face turned pink at this high honour. It had not been too long ago when I had been an ignorant and terrified pupil of his.

We continued our trek through the high snow reaching a spot that Tan said was Bel Gaon. It was my first heartbreak point. I told Tegh that this is where we would have to part. 'Tegh, you are the bravest and the most fearless friend that I've had in my life.' With his brawny arms crossed across his chest, he accepted my decision, his eyes misty with tears. We shook hands like warriors and then hugged each other goodbye. The rest of the boys saluted him. 'Don't forget to keep reading,' said Hafiz as a parting shot, but unlike the other times, it was tearfully painful.

The rest of us proceeded further and reached Chandanwari. It was time again. 'Dear, dear Tabah! What can I say? You are so different and yet so much like me. Without you, I would have never succeeded. You risked your life by living in the lion's den.' Tears came to Tabah's eyes, flowing freely down his cheeks. With an actor's practised flourish, he bowed to us. Cupping my face with his gentle hands, he kissed me on my forehead and bid me goodbye and left.

Then came Sheshnag Lake and it was time I parted with Hafiz. 'Hafiz, your mind left me in awe. Your knowledge can change the world. But never forget me, will you?' He turned his face away with lips compressed, nodding his head at us, saying he was going to be okay. He started to walk away, but then he turned, 'Dawn, there is no limit to scientific and technological knowledge, but you showed me that the world and ultimately life is the supreme teacher.' I ran to him and pressed my hands in his tightly.

At Mahagunas Top, Yuva stopped me. 'What happened?' I asked him. 'Won't you accompany me up on our ascent?' But he shook his head, 'My father left me here and I can go no further. Goodbye Dawn, my Niti warrior princess.'

'Yuva . . .' I felt that I would collapse. Never did I think that in our journey, he would leave me midway. 'Yuva, after my mother, you have made me who I am. What will I do without you?' I cried openly. 'Will . . . will I ever see you again?'

'I am always with you, my child. I told you that I am music. You will hear me as sound, in the flowing river, in the conch, in the bell . . .' he said, winking, and tapping his trunk on my head like old times.

This made me laugh. I embraced him. 'Thank you, my supreme teacher. You always found a way through every obstacle that I faced.' Wiping my tears, I whispered, 'Goodbye, my kick-starter.'

It was only the three of us now who trekked through the mighty valley and then up the mountainside that was covered with high snow. We had to use our antigravity belts now to float up, the blue flames invisible in the white ice. We were silent most times as none had the heart to speak. After what seemed like hours at a stretch, we reached Panchtarni. 'I know, I know, it's my turn,' Yaniv said with a sad laugh. 'I will miss this humour when I am alone, Yaniv, and your delicious food,' I added, smiling. 'You always made us feel happy. My thrice-born doctor, you were so caring of us. It was all part of your oath and you fulfilled it.'

'Dawn,' he said, taking my hand, 'If I have been of help and truly made you smile, then I have done my duty. Your love merely reaffirms what was from my side. I am always at your service.' And so, Yaniv walked away.

It was only Tan and I now. The trek had become impossible at this point and we were slowly floating up the hill. I had reached the entrance to a cave. 'Amarnath,' said Tan, as we looked at the all-white expanse. The peaks were jutting high into the sky with the white mantle reflecting brightly. And so, it was time for the last heartbreak.

'Tan, what can I even say that you don't know already? Your depth of wisdom, positivity and calm has carried me to the final ascent. Without you, I am now left alone.' He only smiled at me. Saluting me with his hands folded, he simply said, 'It was you who taught me many things that books cannot teach, Dawn. You showed me that the power of love will triumph over the love of power. I salute Maha inside you. Namaskar, Dawn.' Then he walked away as I stood at the mouth of the cave, silently mourning the loss of all my friends. The only friends that I ever had.

I snapped on Kota Rani's dejhoor and prepared to enter the cave. The dejhoor were a part of me just like my mace, Yuva had explained as I'd told him about the last teacher. I braced myself and walked in. It was terribly dark and damp and I was suddenly anxious, but I walked in fuelled by the desire to find the way to face the evilness of Dushita, armed with the memories of my friends, my mother and the stories that I now carried inside me. Inside, I found on the ground the skin of a black antelope. I placed the mace in front of me and sat on the antelope skin. Outside, the temperature was a frigid minus 20 degrees, but inside, it was a little warmer.

I saw two white pigeons on the rafters. The female snuggled to the left side of the male and watched me intently. There was a light coming from her eyes that was more intense than any lamp could produce. She reminded me of Kira a lot. Pigeons were the first birds that humans had domesticated, my mother had once told me. It now seemed like it had happened years ago—a distant past. I wondered if they were the pets of whoever had lived in the cave. Sitting there, somehow, I felt that I had come home. Amarnath cave gave me the same feeling that I had when I was growing up in the sanctuary cave in Kailash. I wondered whether there was any connection.

I composed myself and focused. I had renounced everything and sought guidance on how to face Dushita. There was nothing but silence. The female pigeon watched me attentively. I was all alone in the world. There was nobody else—man, woman or child. My mind melted like a snowflake as thoughts disappeared. I waited and waited for a signal, but nothing was forthcoming. If Maha was there, I did not see him. Then it hit me. The brave front that I had put on while saying goodbye to Yuva and the Pandavas finally gave way. I was alone in the world, no, alone in the Universe. What would happen to me? To the world? I broke down and wept out of desperation, knowing that Dushita awaited me outside. My chest heaved with emotions. My tears became the offering to Maha. I felt myself melting as I cried in a state of complete dissolution, which I thought would cause me to collapse. Slowly, I managed to steady my heavy sobs. My mind had stilled, and the toxicity of my anxiety washed out. I felt better and was ready to go out and finally, aggressively confront Dushita.

Then my eyes fell on the mace that my mother had given me. It had the name Usha engraved on it. I was reminded of what my mother had told me. *The mace is now bonded with you. You can will it to come to you in your hour of need. But give it freedom and don't overthink for it. It knows its Dharma quite well.* The mace had come to me. Yuva had told me that I could have any name that I wanted. And so, I, Dawn, decided my future name.

Usha, the life of life and the death of death.

Sarga 16

Innerverse

Nishat Bagh, Srinagar

I sat in the great Samadhi posture concentrating on the Dushitacharya temple from my vantage point above Ishber at the residence of Gopi Krishna, the sage scientist whose writings my mother had shared with me. I could see Suaresvara Lake below. There was an energy there that was palpable. Gopi Krishna had meditated there and given great discourses. The amazing story of Lila that mother had shared with me as to how to face Dushita gave me strength. I had seated myself inside a circular mandala with mustard seeds scattered around it. My left hand rested in my lap, palm facing upward. The right hand rested on my right knee, fingers dropping downward. The faint light of dawn raced across the sky, chased by the sun. Where my concentration would be, there would be formation, Yuva had trained me.

There was a slight movement. A figure started descending from the temple. He was flowing down the slope of the hill. The birds and sound of animals became still, the wind rose as if approaching to listen, the sun went into nothingness as if to consider what had been taught and the shadows grew longer as if stretching their necks to watch.

He came closer.

In his one eye, there was anger and in the other eye, attachment. His forehead bore the seal of a dog's paw that had been burnt deeply in. Yet, he carried the glow of wisdom and the perfection of beauty made even more desirable by the scar. His face had a cherubic smile. Living on top of Dushitacharya Hill, he was in Eden, on the holy mountain of the supreme. Every precious stone was in his covering— ruby, topaz, diamond, beryl, onyx, jasper, lapis lazuli, turquoise, emerald and, lastly, gold. But topping off his turban, where the bun of his hair was coiled on the left side, was a giant sapphire. As he walked and approached me, a carpet unfolded in front of him. It was a carpet of stones of fire on which he stepped firmly, the stones sizzling amid the snow and ice.

If Dushita was unrighteousness, then how could everything about him be so right? I thought. He seemed blameless. He seated himself across from me on top of the red-hot coals. Then I spotted his slightly open mouth with a leer and there was his mark, the fangs. I knew he was formless and that it was only his projection into my mind that was giving him his image.

'Usha,' his voice boomed but was eerily calm. 'Prepare to hate yourself—the greatest punishment.' He was singularly abrupt.

'I am not afraid of you.'

'There is no *you*. I am within you.'

'An impurity, an accident of birth.'

'Your impurity knows you better than you know yourself.'

'My impurity will be expelled.'

He was haughty and dismissive. 'Nobody achieves that level of purity.'

But I was resolute, the memory of my mother, my friends and Yuva reeling inside me. 'Those who unite with Maha do.'

'Maha is the great lie. It does not exist.'

I laughed. 'Maha lies beyond you. I will find Maha, for my will is supreme.'

'*Your* will, little girl?' he sneered. 'Desire is *me*.' His laugh echoed as the mountains joined in.

'Then my only thought will be to renounce desire.'

'Desire can be emptied out, but I will fill it up repeatedly.'

'Not if one's last desire is Maha. Just like Bala.'

'Fools' gold!' he thundered. '*Look at me*,' he commanded. 'I *am* your last desire.' Suddenly, his voice became calm, business-like, a soothing poison. 'Prepare to die.'

I was not prepared to lose after losing so much. 'No,' I said simply, '*You* look at me. I am justice for all the women you have hurt since the dawn of history.'

This was it. I waited for him to act. I waited and waited and waited.

Then finally, he spoke, irritably, for what felt like hours and hours had passed by. 'It seems that you have no karma. I cannot kill you. Never mind, you scheming girl, you will not escape a living death.'

'I have no karma, but you do. I am the death of death.'

He smirked, 'I have paralyzed you and erased your memory, imagination and conception. There is no movement left in you. There is thus no Time for you. You are now in a suspended state of animation and will remain disconnected until you run out of energy.'

I had just started to panic when I remembered my last teacher, the blind storyteller who had told me about Kubjika and Bhairava. *Exhale, inhale, exhale*. All that I could do was breathe like Kubjika. Everything else was paralyzed. All I could do was to breathe to the rhythm of *Namah, Namah, Namah, not mine, not mine, not mine* . . .

Time left me untouched with Dushita as my internal witness. The snow fell and a blizzard howled as the winter got harsher. I was my own prisoner and there was nothing that I could do.

Dushita whispered inside me, his voice tempting like a sweet fruit, 'Little girl, you do have a choice. Join me. Focus on the right side of your spinal cord at the base of the spine, where your back hurts. The harder you concentrate, the more your heat energy will rise. When the temperature of your base matches mine, we will unite.'

I tried to block his voice, but he got in, now soothing like the koori lullaby.

'You will be the first woman to become the centre of the Universe, brighter than the blazing sun. What Maha has withheld from humanity since the creation of the Universe will become yours because of me.'

I blinked mentally. The liar with honey on his forked tongue was trapped in his own web of deceit. So, Maha did exist.

'Your canine teeth give you away. Your promises are all for after-death. With Maha, it is all while alive. I will stand with him.'

Having been exposed, he fell silent and his chatter ceased.

I rested my mind instead on the left side of my spine. And continued to breathe. Time sped by carrying the spinning planets, galaxies, black holes and universes along with it, but Dushita and I were unyielding and immovable.

I had now shrivelled into a stick. My breath was getting weaker and had slowed to a point that it did not even reveal itself as a foggy mist. My body turned into cold ash barely held by my now-ancient body suit, which was vainly trying to keep me stable and warm. I had turned into a ghost in the wintry waste.

My open left hand's wrist was on the wrist of the open right-hand, seeking grace as it rested in my lap. Slowly, my right hand, now weakened and shrunken fell and touched the earth. It encountered firmness in the touch of Bheema Garbha; there was a small movement, something stirred, a cool current seemed to flow from the left side into the central channel of my spinal cord. It had a healing aspect to it as it released the burning sensation that I used to feel. Inside my body, I heard the *anahad* vibrations with their deep sonorous sound. It was Yuva! And it was then that I heard it . . . Kira's song:

Look to this day!
For it is life, the very life of life.

There was a snapping sound of ignition as if Yuva was moving inside me. A silver streak zigzagged through my spinal cord. It was exactly like the graceful movement of a white serpent in rapid flight, a veritable helix DNA that was reminiscent of Patanjali's serpent pouring a radiant, cascading shower of brilliant vital energy into my brain, filling my head with a blissful shine in place of the flame that had been tormenting me. It spread like a tonic through my vital organs, pumping my pulse.

All my memory, thought, imagination and conception returned but vastly expanded with the touch of Prana, the Life Breath that creates all.

My excited mind went into ecstasy, and unfortunately, that took my concentration away from the left of my spine. It was enough distraction for Dushita to fight back. He attacked viciously, his burning red flame singeing Yuva and blackening his silver stream. As Yuva fell back, I could feel myself relapsing into a coma from which I could not hope to recover.

With my last breath, I cried out, 'Ma! *Maej!*'

The whistle of a bird sounded. My Life Breath had rebounded. There was a sound of a million bees coming to meet a ray of light. There was a roar of a waterfall and a stream of liquid light as my Life Breath rushed up and entered my brain. It crossed out of my skull through the kalaposh cap and began to expand into a circle. The waves of light expanded outwards while my body became smaller, and the oceanic waves carried me out further and beyond. I was aware of every point in the Universe without any inputs from my sensory organs. I was no longer conscious that my body existed. I had expelled Dushita.

I had become one with Maha!

But Dushita was not finished. With a shriek, the red streak that was him dashed out of me and arched straight into the lake.

A loud voice crackled, 'Usha, know that I, in the form of Jalodbhava, was born here in the water. I have the triple boon of magical powers, unparalleled prowess and immortality in the water.

I will be back inside you forever since more than half of you *is* water. I, the flesh-eater, will finish all, you included.'

In response, the silver streak above me grew and grew. It took the form of a mighty serpent with a raised hood of 1,008 heads, each wearing a crown. He had the lustre of the full moon. He was dressed in blue, his diadem fastened in gold. He had a plough that seemed to have the faces of the ancient gods. With it, he broke the mountain. The icy water in the lake flowed out with force through the opening. There was a terrifying rush and sound as the waves overflowed the lower peaks.

With the water receding, Dushita in the form of Jalodbhava was uncovered and no longer immortal. But he was not done. He saw the disappearing water, and so, he darkened the sun and the moon so that he could not be visible. His magical powers came from his paradox bombs—the viruses—but then suddenly, Kira appeared in the sky. She was highly excited and her sharp whistles filled the expanse. She dove to the ground, picked up a pebble and flew straight up. Dushita saw her and rose into the sky to stop her. But Kira flew higher and Dushita followed her into the sky, growing effortlessly and unboundedly. Then, when Kira was no more than a dot in empty space, she turned and dropped the pebble. It fell quietly, but as it fell, it expanded in size. Dushita let out a roar and raised his fists to smite away the pebble, which had now turned into a rock. The rock now grew into a meteor and was expanding at a fierce rate. When it smashed into Dushita, it was the size of a huge mountain. It crushed his manifestation into smithereens, every single particle of his being penetrating deep inside the earth.

I witnessed it all.

First came the rumble of the earthquake, then my awareness picked up the sound of hideous blasts of the earth smashing into itself. Then, the tortuous cries of animals, then the screaming and moaning of the wind as it was twisted and contorted beyond Nature's laws. And then the neutrinos and anti-neutrinos buried deep inside the earths' crust were unleashed by the touch of Dushita's smashed death particles. Unlimited quantities streamed out as earth's natural nuclear fusion accelerated. From generating 24 terawatts of heat and energy, the number doubled and then tripled and multiplied rampantly thereafter. Soon, the entire earth became a raging ball of radioactive fire. The cascading number of outcomes and a rise in temperature caused Planck's constant wall to be hit. Planck's constant was the determinate of action, the energy of a photon divided by its frequency. The frequency crossed gamma rays and with the rise in energy continued to rise exponentially.

I experienced it all.

In the darkness emerged a five-headed, ten-armed and three-eyed being. One eye was the light of the sun, the second eye was the lustre of the moon and the third eye was the flame of fire. He started to dance amidst the inferno, a dark form that filled the ten directions accompanied by a cosmic sound. From his body arose the black shadow of Kaalaratri. The shadow became the Planckian black hole, sucking my dead body with the mangled remains of Dushita's Jalodbhava. Then went the planets, the sun, the galaxies and other black holes.

Kaalaratri grew smaller, spiralled into a particle, then an atom and finally disappeared. My awareness went with it. Dushita was slain. Nothing remained. The Sarvanash Great War was over. There was no light, no time and no space.

The universes had become the sound of Mahashanti, great peace. AUM. AUM. AUM.

Sarga 17

Resurrection

Anno Usha 11
Daughter Universe

The storytelling hour was over.

I was in the nursery with my five blessings! The youngest one was nestled next to me, clutching my hand with her tiny fingers. Some parts of my story were scary for the younger children, and some parts they would fully understand only once they were grown up. *The Grimms' Fairy Tales*, a few drawn from the *Kathasaritsagara*, were grim indeed for a very good reason. My story was to teach our children that even if the most terrible evil befell them, within the safety of their nursery, they would come out alive as a winner and live happily ever after. But for that they had to follow the Niti way, the way of the wise conduct in life.

All I could tell them about the last moment for me was that, biologically, I had been reduced to mere Life Breath, which became space within space. Then the Life Breath's imagination conceived it to be contained inside something physical, and so, the breath energy became mass and acquired a body with Life Energy. It then acquired time, a virtual pre-history, such as parents, age and so on, and thus the movement began. Whatever I imagined in detail became real.

It was interesting and not surprising to me that my name Usha had in my previous birth and world morphed into Easter, which was the greatest resurrection story ever.

My rebirth began with the first activity of this rebooted form. My last wish—a *dohada*—when I clipped on the dejhoor earrings had been that I would be 'creation', just as my mother had wished for me. It was the one attachment that I had not cast away before entering the cave, and yet, Maha had understood. Or was it Kira?

So, I was reborn along with a new Universe, or correctly, a Daughter Universe. My heroine in the stories that maej had told me had always been Draupadi. So, it was natural that I selected the Pandavas to be alongside me. They were part of my life and I felt responsible for them in the same way that they had felt responsible for me. I trusted my feelings and let them guide me. I must have inherited this trait from my mother who had done what she believed in, and in the end, my mother had won. United Life triumphed over United Intelligence! And I had become part of the story that had won.

In my new world, I choose to restart life at the point that we had assembled in Ishber. I choose Ishber because I was Kashmir. There was no rule to restart as a newborn baby. There was no compulsion to follow anyone else's resurrection story, especially the ones inventing false dying, judgements and heaven or hell. I became the programmer of my own dream and did not bend to the rules of some male fossil that had come before me. And yes, in my programme, Muladeva and his wife became part of us also because he is such good company.

What I have done here is to provide an accurate biological description of my experience to my descendants so that they would have the roadmap of the innerverse. I experienced death, but all along, I stayed stubbornly and one-pointedly aware of what was happening to me because the knower of the world cannot match the knower of the Self.

I am no longer blind to Maha. There is still a silvery lustre, a glow to every entity that I see. It took me a long time to realize that it was a projection of the pure, awakened Life Breath radiance that is within me.

It is not just science seeking truth that is evolving but also the human brain. It will take enlightened scientists of the Usha race thousands of years to completely figure out what had happened to me spontaneously: The gift of the experience of the death of death coming from the life of life, which is Maha realization. Maha gave me the gift of being a creator and the power of making anything possible. But what I got is also everyone else's birthright to choose—a birthright to expand and realize that Maha is us.

The future Truth Keepers will be the Life Story Scientists. They will reveal with greater clarity, the mysteries of the miracle that is life in its totality. These life story scientists will entertain, educate, empower and enable ignition the way the Granthikas did. What my own life story did teach me is that a woman or a man is her or his sole friend or enemy. We are responsible for what happens to us because of our desires, thoughts and actions. One should be dispassionate, and if one is passionate, then in each action one should first purify one's desire because that is where Dushita resides. The glide path of purification is the willing path of an increasing freedom and acceptance leading to complete fulfilment.

My oldest son sleepily asked me, 'Ma, who is Maha?'

Children ask the most difficult questions, which need simple but honest answers. I repeated what I had been told, 'For now, think that he is my true father who permitted me to be me, gave me the right to have unbounded experience.'

'And who was Kira?'

'She is Maej, the mother of all.'

That satisfied him for the moment and then he continued, 'If there are no rules in life, then what is Niti?'

'The Niti warrior's way of life is so simple yet so powerful. You will get all you want from learning deeply, acting bravely but kindly, and having five very close friends.' I smiled.

"It is that simple. No rules?'

"It is that simple. You make your own rules.'

'Are there any more Niti stories?'

'Yes, there are thousands of amazing Niti stories.'

'Good,' my little girl said. 'I want to hear them all. Also, I want Yuva as one of my five friends.'

'Your wish will come true.'

'And I want the mace also.'

'It will come on its own to you when the time is right.'

'And I want your dejhoor too.'

I laughed and cradled her in my lap and sang the koori lullaby. My daughter wanted it all. It was so with my mother, and so, it is with me now.

'Zuv vandmaye. My life is yours,' I whispered.

Acknowledgements

I was pottering around through the fog that surrounds my daily existence when the phone rang. A young woman on the other end told me that I had been recommended to her by a mutual friend, Aaditya Kitroo. Her brief was simple. Would I write a book on Kashmiri folk tales for young adults?

I am like you. We all try so hard to say yes whenever a member of the next-generation makes a request of us, especially if a common friend is involved. I suppose we all think that, after all, it is for them that we exist.

'But, but,' I spluttered, 'nobody reads that stuff. Not the adults and certainly not the young adults. They are armed with Google, so what's the need for obsolete stories?'

'Oh,' she said. 'We have folk tales from all parts of India but hardly any from Kashmir. Plus, Aaditya said that if there was anyone who could do this right, it would be you. Please . . .'

I sensed the disappointment in her voice. I thought about how I would have felt if the daughter that I never had would have been the one making the request of an author and got turned down. I weakened momentarily, overcome by a dohada wave that swept within me.

'Okay, let me send you a short synopsis of what I could do. It will not be folk tales; it will be ancient folk tales. I warn you that it will be very different. I only do stuff that others are afraid to take on. If you like it, then we can move forward, and if you don't, then I will not feel bad that I turned you down.'

We agreed to the pact, and in due course, I put some thoughts together. As part of it, I sent the outline to my adviser Amitav Kaul. As always, he gave it spine and coherence. Then I forwarded it to the young lady who had approached me, fully expecting that she would blanch on reading it and beat a hasty retreat.

Imagine my surprise when Arpita Nath, the commissioning editor for young adults at Penguin Random House India, responded positively and with great enthusiasm!

Thus was born *Dawn: The Warrior Princess of Kashmir.*

Arpita was not only the inspiration for the ambitious literary effort here but also an extraordinary cheerleader. She expanded my ability to write complex concepts in a simpler manner to make the book accessible to a younger and broader audience. She pulled me back from the edge whenever the story was at risk of veering off. She brought the inner emotions to life and the characters and their interplay become real. It was a literary *jugalbandi* between the author and the editor. For this, I am truly grateful.

The next impact players from the publisher's team were Rujuta Thakurdesai, the cover designer who guided the incredibly talented artist Kalyanjyoti Mohan. He was the one to manifest the power and beauty of Dawn, the Niti warrior. While his creativity is unique, he exercised it completely conforming to the canonical inputs that he was provided. The smart book cover is a tour de force in that each aspect carries intelligence within it even as it pleases aesthetically.

Vijesh Kumar and Sameer Mahale, the latter of whom I had known from before got involved in the story from early days. Representing Sales, they were an extremely reassuring proxy signal for a novel, which was going to straddle Time and Space. Aditi Batra, the copy editor, was veritably hawk-eyed. Much as I thought that as a result of many revisions, I was submitting perfection, I learnt that my blind spots will always limit me, needing an editor like her. Srishti, marketing publicist, took the story to the world and popularized it. All authors love apostles and Srishti's case is no different.

My family has remained supportive of this late blooming tangent to my professional career. To our sons, Shiva and Dhruva, my hope is that this story will reveal to them how to face the world in a manner that enables them to have it all. My wife, Sushma, has opened new worlds for me, which helped shape considerable portions of this novel. Sushma has been a great teacher of the Maha pathway and a joyful life companion. This novel would not have been possible without her support and understanding.

I have memory and therefore I am free. My late parents, Radha Krishan and Ragya Kaul were always uppermost in my mind when I thought of the cultural context of the stories that I wrote. My brother, Rajiv Kaul, is a profile in courage and grit.

The ancient, Niti storytellers of my land were constant sources of inspiration. Some are known like Pandit Vishnu Sharma whose stories remain the most widely translated in the world. Somadeva, Kalhana, Jonaraja, Srivara are a veritable treasury. Hatim maintained the tradition of oral storytelling until British times. Then there are the unknowns, the author of *Yoga Vasistha*, the *Nilamata Purana* and many others. What amazing alchemy did they weave!

Finally, as I look at this novel, one conclusion is inescapable. I did not write it. Whoever or whatever guided me in this writing, I offer my salutations. May the muse of Kashmir accept this wondrous literary manifestation with a smile from the lucky and humbled recipient of her gifts.

Selected Bibliography

❧ Edited by Yigal Bronner, David Shulman, and Gary Tubb. *Innovations and Turning Points: Toward a History of Kavya Literature*. Oxford: Oxford University Press, 2014.

❧ Edited by Christopher Key Chapple and Arindam Chakrabarti. *Engaged Emancipation: Mind, Morals, and Make-Believe in the Mokṣopāya (Yogavāsiṣṭha)*. New York: State University of New York Press, 2015.

❧ Chaudhury, Bani Roy. *Folk Tales of Kashmir*. New Delhi: Sterling Publishers, 1983.

❧ Chung, Tan. *Himalaya Calling: The Origins of China and India*. Singapore: World Scientific, 2015.

❧ Das, Rahul Peter. *The Origin of the Life of a Human Being: Conception and the Female According to Ancient Indian Medical and Sexological Literature*. New Delhi: Motilal Banarsidass, 2003.

❧ Edited by Harsha V. Deheja and Makarand Paranjape. *Saundarya: The Perception and Practice of Beauty in India*, New Delhi: Samvad India Foundation, 2003.

❧ Dhar, Somnath. *Tales of Kashmir*, New Delhi: Anmol Publications, 1992.

❧   Ganguli, Kisari Mohan, trans. *The Mahabharata of Krishna-Dwaipayana Vyasa, Vol I–IV*, New Delhi: Munshiram Manoharlal Publishers Private Ltd., 1993.

❧   Edited by Brenda E. F. Beck, Peter J. Claus, Praphulladatta Goswami and Jawaharlal Handoo. *Folktales of India*. Chicago: University of Chicago Press, 1987.

❧   Handoo, Lalita. *Structural Analysis of Kashmiri Folktales*. Mysuru: Central Institute of Indian Languages, 1994.

❧   Hanneder, Jürgen. *Studies on the Mokṣopāya*. Wiesbaden: Harrassowitz Verlag, 2006.

❧   Edited by Jürgen Hanneder. *The Mokṣopāya, Yogavāsiṣṭha and Related Texts*. Aachen: Shaker Verlag, 2005.

❧   Hariharan, Ramesh. *Genomic Quirks: The Search for Spelling Errors*, Bengaluru: Strand Life Sciences, 2016.

❧   Kak, Subhash. *The Loom of Time: On the Recursive Nature of Reality*. New Delhi: D.K. Printworld, 2004.

❧   ———. *The Architecture of Knowledge: Quantum Mechanics, Neuroscience, Computers and Consciousness*. New Delhi: Centre for Studies in Civilizations, 2004.

❧   ———. *The Nature of Physical Reality*. Ontario: Mount Meru Publishing, 2016.

❧   ———. *Mind and Self: Patanjali's Yoga Sutra and Modern Science*, Ontario: Mount Meru Publishing, 2016.

❧   Koul, Omkar N. *A Dictionary of Kashmiri Proverbs*. New Delhi: Indian Institute of Language Studies, 1992.

❧   Kumari, Dr Ved. *The Nilamata Purana* (Vol II). Srinagar: Jammu and Kashmir Academy of Art, Culture and Languages, 1968.

❧   Knowles, J. Hinton. *A Dictionary of Kashmiri Proverbs & Sayings*. New Delhi: Asian Educational Services, 1985.

❧   ———. *Folklore of Kashmir*. New Delhi: Anmol Publications, Reprint 1993.

❧   Krishna, Gopi. *Kundalini: The Evolutionary Energy in Man*. Colorado: Shambala Publications, 1970.

———. *The Dawn of a New Science*. New Delhi: Kundalini Research and Publication Trust, 1978.

———. *The Biological Basis of Religion and Genius*. New York: Harper & Row, 1971.

Kutumbiah, P. *Ancient Indian Medicine*. New Delhi: Orient Longman, 1962.

Lakshmanjoo, Swami. *Bhagavad Gita: In the Light of Kashmir Shaivism*. Edited by John Hughes. Culver City: Lakshmanjoo Academy, 2013.

———. *Vijñāna Bhairava: The Practice of Centring Awareness*. New Delhi: Motilal Banarsidass, 2003.

Langoo, Dalip, trans., Koori lullaby. Edited by Rakesh Kaul, 2018.

Naidu, Bijayetti Venkata Narayanaswami. *Tandava Laksanam: The Fundamentals of Ancient Hindu Dancing*. New Delhi: Munshiram Manoharlal Publishers Private Ltd., 2015.

Edited by N. M. Penzer. *The Ocean of Story translation, Being C.H. Tawney's Translation of Somadeva's Katha Sarit Sagara Vol I–X*. London: Chas. J. Sawyer, Ltd., Grafton House, 1924.

Polanyi, Michael. *The Tacit Dimension*. Chicago: University of Chicago Press, 1966.

Pollock, Sheldon, trans. and ed. *A Rasa Reader: Classical Indian Aesthetics*. New York: Columbia University Press, 2016.

Randall, Lisa. *Warped Passages, Unraveling the Mysteries of the Universe's Hidden Dimensions*. New York: Harper Perennial, 2006.

Ramanujan, A. K. *Folktales from India*. New Delhi: Penguin Books India, 1994.

Ryder, Arthur W., trans. *The Panchatantra*. Chicago: University of Chicago Press Ltd., 1925.

Stein, Sir Aurel. *Hatim's Tales: Kashmiri Stories and Songs*. New Delhi: Gyan Publishing House, First Reprint, 1989.

Tipler, Frank J. *The Physics of Immortality: Modern Cosmology God and the Resurrection of the Dead*. New York: Doubleday, 1994.

❀ Vatsyayan, Kapila. *Bharata: The Natyasastra.* New Delhi: Sahitya Akademi, 1996.

❀ Venkatesananda, Swami. *The Supreme Yoga: Yoga Vasistha.* New Delhi: Motilal Banarsidass Publishers, 2006.

❀ Tompkins, Chris, trans. *Chakra System of the Universal Mother.* Preserved as a scroll at the Victoria and Albert Museum, London.

❀ Wallis, Christopher, "The Blossoming of Innate Awareness", tantrikstudies.org, 9 March 2018. Accessed 14 August 2018. https://hareesh.org/blog/2018/3/9/the-blossoming-of-your-awareness?rq=svabodh.

❀ Wolf, Fred Alan. *The Yoga of Time Travel: How the Mind Can Defeat Time.* Wheaton: Quest Books, 2004.

❀ Mahadevan, Lakshminarayanan and E. Hosoi, A, "Flexible Flying Carpets," Research Gate, 1 November 1999. Accessed 20 November 2018. https://www.researchgate.net/publication/252188425_Flexible_Flying_Carpets.

❀ *Bala Kavacha*, 'Protection of the Young Woman Goddess'. Shri Bālā, daughter of Tripurā, belongs to the retinue of indigenous Kashmir Goddesses, worshipped in the *Agni-karya-paddhati*, *Devi-rahasya*, etc.